The Lesser of Evils

Tony Frank

Writer's Showcase
San Jose New York Lincoln Shanghai

Writer's Showcase
an imprint of iUniverse.com, Inc.

For information address:
iUniverse.com, Inc.
5220 S 16th, Ste. 200
Lincoln, NE 68512
www.iuniverse.com

ISBN: 0-595-17139-7

Printed in the United States of America

The Lesser of Evils

In loving memory of Ruby

ACKNOWLEDGEMENTS

I might not have started this book without help from Scott Chasin, or finished it without the assistance of Chris Goggans. Computer insecurity aces both, and masters of their craft.

For perspectives from the other side of the fence, I was expertly set straight on how the law enforcement community battles computer crime by Byron Sage and Sykes Houston of the FBI's resident agency in Austin, and by David Icove of the Tennessee Valley Authority.

My hopes were surpassed not only by the generous time the aforementioned took from busy schedules to humor me, but also the gentlemanly manner in which they did so.

"We must indeed hang together, or, most assuredly, we shall hang separately."

—JOHN HANCOCK
July 4, 1776

PROLOGUE

April 12, 1996, Department of State, Washington, D.C.

A strained silence filled the room. The two visitors exchanged uncomfortable glances, then turned their eyes back to Ed Harkutlian. The secretary of state reacted by rising from his chair, signaling the discussion was over.

"It'll be an almighty stink if word of this ever gets out," Lee Trujillo said somberly, straightening the jacket of his uniform as he stood up. As chairman of the Joint Chiefs of Staff, and a career military man, the decision had been most difficult for him to accept.

Robert Carlson also got up, nodding in agreement. He would not normally have been party to a decision of such poignant ramifications. But as deputy secretary of defense, the burden was his to bear while his superior convalesced from an appendectomy. "I can just see the headlines," he said, unable to mask his anxiety. "POWGATE!"

The word hung for a few seconds. Then Carlson added with a shrug: "But bad as it stinks, it's still the lesser of evils."

"Gentlemen," Harkutlian said. "Let's keep things in perspective here. We're entrusted, first and foremost, with acting in the best interests of the United States of America. As difficult as this circumstance may be, I believe we have decided in a manner consistent with the exigencies of the country's national security."

The two visitors concurred with the secretary of state's remark. He was a tall, imposing man, still remarkably fit for his fifty-seven years, well renowned for his tenacity, and reputed never to lose an argument. In the matter at hand, his reasoning was typically sound. Harkutlian had dissected and analyzed all elements of the situation with seemingly irrefutable logic.

As they shook hands and prepared to leave the State Department, Robert Carlson and General Lee Trujillo conceded that all the angles had been covered. All there was to say had been said. It was time to cast the hapless die.

*   *   *

Two hours later, the Pentagon, Arlington, Virginia

The memorandum was potent, enough so to cause Robert Carlson to stop and ponder the consequences several times as he composed it. There was no question in his mind—if the substance of what he had written were to fall before the wrong eyes, there was no saying what the political cost would be.

As concerned as he was for himself, Carlson felt even greater angst for Lee Trujillo, his friend of many years. In Trujillo's case, a brilliant military career would be overshadowed by the inevitable controversy, forever tarnishing the reputation of a man that had long served his country with pride and honor. Trujillo had fought in three wars and had the scars to show for it. Countless times throughout a distinguished career he had led men into battle. Not once had he done anything to unnecessarily jeopardize the lives of men under his command. Yet, as Carlson sat pensively in the comfort of his third-floor office, he knew that the issue consuming their undivided attention for the better part of a week bore heavier on Trujillo's conscience than any line the general had ever crossed on the battlefield.

Carlson proofed the draft twice, placing the pages neatly on the desk, face down to his left. As he reached the concluding paragraph on the third page, he sighed deeply and cursed the world he lived in. The brief would make poignant reading for the secretary of defense. It involved the lives of two soldiers. Just two men out of a nation of over two hundred and fifty million. But it would put at risk the lives of thirty-seven thousand others.

His confidential assistant appeared within seconds of him summoning her. Ellen Rundle stood at the edge of his desk, empathizing with the man she'd served loyally for the last three of her fourteen years at the Pentagon.

"Just a couple more changes," he said, uncharacteristically avoiding eye contact. "When you're done, I want a clean copy for Hackelman. Shred this one, and…" he hesitated for a moment, for him a sure sign of nerves, "no other copies anywhere."

She nodded quietly as he handed her the draft. As Rundle left the room, Carlson leaned back in his chair and closed his eyes.

Ellen Rundle made the corrections to the text and printed a fresh copy of the brief for Secretary of Defense Roone Hackelman. After securing the copy inside an official Department of Defense binder, she went back into the larger office and placed the binder on the desk, eliciting a nod of acknowledgment from Robert Carlson. The clock on the wall of his office read 10:59.

Back at her office, Rundle ran the marked-up draft of the brief through a paper shredder. By the time she had destroyed the document and discarded its remains in her trash basket, Carlson's clock read 11:02.

Later that morning, a few minutes after Ellen Rundle left her office for lunch, Robert Carlson stepped cautiously into her office, slipped into her chair and swiveled it around to face her computer. The machine was on, and he quickly accessed Rundle's directory at her local network's file server. After checking the reference code in the binder Rundle had left him, he found the correct sub-directory, then the file he sought. He confirmed it was indeed the right one, then proceeded to delete it.

Satisfied that the text of the brief could no longer be retrieved, the deputy defense secretary returned to the system's main screen. He carefully collected the shredded remains of the draft copy out of his assistant's trash basket, and deposited them in a large envelope that would later burn to ash in his fireplace at home. Finally, glancing around to ensure he'd covered his tracks, he restored Ellen Rundle's chair to the position in which he'd found it and returned, binder in hand, to his office.

               *   *   *

Twenty-six feet under the ground, in a bunker-like basement suite in the building's West Wing, the remote field office occupied by the Disaster Recovery Group was abuzz with activity. A quasi-autonomous spin-off of the Defense Information Systems Agency, DRG was a small but highly specialized team of digital and magnetic media experts with a crucial mission. Every hour on the hour, automatic backups were made of every new or revised file in every directory of every personal computer, minicomputer, workstation, file server and mainframe on the entire Pentagon electronic data network. As the tapes containing the backups filled up, they'd be transported via military armored trucks and aircraft to their eventual resting-place under a salt dome deep in the heart of the Nevada desert. There, in what was euphemistically referred to by DRG personnel as data cemeteries, the tapes would be stored in the safety of large underground concrete vaults built to withstand the most powerful surface nuclear explosions known to mankind. The purpose was simple. Should any disaster, natural or man-made, ever cause the loss of data from the Pentagon's massive digital information network, the underground tapes would allow for complete data reconstruction by DRG staff.

A system is only as good as its weakest link, and frequently that link is human. On the afternoon of April 24th, beset by worry over the negative reaction her ailing brother had shown to his first dose of chemotherapy, Ellen Rundle absentmindedly ignored the warning that appeared on her computer screen, and with the stroke of one key, erased all the information from her directory on the file server.

It was the first time she'd made the mistake, but she didn't panic. She was aware of the available remedy, and with the deputy defense secretary away in the Pacific for the better part of a week, there was no reason for him to know. All it took was one quick telephone call to DISA's Information Services Control and help was on the way. Rundle's security clearance enabled her to sign the necessary requisition forms, thus authorizing the reconstruction of her lost data. Within two days—well before Robert Carlson returned from Hawaii—every file that had been saved to Ellen Rundle's directory at any time during the previous twelve months had been restored. All, without exception, in perfect condition.

CHAPTER ONE

September 2, 1996, Austin, Texas

The pager startled everyone assembled for the early morning lecture. The bearded professor manning the projector shot an irritated glance at his teaching assistant, who in turn fiddled with the black box clipped to his belt in a hurried effort to silence it. He checked the number on the digital display.

Twelve minutes later it happened again. This time, as a murmur broke out among the computer science seniors, the professor's expression implored his Ph.D. student to ensure there would be no more distracting interruptions. Brad Renberg hastened out of the room, checking the pager as he left. It was the same number again.

He made his way downstairs to the building's basement and reached into his pocket for a quarter as he approached a payphone. He cursed under his breath and dialed.

"Brad?" Richard Harding answered expectantly.

"Dick?"

"Yeah."

Renberg's ire jumped a notch. "What the hell are you beeping me in the middle of a lecture for?"

"Hey, you didn't answer at home," Harding replied. "I didn't know you were in class."

"So what's so important?"

"I need to see you. Have you got a few minutes?"

"What for?"

"I'll tell you when I see you."

"It'll have to wait till later," Renberg said. "Come by my place about five-thirty."

"Brad, it can't wait. Please!"

Renberg sensed Harding's urgency. "Okay," he relented.

"I can be there in fifteen minutes. Are you at Taylor?"

"I'll be in the basement, next to the vending machines."

Harding's spirits perked. "Fifteen minutes."

Renberg hung up, wondering. He checked his watch and headed back to the lecture room.

*   *   *

The sun was cracking the horizon when James Marshall drew the vertical blinds in his plush corner office. It wouldn't be long before traffic clogged up Mo-Pac Boulevard, four floors down from where he stood. The cars, trucks and eighteen-wheelers were already roaring past, a sure sign the inevitable buildup had started. As he sipped his steaming black coffee, Marshall's eyes were on the sunrise, but his mind was elsewhere. He fished a cigarette out of his breast pocket and brought it to his lips in time to meet the flame from his lighter.

"Did Harding make any progress yesterday?" he asked, exhaling smoke.

Barry Neale cleared his throat. "No."

Marshall nodded. "The bids are due in a week."

"I know. He's trying. We were up here late."

Marshall sighed. "It's amazing what these guys can do. Did you hear about the Swedish hackers on the news yesterday?"

Neale shook his head.

"They got into the CIA's home page on the web and changed the heading from Central Intelligence Agency to Central Stupidity Agency."

Neale chuckled. "Something similar happened a couple of weeks ago," he said. "Somebody messed with the heading on the Department of Justice home page. Left it reading United States Department of *In*justice."

Marshall turned away from the window and returned to his desk. "You've got to admire the bravado."

"Not to mention the skill," Neale quipped.

"Well, that's something you'd appreciate more than I." Marshall leaned forward and flicked his cigarette above an ashtray. "For God's sake, Barry, keep an eye on him."

"Don't worry," Neale replied. "I'm watching him. That's why I insisted he work out of here."

"What happens on days like today? How can you watch him when you're tied up in meetings all day?"

Marshall had a point. "I'll take care of that," Neale replied. "There's a sniffer program I can download off the Internet that will capture all his keystrokes and save them on my machine. That way I can periodically spot check what he's doing."

Marshall stared at Neale. "Won't he know he's being sniffed—if that's the right term?"

Neale thought about it. "No. He might if he was dialing out of a modem dedicated to his computer. But he goes through a modem on our network server, and *that's* where I'll capture his keystrokes. He won't know."

Marshall looked skeptical.

"In fact," Neale added, "I'll set it up so that I watch him on a monitor in the computer room. He comes into my office, but he's got no business going into the computer room. Even if he did, I'd see him and have enough time to kill the screen."

Marshall wasn't quite satisfied. "Won't that impact our online connection with the Pentagon? We're expecting the contract amendments today."

"No problem. The sniffer operates in the background. It won't interfere with normal operations. We'll get the amendments as soon as they're sent."

Marshall was still anxious. "This whole business scares me. I'm not sure we should be doing this. I wouldn't want him turning against us."

"Don't worry, Jim," Neale insisted. "Harding's under control." He got up off the couch. "Was there anything else?"

Marshall hesitatingly shook his head. "Just watch him."

*   *   *

The forecasted front was still two days away and the wind was southerly and warm. Richard Harding drove north along Lamar Boulevard for four miles, then turned east on West 24th Street, towards the University of Texas. He parked at a meter at the corner of 24th and Speedway before making his way on foot to the basement level of UT's Taylor Hall Computation Center. Renberg was waiting.

"Let's go outside," Harding said when he found him. Renberg wasn't surprised. When he and Harding talked, the walls had ears.

"Let's walk," Harding suggested when they exited the building.

"Okay," Renberg replied. "Now what's this about?"

Harding glanced around to ensure no one else was close. "I need into the Pentagon," he said. "ASAP."

Renberg stopped in his tracks.

"Keep walking," Harding said, a nonchalant smile masking his anxiety.

"*What?*" Renberg asked incredulously.

"You heard me."

It was Renberg's turn to look around. "What the hell for?" he demanded. "What are you up to?"

"Nothing that'll ever get back to you." The smile was still there, but now obviously contrived.

They had stopped walking and faced each other awkwardly. Renberg shook his head.

"Come on, Brad," Harding snapped. "You owe me. I've never asked for anything until now. Get me into the Pentagon and we're even." The smile had disappeared.

"Settle down," Renberg countered. "Tell me what you're up to."

"Why?"

"Because I want to know."

Two students rode past on their bicycles, giving Harding time to think. "All right," he said reluctantly. He started walking again and Renberg kept pace beside him.

"Have you heard of Pantheon Telesystems?"

"No."

"Small defense contractor. They design and build satellite-based telemetry systems. They're bidding on a Pentagon contract. Some carry-over from SDI. I don't know the details, but the way I understand it, even though expansion work on SDI was scrapped, this is a final piece that completes a stage that's otherwise already deployed. So much money's already been spent on it that the government's going to finish it."

Renberg was listening intently.

"The contract's for something called SMARTS. Strategic Missile Attack Repulsion Telemetry System. Some kind of fancy satellite-based signaling system that monitors how successfully our missiles intercept incoming missiles, and then sends the information back to earth. It's like…the Patriot missile meets SDI, or something." He shrugged his shoulders. "That's all I know."

Renberg stared at him. "So why do you need into the Pentagon?"

Harding waited until another student walking towards them had passed. "Pantheon's chasing the SMARTS contract. They're concerned about the competition—a company in California called Systek." He lowered his voice and looked away from Renberg. "I'm trying to find out what Systek's going to bid."

"Jesus!" Renberg exclaimed. "Are they paying you?"

Harding nodded.

Renberg bristled. "What are you doing getting involved in shit like that?"

Harding shuffled his feet. "I need the cash. I'm butt-bare broke. But that's beside the point. You wanted to know, I told you."

Renberg sighed disapprovingly. "Why the Pentagon?" he asked again.

"Because I've tried everything else to get into Systek, and nothing's worked. Defense contractors like Pantheon and Systek are online with the Pentagon. I want to try getting to Systek through the Pentagon."

"That's crazy," Renberg scoffed.

"Not impossible," Harding replied.

"Not impossible, just…crazy!"

Harding didn't respond.

"You're already exposed enough as it is with that phone cloning bullshit," Renberg protested. "Now you want to spy on a defense contractor by going through the Pentagon? Forget it, man. That's no needle in a haystack. It's a pinhead in a hayfield!"

Harding was adamant. "We've found weirder things in stranger places. You know that."

Renberg turned away in disgust. "This is bullshit! Dammit, you know what my situation is. I can't get involved."

"You won't be. Come on, man, I'm out of time. I'm asking you 'cause you know and you owe me. We made a deal and I've done my part. Now tell me and forget you ever heard about it."

Renberg stared into the distance.

"Come on, Zube," Harding urged.

"Don't call me that any more," Renberg snapped. "That shit's in the past as far as I'm concerned."

Harding shrugged his shoulders. "Whatever."

"What the hell's going to happen if it's traced back to you?" Renberg asked.

"It won't be," Harding argued. "I'll dial from Pantheon. They do it all the time in the course of doing their business with the Defense Department."

"So get a dial-up from them."

"You and I made a deal. Are you going to keep your side or what?"

Renberg glared at Harding. "Damn you, Richard. If this comes back to me in any way, I'll say you stole the numbers."

"Fair enough," Harding said. He would take what he could get.

It was a ten-minute walk to Renberg's apartment, a few blocks west of the campus. Not a word was spoken on the way.

"Here's what I've got," Renberg said, handing Harding a single sheet of paper that he extracted from a folder in the living room. It was a list comprising four prefixes, each followed by approximately eighty telephone numbers. Some had notes scribbled next to them, words like *fax*, *computer*, *disconnected* or *always busy*.

"It's been a while since I used this," Renberg said curtly.

Harding glanced at the list. "Do I need to make a copy?"

"It's yours," Renberg replied. "You stole it, remember?"

"Pinhead in a hayfield," Harding murmured softly. He folded the paper twice before looking up at Renberg. "Thanks," he said with a glint in his eye. "We're even."

"For God's sake, Dick," Renberg pleaded. "Be careful."

Harding responded with a straight-faced wink. He turned and walked out of the apartment.

*   *   *

Sadie Harding groaned as she stumbled out of bed. The digital clock at her bedside showed it was almost eight, leaving her just over an hour to shower, dress, grab some breakfast, and drive across town to make her appointment.

She kept the shower brief, barely in and out, just enough to jar the sleep out of her senses. Her short hair was a definite plus at times like this, as she could pass on the blow-dryer yet still get the wind-ruffled look she favored by driving with the Golf's top down. Makeup was no problem. She didn't need much, and what little color and liner she did use she'd apply at the traffic lights.

With practiced ease she slipped on a garter belt, G-string, bra and black stockings, wrapping them in a tight, mid-thigh-length black leather dress. It took twenty minutes to satisfy her need for food, coffee, and cocaine, all pre-requisites for the morning's activities.

It was a clear morning, perfect for driving with the top down. After skipping down the steps, she turned left towards the single covered parking space assigned to apartment 202, only to come to an abrupt stop. Her car wasn't there. She hurried back to the apartment and checked Richard's bedroom. The bed was empty and, like the rest of the room, a mess. Back in the kitchen she found the message, scribbled on a piece of paper under a magnet on the refrigerator: *Sade, I borrowed the car. Call me when you need It—Dick.*

"Damn you, Richard," she hissed, picking up the phone. She dialed his pager, yelled out her message, and hung up.

When ten minutes passed without him calling back, Sadie turned livid. She tried his pager again and got the same response.

"Son of a bitch!" she fumed.

Her options were few. She could catch a cab to the hotel, but she'd probably be late. She would straighten her brother out later.

*   *   *

Richard Harding could barely contain his excitement. In the two years since he'd caught the bug, he'd cracked a variety of corporate, institutional and government computers. For the most part he'd break into a system for the sheer thrill of it, browse around, then get out, leaving no trace. It was part addiction to the technology, part egotistic power play, and part rebellion against the arbitrariness of society's rules. He thrived on the intoxicating exhilaration of cracking a code, figuring a password, or discovering a user ID. More than an obsession, it was, pure and simple, a lifestyle. But for all his brazen forays into proprietary information systems, he'd never before ventured inside the Pentagon's network. Now that he was on the verge of doing so, he felt the familiar rush, the onset of a high so powerful its mere anticipation was itself a high.

His excitement ebbed as he pulled into Pantheon's parking lot. He was going to have to keep his strategy under wraps. Despite their readiness to cross a line to see what the competition was bidding, the people at Pantheon would never condone his approach. Penetrating Systek's computer network was one thing. Violating the inner sanctum of America's defense establishment was entirely another.

Harding flashed Rosie Eisen a smile as he approached her desk. "Is Barry in?" he asked.

Neale's secretary pointed at the ceiling. "He's upstairs. Department heads meeting."

"I just wanted to check in."

"I'll tell him."

Harding waited at his assigned cubicle. Within minutes Barry Neale appeared at his side.

"I'm going to be in meetings most of the day," Neale said. "Let Rosie know if anything happens."

"I will," Harding replied, watching him go. The meeting suited him just fine. With Neale gainfully employed on another floor, the coast would be clear.

He gave Neale time to get back upstairs, then installed a floppy disk into the computer and activated the PC's capture function. It was standard modus operandi that ensured everything appearing on his screen would automatically be saved on the floppy for later review. He glanced over his shoulder, reached into his pocket and retrieved Renberg's numbers.

His pulse quickened as he ran his eyes down the list. Starting at the top, he decided initially to try only those numbers next to which Renberg had scribbled the word *computer*.

The first two numbers resulted in a *This number has been disconnected* message on his screen. It was par for the course. The third number prompted him to transmit his facsimile message. He'd connected to a fax machine, probably located somewhere within the Pentagon. Under different circumstances he might have transmitted some obscene message signed by Saddam Hussein, but this was no time for games. He moved on.

The first response of interest came when he tried the seventh number on the list:

```
THIS IS GATEKEEPER
UNAUTHORIZED ACCESS PROHIBITED
PENTAGON SECURE ID
CHALLENGE: 35578164
RESPONSE:
```

Harding's eyes were glued to the screen. The message told him he was knocking on the door of a Pentagon computer. He had no idea which one, what it was, how big it was, what kind of information it contained, which departments accessed it, or anything else. But he knew two things. It was a computer at the Pentagon. And SECURE ID told him he wasn't about to get through this particular door.

"Fuck," he murmured softly, folding his arms as he leaned back in the chair. He stared at the screen in silence and reached for the keyboard. He disconnected the line, consulted Brad Renberg's list, and proceeded to dial the next number.

*   *   *

The visitor to Austin stepped out of his Four Seasons hotel room and turned right, towards the elevators. He'd barely taken four steps when he heard the first moan. Stopping abruptly, he strained his ears, took a step back, and glanced to his left at the door to room 1224. The moaning came again, this time synchronized with the creaking of a bed. The visitor checked both sides of the corridor and held his ground, mesmerized by the sounds of live sex on the home stretch.

The couple in the room was oblivious to the world outside. The man suddenly relaxed on top of his partner and they lay still, his panting subsiding as the sweat trickled off his body onto hers before soiling the sheets. They never heard the soft chuckle outside the door, or the sound of footsteps fading down the hall.

"Damn," he whispered, rolling off her onto the bed. "It's already ten-thirty."

She was still lying in bed, smoking a cigarette when he came out of the shower.

"You need to kick that," he said, drying himself in front of the mirror. "It makes you smell like an ashtray."

"Don't talk to me like that," she said.

"You're on my time, remember? I'll decide how we talk."

She ignored the remark. Some were just more abusive than others. She watched him zip up his pants and buckle his belt. He picked his jacket off a chair and slung it over his arm as he turned to face her. "Be out of here in ten minutes," he said firmly. He unlocked the door, stepped out, and let it swing shut behind him.

She waited a few seconds before locking the door again. She took a final drag on the cigarette and exhaled the smoke as she reached under the bed for her purse. She took out the micro-cassette recorder and pushed its rewind button before tossing it on the bed beside her. In the couple of minutes it took to rewind the tape she helped herself to two snorts, one in each nostril. She leaned back against the pillows stacked behind her and slipped on the lightweight headphones. With the moans and grunts of fornication filling her ears, Sadie Harding smiled wistfully and shook her head.

She was oblivious to the turning heads as she strode out of the Four Seasons Hotel. Two middle-aged couples getting out of a rented Cadillac were being tended to by a bus boy as a valet took care of the car. The men had *Wow!* in mind as their wives thought *Bitch!* Accustomed to the attention, Sadie ignored them and climbed into the waiting cab.

The ride home took ten minutes. The first thing she did when she walked in was check the answering machine. There were no messages. She paged her brother again.

"Richard," she said in a gentler tone than before. "Sorry about the earlier message. It's twelve ten and I'm at home. I need the car. Please call me."

Twenty minutes later she left the apartment again, angrily slamming the door behind her. The little shit still hadn't called.

*   *   *

Richard Harding was flustered by his lack of progress. It was already lunchtime and he'd tried fifty-six numbers from Renberg's list, all to no avail. It was time to improvise. He cleared his screen and wandered over to Rosie Eisen's desk.

"Is Barry still upstairs?"

"Yes," she replied from behind a sandwich. "Do you need him?"

"Oh, it can wait." He glanced inside Neale's office. The screen saver on Neale's monitor was one Harding hadn't seen before. The head of a great white shark came out of a murky ocean surface and locked jaws around a piece of meat tethered to a rope. It shook from side to side before disappearing with a splash.

"Neat screen saver," he mused. "Say, y'all go on line with the Pentagon don't you?"

Eisen nodded. "Mr. Neale logs in every morning."

It was as he had figured. "That sandwich is making me hungry," he said. "I'm going to get some lunch. I'll be back in an hour."

As soon as Rosie Eisen informed him of Harding's departure, Barry Neale skipped downstairs to set up his electronic peephole. He stopped short of testing it, fearing Harding might notice his computer had been tampered with in his absence. But Neale had used the sniffer before and didn't need to test it. Once he had it up and running, he knew it would perform.

Richard Harding, on the other hand, skipped lunch. After calling ahead to make sure Sadie wasn't there, he drove home, spent a few minutes in his bedroom, then took the most direct route back to Pantheon. He returned to his cubicle with a black Nike gear bag slung over his shoulder. He slid it under the desk and checked in with Barry Neale. He found Neale busy at a monitor in the computer room. When Harding stuck his head in and announced he was resuming the hunt, Neale acknowledged him and wished him luck.

Back at his desk, Harding proceeded with his charade. Knowing that Systek's telephone number was 619-468-6888, he ran a program that automatically dialed every possible telephone number that started with the 468 prefix in the 619 area code. He sat back and watched as his computer dutifully responded, dialing all the numbers in succession while highlighting all combinations that were connections to computers. It was an exercise he'd already been through a few days earlier, but repeating it served his need to look busy while buying time.

Barry Neale was ready. As his monitor displayed Harding's keystrokes, Neale felt a thrill ripple through his body. It was awesome to be surreptitiously one up on a hacker. Moments later, satisfied the sniffer was doing its job, he left the computer room, informed his secretary he was rejoining the staff meeting, and headed back upstairs.

Richard Harding waited until the computer department's double-doors swung shut before going about his real business of the afternoon. He retrieved the Nike bag from under the desk, set it on his lap, and emptied it of its contents.

First out was a laptop computer that he laid on the desk. Next he fished out two identical homemade receivers, each the size of a car radio and with a single plastic knob on its front. A pair of smaller boxes sporting a small digital display followed the receivers. Last out of the bag were a handful of cables and a roll of wire.

He interconnected one receiver to one of the display boxes and the laptop. He screwed one end of the wire into the antenna terminal on the back plate of the receiver, uncoiled the remainder, and taped the other end to the metal frame of the window. After plugging the receiver into a 120-volt outlet, he settled back, his eyes on the laptop's screen, his thumb and forefinger gently rotating the tuning knob on the receiver.

Within moments the screen displayed neat rows and columns of numbers in what appeared to be a spreadsheet. With a few twists of the knob the image was replaced by what Harding was looking for. The head of a great white shark rose out of the water, its jaws snapping shut around a large cut of raw meat on the end of a line before it disappeared under the surface. A thin smile broke on his face as he watched the sequence repeat itself. He glanced at the frequency counter and committed the displayed number to memory. Then he set the receiver, counter and laptop in the empty hanging file drawer at the bottom of the desk. As best he could, he concealed the power cord and antenna wire between the desk and the wall. The spare receiver, frequency counter, wire and tape all went back into the gear bag.

With his surveillance gear safely stowed, Harding relaxed. He stepped out of the cubicle and turned left, away from Rosie Eisen's station. Feigning interest in the computer equipment behind the smoked glass wall of the computer room, he walked to the far wall, then turned and walked back, sneaking a glance inside the three other cubicles as he passed them. Two were vacant, their normal occupants hunched over a printer in the computer room. Stan Gertner, the programmer in the third, took his eyes off the spreadsheet displayed on his monitor long enough to acknowledge Harding with a casual nod, then turned back to his work. Satisfied, Harding headed to Barry Neale's office. By the time Rosie Eisen told him Neale was upstairs, Harding had already glanced at Neale's monitor.

"Ah…it's not important," he said, turning to face her. "It can wait."

Back at his desk Harding took the laptop out of the drawer and flipped the screen up. The great white shark was doing its drill. Harding typed two commands on the keyboard, tilted the screen down, placed the laptop back in the drawer and slid the drawer shut. Having confirmed that of the desktop machines in the computer department only Barry Neale's displayed a shark on its monitor, it was now a simple waiting game.

Several times that afternoon Barry Neale slipped into the computer room and checked a monitor. Each time he surmised that, despite his best efforts, Harding had made no progress.

*   *   *

It was 6:15 that evening when Brad Renberg's doorbell and telephone rang simultaneously. As always when someone was at the door, Mutley started barking.

"I'll be right there!" Renberg yelled in the direction of the door. After noting the telephone number on the caller I.D. display, he picked up the phone. With a hasty "Hold just a sec, Dick," he put the phone down, told Mutley to stop barking, and opened the front door.

Kelly Calloway brushed past as Renberg stepped aside to let her in.

"Hi Mutt!" She leaned towards the white German shepherd and let him lick her face.

"That smells good," Renberg said, his eyes on the casserole in her hands. He closed the door as she walked into the kitchen. "Let me just get this," he added, reaching for the phone.

"What now?" he said into the mouthpiece.

"It's Sadie, Brad."

"Sadie! I'm sorry, I thought it was Richard."

"I'm looking for him. You wouldn't know where he is?"

"Uh…no," he replied warily. "Is anything wrong?"

"He's had my car all day. I need it and I can't find him."

"Have you tried paging him?"

"Several times. If you hear from him, tell him I need my car."

"Ok," Renberg replied. He hung up the phone as Kelly set plates down on the table.

"Is everything ok?" she asked, noticing his frown.

"Yeah, fine."

He could tell from her expression she didn't quite believe him.

"Just starving," he said, patting his stomach.

"Good. I'll go get the salad."

As Kelly skipped across the landing to her apartment, Renberg's thoughts returned to Richard Harding. Not for the first time that day, he felt distinctly uneasy. Giving Harding the dialups had been a bad idea. He hoped it wouldn't come back to bite him.

"You look a million miles away." Kelly observed when she returned. "What's troubling you?"

"Oh…nothing. The usual. Life. Schoolwork."

She turned to face him. "Do you want to be alone, Brad?"

"Hell, no," he replied, snapping out of it. If anything was going to get his mind off Richard Harding, it was the sweetness of Kelly Calloway's face. In the few weeks since she'd moved in next door, he'd grown to appreciate more about her than just the obvious physical attributes. The fact that she'd kept him at bay only heightened the air of intrigue about her. "Do I want to be alone…" he muttered in jest.

"Well, you just seem so…preoccupied."

"I am," he conceded. "I need to remember to go check on my mom tomorrow."

She pulled a chair out and sat down. "Check on her?"

"Mom's diabetic," he explained, "and she can't be trusted to take her daily insulin shots by herself. She lives with my Aunt Charlene—her sister—who takes care of her. Charlene's leaving tonight and she won't be back till Wednesday evening. I just need to make sure mom takes the insulin."

Kelly reached for the salad bowl. "Where's your dad? By the way, do you mind if we turn this off?" She gestured towards the muted TV.

"Hold it!" He grabbed the remote and switched the volume on. She turned to the television in time to catch the tail end of a Pentagon spokesman in front of a microphone in what looked like a press briefing. As Renberg increased the volume, the picture reverted to the evening broadcast's anchor and the next item on the news.

"Shit!" Renberg hissed.

"What?" Kelly asked. "What is it?"

He didn't respond and Kelly looked back at the TV. The Pentagon story was gone, an item about doctor-assisted suicide in its place.

"What was so important?" she asked, stepping into the living room next to him.

"Nothing," he replied, tossing the remote back onto the couch.

"Are you sure?" she persisted.

He went back to the table and sat down. "Let's eat."

She was dying to ask again but thought better of it. When he looked up at her, there was a look in his eyes she hadn't seen before. A distant, detached look that she couldn't put her finger on. It reminded her just how little she actually knew Brad Renberg.

Thirty minutes later he was waiting and she was watching. As CNN's Headline News recycled, the Pentagon story played over. The Pentagon spokesman insisted there was no evidence whatsoever that United States Armed Forces personnel had ever been exposed to biological or chemical weapons during the Gulf war. The Pentagon had conducted its own conclusive tests, the spokesman asserted, that failed to lend credence to the claims made by a growing number of Gulf War veterans. It was the Pentagon's position, he continued, that there was no such phenomenon as the so-called Gulf War Syndrome.

"Liars!"

Calloway was taken aback by the venom with which Renberg punctuated the word. It was the first time she'd had seen him display such emotion.

He caught the surprise on her face. "Leave it alone," he whispered.

Despite her gnawing curiosity, Kelly Calloway knew enough to do just that.

*   *   *

Leaving Harding alone at Pantheon after hours was out of the question. Barry Neale stuck around, busying himself in his office and occasionally checking a monitor in the computer room. Harding patiently played out his act, doing enough to convince Neale he was still searching for the elusive cyber-trail, while quietly buying time and keeping his fingers crossed. Just after eight-thirty, while focused on the sound of Neale tapping away on his keyboard, Harding retrieved his gear bag and deftly interconnected the second receiver and frequency counter to the desktop machine. In the same manner as before, he clipped a length of wire off the roll and connected it to the receiver. He adjusted the frequency until the desktop monitor displayed a new screen of text. A quick check of the laptop in the drawer confirmed it was the text on Neale's monitor. For last good measure, Harding checked that the two frequency counters displayed different numbers. Then he smiled, concealed the tools of his trade, and decided to call it a day.

A few minutes later Harding reported to Neale that his effort to uncover details of Systek Corporation's SMARTS bid had borne no fruit. As they left the offices of Pantheon Telesystems, the two men parted ways reminding each other that there was always tomorrow.

CHAPTER TWO

Tuesday, September 3

"You want to know why I'm mad?" Sadie Harding scowled at her brother across the breakfast table. "First you take my car without asking, which is bad enough, then you disappear all day and half the night, I have no idea where you are, and you don't call back when I page you! You show *no* consideration for my needs! Asshole!"

Harding winced and looked up from the bowl of cereal. "You were asleep when I left and I didn't want to wake you."

"Why didn't you call back when I paged you?"

"For fuck's sake, Sadie, I forgot to turn my pager on yesterday. And I told you, I'm working on something important."

"And my life isn't important?" she shrilled. "Who pays the bills around here?"

"Oh, man!"

"Don't you ever...*ever* take my car again without asking."

"I'm sorry, Sade. You were asleep. Pretty soon here I'll be able to pay my share of the bills for months."

She turned away and yanked open the refrigerator. "That'll be the day."

He finished his breakfast in silence, giving her time to drink her coffee and calm down. "What time did you get in?" he eventually asked.

"Five."

"Did you have a rough night?"

"I've seen worse."

He decided to wait a little longer. He left her with her coffee and went to take a shower. When he returned twenty minutes later she was nibbling on a piece of toast and he decided to go for it.

"What have you got going today?" he asked amicably.

"What's it to you?" She was obviously still steaming, but the clock showed 7:42 and he needed to get rolling.

"I'm wondering if I can…I'm wondering if you need your car."

"I don't believe this, Richard!"

"Sadie, this job is worth ten grand to me, okay? I'm close to being done."

She stared at him in alarm. "What the hell are you doing that's worth ten grand?"

"Don't worry. It's a legitimate job with a real company. They need my expertise, and I need the cash."

"Ten grand?" she asked incredulously.

"You've always said I need to stop screwing around and start earning some real money. Well, this is it."

"*Ten grand?* For how much time? And what about school?"

"It shouldn't be more than a couple more days. School will be there when I'm done. And I'll be able to pay some bills. Besides, this should open some doors for me."

A familiar empathy welled up inside her. Ever since the day—now almost ten years ago—when she'd watched Richard force his way between their mother and the barbarian that passed as a stepfather, watched the big bastard beat up on her nine-year-old brother like he was a punching bag, she'd never overcome her weakness for him. And when their mother had died two days later of head injuries, and the state had locked the barbarian up where he belonged, Sadie and Richard Harding had found themselves with nothing left in life but each other. She had done what it took to support them, and he'd never let her down. She was eternally grateful that when he did get addicted it was to computers, not dope. She'd long hoped it would be their ticket to a better life. If this really was the beginning …

"I need to go to the gym this morning," she said reluctantly. "Wait a few minutes till I'm ready and drive me there. I'll catch a cab back."

"Jeez, thanks, Sade."

"Have it back here at noon."

"Whatever you say."

"And turn your pager on."

"Love you, Sade," he said, pecking her on the cheek. "I'll be in my room. Holler when you're ready."

"I love you too," she whispered after him.

*   *   *

After dropping his sister off at the gym it was a twenty-minute drive to Pantheon, and again Harding kept his fingers crossed. He pulled into a visitor space in the parking lot at 8:16, and presented himself at the door to Barry Neale's office a few minutes later.

"Good morning," Neale said, looking up from his desk.

"Morning," Harding replied, his eyes on Neale's monitor.

"I'll be upstairs in Engineering most of the morning. Tell Rosie if you need me."

Harding turned to leave.

"Good luck!" Neale called after him.

"Yeah," Harding muttered. "We're gonna need it."

Back at his cubicle, Harding switched on the desktop monitor and stole a furtive glance inside the bottom drawer. Everything was as he'd left it the night before. He was eager to see what it had in store for him, but he waited. It didn't take long. The first time he heard the department doors it was one of the programmers arriving for work. The second time it was Barry Neale heading for the elevators.

Harding sprang into action. The laptop was out of the drawer in an instant, on the desk, screen up, keyboard at his command. He scrolled backwards, his concentration on the screen total. Within seconds he had highlighted seven rows:

```
Dialing Pentagon Gatekeeper port 35 (202-555-4735).
Connected
THIS IS GATEKEEPER
UNAUTHORIZED ACCESS PROHIBITED
PLEASE IDENTIFY YOURSELF: B. Neale 44853
PASS KEY: XXXXXXXXXX
Last login September 3, 1996 @ 7:37 a.m.
```

Harding scribbled down the telephone number on the first row, then the letters and digits following the first colon. He switched on the desktop monitor and scrolled back one screen. He scribbled down the nine key entries in the row under B. Neale 44853, noting with exactitude the spaces, periods, upper and lower case letters, and exclamation mark. He put the laptop back in the drawer before turning back to the desktop machine.

Using the keyboard's number keys he instructed the computer to dial 202-555-4735. The screen displayed:

```
Dialing Pentagon Gatekeeper port 35 (202-555-4735)
```

Moments later, the on-screen message grew:

```
Connected
THIS IS GATEKEEPER
UNAUTHORIZED ACCESS PROHIBITED
PLEASE IDENTIFY YOURSELF:
```

Harding glanced at the notepad, hit the spacebar once, and typed in:

```
B. Neale 44853
```

In response to the PASS KEY prompt he again referred to the notepad and, taking care to get it right, entered:

```
Gr8 Whyte!
```

Another line immediately appeared on the screen, telling Harding that the last login was on September 3, 1996, at 8:22 a.m. He understood the message to mean he was through the first door—to him the most important one. In response to the GATEKEEPER> prompt that appeared next, he typed the words *show hosts*. A list instantly appeared on the screen, representing all of the computers he could access from his current position in the system. The first entry was:

        PENDIT2—Military Affairs Division 5.3.

He highlighted it and pressed the *Enter* key. The monitor screen cleared to show:

        SUNOS—V4.1.0
        LOGIN:
        PASSWORD:

"Yes!" Harding hissed to himself. To his skilled eye, the banner on the screen identified the PENDIT2 computer as having a UNIX operating system, the one favored over all others by hackers. He immediately responded to the LOGIN and PASSWORD prompts by typing *SYNC*. The message on the screen told him his attempt to log in to the computer was incorrect. With nary a second's hesitation, he tried *NUUCP*. The result was the same. He tried TROUBLE, ADM, and SYSADM, each time failing to log in. But now he was brimming with confidence. It was just a matter of time.

A few seconds later, with UUCP, he finally scored. He felt the rush of euphoria as PENDIT2's *Message of the Day* appeared, indicating he was in. The screen filled with information about the computer he'd logged in to, including its uptime, downtime, its scheduled maintenance, who to call with problems, and the system administrator's telephone number. As if needing to pinch himself to confirm he wasn't dreaming, Harding reached for his cell phone and dialed the number. He waited tensely until a male voice answered.

"Military affairs information systems support."

Harding immediately hung up, leaned back in the chair and closed his eyes, an ear-to-ear smile on his face. *"Yes!"* he hissed again, pumping a clenched fist in triumph. *"Yyyes!"*

*   *   *

Just as Richard Harding's spirits were stoked by the positive start to his day, Jim Marshall's were dampened by Barry Neale's no-progress report.

"All he's been able to come up with is e-mail addresses at Systek, but that doesn't do us any good. He hasn't been able to connect to their mainframe. Yesterday he was knocking on the door, but we don't have the magic word."

"How do we find it?" Marshall asked impatiently.

"If I knew I wouldn't need Harding."

"Yeah," Marshall said. "Okay. Do we have those amendments yet?"

"They hadn't been sent when I checked late yesterday," Neale replied. "They should be here this morning."

"Get them to me as soon as you see them," Marshall instructed.

"You'll be the first to know," Neale said as he walked out of the office.

*   *   *

To manually go through every file in PENDIT2 was unthinkable. Instead, Richard Harding used GREP, a UNIX operating system command that conducts a near-instantaneous search of the computer's memory for every occurrence of any specified word.

Harding started by seeking any file with the word *Systek* in its name. The search, which took a blink of an eye, came up empty. He next commanded an expanded search, covering all the contents of all the files stored in PENDIT2's memory for any mention of *Systek*. Although it took longer, the effort was again fruitless.

Once again he commanded a search of PENDIT2, this time for *Systek* spelled backwards. The result was the same as before. Pressing on, he tried *contract*. The screen immediately filled up with rows of text culled from different files. Harding hastily scrolled through the information before him, looking for anything remotely connected to Systek. Still he found nothing. Brad Renberg's description of the pinhead in a hayfield flashed through his mind. Succumbing to his suspicion that he was better off doing a quick sweep of the computers on the network—the hacker's equivalent of channel surfing—than wasting too much precious time on PENDIT2, Harding manipulated the operating system, recalling the LIST command. Less than a minute later, he had left PENDIT2 and accessed another machine, NAVTAS.

When an identical series of searches on NAVTAS bore the same results as on PENDIT2, Harding moved on to a third machine, PACTAN3. As he prepared to repeat the search routine, he glanced again at his watch. Just over twelve minutes had elapsed since he'd assumed, as far Pentagon Gatekeeper Port 35 was concerned, the identity of Barry Neale.

           ★   ★   ★

Neale's entry into the computer room was greeted by Stan Gertner's announcement that the SMARTS contract amendments had downloaded. Relieved that at least one of the day's objectives had been achieved, Neale asked Gertner to print them.

"It's already done," Gertner said, pointing to a wire basket adjacent to the printer.

Neale reached for the hard copy. As could be expected from the United States government, a full set of the revised General Conditions had printed—one hundred and sixty eight pages in all—despite the fact that only four pages, those addressing required documentation for contractor requests for payment, had actually been amended. All it is is taxpayer money, Neale mused as he thumbed through the sheets.

Aware that Marshall and the bid preparation team were all anxious to review the amendments, Neale decided Harding could wait a few minutes. With the document in hand and a word of thanks to Stan Gertner, he headed back upstairs.

           ★   ★   ★

Computer hackers are nothing if not systematic. Below the often-unkempt disarray of their physical appearance lies a well-structured, vivid understanding of the operating systems that run computers. Even the most intricate and complicated software is essentially no more than an array—albeit vast in scope—of simple instructions: If A happens, do X; if B happens do Y; if both A and B happen do Z; if neither A nor B happens…and so on. So by its very nature, the successful composition of software demands a rigidly systematic approach. To understand it to the point of being able to manipulate it, as hackers do so adroitly, requires a comparable measure of intellectual discipline. Richard Harding was therefore only being true to his nature when, just over two minutes after moving on to PACTAN3, he re-visited PENDIT2 and NAVTAS.

Having just concluded another fruitless search through PACTAN3, he'd paused, anxiously contemplating proceeding to the next machine, when it had suddenly occurred to him that he'd left out the most obvious word of all.

As a self-deprecating smile broke across his face, he once again ran the GREP command through PACTAN3, this time for SMARTS. The smile persisted when nothing came up. Relentlessly pressing on with the familiar routine, Harding repeated the process for STRAMS. When that, too, brought naught, he backtracked to PENDIT2. Once more, the result was the same. He turned again to NAVTAS.

The search for SMARTS ended as before. But when Harding ran a check for STRAMS in NAVTAS, the monitor suddenly displayed two separate rows of text, each containing one occurrence of the word. Harding sat motionless, only his eyeballs moving as he read the two rows over several times. Both rows started with the word *KORPEN*, followed by a colon, a single space, then the line of text. That told Harding that the two lines came from the same file, named KORPEN. His eyes shifted to the prompt and he typed: *more KORPEN.*

NAVTAS responded. The screen filled up with text. A message at the bottom of the screen told him what percentage of the document was currently displayed, and he quickly estimated its total length to be about three single-spaced letter-size pages. He started reading. When he reached the bottom of the screen, a single tap of the space bar moved the text up, enabling him to read on.

Six screens into the document, just as he was beginning to lose interest, Harding suddenly stiffened. He jabbed at the keyboard with his index finger, his eyes flicking left and right across the screen as they soaked in the rolling text. He sat transfixed, scrolling forward, backward, then forward again, now totally riveted to the information before him. His senses jarred, he read on until the concluding paragraph jolted him breathless. He paused long enough to check that the floppy disk was still recording everything in the external drive. After a nervous glance over his shoulder, he turned back to the screen.

*   *   *

Barry Neale watched Jim Marshall leaf through the amendments and offered his unsolicited opinion that they favored the government, not the contractor. When Marshall called his secretary in and asked her to distribute copies to the bid team members, Neale excused himself and returned to his department. He went directly to the computer room. Stan Gertner was still there, holding vigil next to the printer as it churned out another document. Neale slid into a chair, adjusted the monitor in front of him away from Gertner's line of sight, and hit a few strokes on the keyboard. He leaned back in the chair, then abruptly snapped forward again, squinting at the screen. He peered to his left, through the smoked-glass partition towards Harding's cubicle, and a hollow sense of dread overcame him.

"What the *fuck...*" he started in alarm. "*Son of a bitch!*"

Stan Gertner had never seen Barry Neale move as fast as when he shot out of the computer room.

Entranced as he was by the information before him, Richard Harding failed to register the sound of Barry Neale's footsteps until it was too late. By the time Harding saw his reflection on the screen, Neale had him by the shoulders.

"What's this?" Neale demanded, pushing Harding aside. His eyes were on the menu bar at the top of the screen. *"What the fuck is this?"*

"Let me explain," Harding began, lunging for the keyboard.

Neale threw an arm out to keep him back. "What the *hell* do you think you're doing?"

Harding dropped to one knee and reached under the desk. He yanked the floppy disk out of the computer with his right hand, while his left jerked the power plug out of its receptacle.

"What the..." Neale yelled, grabbing Harding by his neck. "Give me that!"

As he sprang up from his crouched position Harding rammed his knee hard into Neale's crotch. Neale doubled over in pain, clutching his groin as he crumpled to the floor.

By the time Rosie Eisen and Stan Gertner responded to Neale's cries and found him curled up in the fetal position where he'd collapsed, Richard Harding was already out of the building and tearing across the parking lot as fast as his legs would carry him.

CHAPTER THREE

"Y'all did *what?*" Bill Davis asked incredulously.

Jim Marshall shook his head and raised a defensive hand to his senior vice president.

"I don't believe this," Davis said across the conference table. He turned to Barry Neale. "Where'd you find this punk?"

Neale swallowed hard. "It was back in December. Harding had approached someone I know…"

"Who?" Davis snapped.

"The guy who oversees computer operations at Fidelity Bank. Harding gave him a proposal to evaluate the bank's computer system security. He said he would demonstrate how easily he could get in, and then charge the bank a fee to plug the holes. When SMARTS heated up, I figured maybe *we* could use Harding."

Davis glanced at Marshall, who looked like he was about to explode.

"Last month I went to a hacker's convention here in Austin," Neale added. "That's where I met Harding."

"A *hacker's* convention?" Davis asked.

Neale nodded. "They hold them once or twice a year. A few hackers and a bunch of hacker-wannabees get together for a weekend. I met with Harding several times over a two-week period, felt him out. He wanted to go legit. He figured he had something to offer corporate

America, and was looking to go into business for himself as a computer security expert. After clearing it with Jim, I offered to contract him to shore up our own system if he could first convince me he had what it takes. I told him about SMARTS, and suggested he demonstrate his skills by getting into Systek's system and showing me their bid."

Davis turned to Marshall. "And you bought this?"

Marshall grimaced and nodded. "It was a calculated risk."

"A *mis*calculated one, evidently," Davis noted.

"We were just thinking of the company, Bill," Neale argued.

"The son of a bitch was supposed to get into Systek's network, copy their bid file, then get out. That's what we agreed on." Marshall stared at the computer printout on his desk. "Instead, he busts into the Pentagon."

"How'd you guys find out?" Davis asked. "And where's Harding now?"

"We don't know where he is. When Barry confronted him the son of a bitch bolted."

Bill Davis was aghast. "Is this something we can just let lie?"

Marshall sighed. He picked up the printout and dropped it on the conference table in front of Davis. "When Barry confronted him, Harding was reading something."

Jim Marshall and Barry Neale remained silent and motionless as Davis glanced at the printout. "Reading what?"

"A file called KORPEN," Marshall said gloomily

"So? What the hell is KORPEN?"

"We don't know." Marshall glanced at Neale, who dropped into a chair opposite Davis at the conference table. He swallowed hard, hating his life.

"Before he ran out…just before he kneed me, Harding took a disk out of the computer." He licked his lips nervously as Davis stared at him. "In all likelihood, he was copying everything. Which would mean he's out there…with a copy of KORPEN. Whatever it is."

"That's great," Davis said in exasperation. He shot a troubled look at Marshall. "What are we going to do?"

"Uh…" Neale started, "for what it's worth, hackers rarely do any harm in situations like this. This isn't some gang busting into the brains of an ATM machine. Harding's probably scared out of his wits right now because we caught him. But I don't think…"

"We need to talk to Harding," Marshall said.

"Harding?" Davis said indignantly. "We need to talk someone at the Pentagon! *Now!*"

Marshall winced.

"So we screwed up," Davis argued. "How bad, we don't know. But I'll tell you what. Harding may not do anything with this, but we can't take the chance. Before this thing gets out of hand, we need to own up and come clean."

"Shit!" Marshall hissed.

"Just a second," Neale interjected. "We don't have to tell anyone the real reason Harding was here. We could claim we hired him to beef up our system."

"We can say what we want but it's beside the point." Bill Davis turned to Marshall. "Jim?"

Jim Marshall had a pained expression on his face. "You want me to call the Pentagon?"

"For Christ's sake Jim," Davis pleaded. "Let's not make this worse."

There was silence as Marshall thought it over. "You said Harding impersonated you to get into the Pentagon's system," he said to Barry Neale. "Let's go back in there and read KORPEN. Let's find out what it is."

Neale pondered the proposition. "I guess…we could do that. I could re-trace his keystrokes and…"

"Bull*shit!*" Davis slammed his hand down hard on Marshall's desk. "Are you guys out of your minds? I'm telling you, we don't touch Korpen or Korpass or whatever the hell it is. We call Bryant *now*, and hopefully nip this thing in the bud."

"Yeah," Jim Marshall said softly, his shoulders slumping. Davis was right and he knew it. "As much as I hate to…"

There was no masking his dejection as he reached for the phone.

                  *   *   *

Don't panic. Neale's ass is on the line. He won't say anything.
Will he?
Fuck! How much did he see?
He must've known it was the Pentagon. Why else would he go crazy like that?
Surely he won't risk implicating himself by saying anything?
Gotta tell Zube. The son of a bitch is gonna get high on this.

                  *   *   *

Brad Renberg instinctively took his foot off the accelerator as he reached to the passenger seat. He silenced the pager, checked the number, and considered what to do about Richard Harding.

On the one hand Harding could be getting himself in trouble. More likely he was still running into brick walls on the Pentagon thing, and needed help. Regardless, Renberg wanted no part of it.

He tossed the pager back on the passenger seat, and checked his watch. San Marcos was just five minutes away. Harding could go to hell.

                  *   *   *

Son of a bitch. Answer, Goddamit!
Harding took the steps in twos.

"Sadie?" he called into the apartment. There was no reply as he locked the door. A quick look in her room told him he was alone.

He reached for his desktop computer's keyboard and noticed the shake in his fingers.

Why the fucking jitters? Neale will keep his trap shut. It would be his ass on the line as much as mine.

Won't he?

He clasped his hands together tightly and closed his eyes. He brought his head down to his hands and rested his forehead on his thumbs, trying desperately to think straight. He played over in his mind the scuffle with Neale. At least he'd logged into the Pentagon as Neale. Technically, there was nothing to tie him to it personally...except fingerprints, maybe. He considered where his prints might be. On the keyboard, the chair, the desk...

"*Fuck!*" he groaned, suddenly remembering his laptop. He sprang up and frantically rummaged through his desk, hoping for a miracle, his laptop computer and the Nike gear bag.

"Fuck, fuck, *fuck!*"

Unable to stem the inexorable sense of dread, he rushed back out of the apartment.

*   *   *

Under the direction of the secretary of defense, the under secretary of defense (Acquisition) acts as the principal staff assistant and advisor to the secretary for all matters relating to the Department of Defense Acquisition System, research and development, production, logistics, military construction, and procurement. The under secretary's functions are carried out with the support of ten key personnel, one of whom, the director of defense procurement, was a mild-mannered fifty-two year old Texan by the name of Wayne L. Bryant.

Banking on the strength of their long standing personal friendship, one that pre-dated either man's involvement in America's military establishment, a chagrined Jim Marshall hesitatingly bounced his predicament off Wayne Bryant, and sheepishly requested the latter's guidance on how to proceed. After asking eight questions, the responses to which served only to progressively heighten his alarm, Bryant instructed Jim Marshall to sit tight and stay by his phone.

Staring at the notes he'd scribbled down while talking to Marshall, Bryant reached behind him for his copy of the 80,000-listing Department of Defense Telephone Directory. It didn't take long to find the number he was looking for, even less to dial and connect to it.

In his cramped office in the building's basement, Stephen Swensson listened attentively, jotted down a few notes of his own, then promised Bryant he'd get right on it. Twelve minutes later, when a panting Wayne Bryant reached the basement suite of offices occupied by the Defense Information Systems Agency, Swensson was hunched over his desk, staring grimly at the document on his desk. His expression didn't change as he stood to shake Bryant's hand.

"Did you find it?" Bryant asked, glancing at the desk.

Swensson nodded and gestured to the visitor's chair as he reached behind Bryant to close the door.

"Here," he said, handing Bryant three pages.

The silence in the room was punctured twice by expletives. By the time he reached the end of the third page, Bryant's face was set in a deep frown.

"How did you learn of this?" Swensson asked.

Bryant hesitated. "Someone stumbled upon it...by accident...and told me to check it out."

Swensson nodded. "What are you going to do?"

Bryant sniffled nervously. "Is it still on NAVTAS?"

Again Swensson nodded.

"Can you get it off?"

"You mean delete it?"

Bryant shrugged his shoulders. "I guess."

"I'd need authorization."

It was Bryant's turn to nod. "Yeah." He stared blankly at the document before looking up at Swensson again. "Let me see your phone book."

Swensson reached into a drawer. "Who are you calling?"

"Tesko. Under Sec Acquisition. I'll let him take it from here." He was stone-faced as he leafed through the phone book. "I'm not into handling fireballs."

Bryant's choice of words was apt. No sooner had he apprised the under secretary of defense (Acquisition) of the situation, than sparks began flying in earnest. Lance Tesko demanded Bryant immediately seal his mouth and accompany him to the office of the deputy secretary of defense. When Ellen Rundle showed the two men into Robert Carlson's office, their grim faces forewarned him of trouble. Their tale delivered a bombshell.

Carlson was appalled to learn they were in possession of a copy of his April 12th memorandum to Secretary of Defense Roone Hackelman.

"Is this some kind of bad joke?" he asked. Tesko had never seen him look so pathetic.

"No joke, Bob," Lance Tesko said dryly as he handed Carlson the document. "Wayne got a call from a defense contractor in Texas, an outfit called Pantheon Telesystems. Apparently they hired a contract computer security expert to work on their system, only he turned out to be more than that. He busted into one of our computers and saw this. Robert, our best information is he's out there with a copy."

Carlson was frozen in stunned disbelief. "No!" he whispered. "That's impossible!"

There was no need for Tesko to respond. The hard copy spoke for itself.

"*Impossible!*" Carlson whispered, rising behind the desk. He went to Ellen Rundle's station and asked to view filenames in one of her directories. When he returned moments later he was on the verge of panic.

"Wayne," he said, a blank hollowness permeating every last vestige of his soul, "I appreciate your diligence in bringing this matter to our attention. I trust, gentlemen, you recognize this is classified material of a…uh, highly sensitive nature."

Tesko and Bryant nodded solemnly.

"Good. I trust, then, you recognize the absolute need for discretion regarding this document."

"I have no knowledge of the document you're referring to, sir," Bryant said.

"Good man. Now tell me how you came to learn of it."

As Bryant recounted his conversations with Jim Marshall and Stephen Swensson, Carlson jotted down their names, adding quick notes next to each.

"You can reach Marshall?" he asked.

"I told him to sit by his phone."

"Good. Call him, right now, and get every last detail of what happened down there. I want names—everyone involved. We need to know exactly who saw what. Most of all, we need to know who—and where—this hacker guy is."

"I understand."

"Now," Carlson said, pointing to a phone on the coffee table next to Bryant.

As Wayne Bryant started dialing, Carlson picked up the receiver on his own phone. "Ellen, I need Ed Harkutlian, ASAP. And get a message to Hackelman…I know he's with the committee—get a message to him to call me. Tell 'em both it's urgent!"

He replaced the receiver and looked over at Wayne Bryant. The director of defense procurement had his ear glued to the phone and was scribbling away on a note pad.

*   *   *

Secretary of State Edward Harkutlian was en route to the State Department when he learned of the unfolding disaster. He was flabbergasted to learn Robert Carlson had documented minutes of their April 12th meeting, more so that a copy of the memorandum had been saved on a Pentagon computer. Harkutlian dismissed as redundant Carlson's insistence that he had personally erased it the day it was written, and focused instead on damage control. He kept Carlson holding and considered how best to react.

Under normal circumstances Harkutlian would have contacted the U.S. attorney general, who would then take it upon herself to call FBI Director Brent Zarbach. But that was under normal circumstances. In this case, two factors held him back. First, the violation had occurred at the Pentagon. The attorney general was bound to find it odd that the secretary of state was calling about a problem at the Department of Defense. Second, in addition to an excellent working relationship, Harkutlian and Zarbach enjoyed a strong personal friendship. Zarbach might not be as prying as the attorney general would surely be.

At the conclusion of their exchange—conducted with scant regard for political decorum and etiquette—Harkutlian told Robert Carlson to call the attorney general and report the attack on a Pentagon computer, but to provide her with no specific information as to exactly what documents may have been violated. He then warned his driver of a possible change of destination. After confirming the director of the Federal Bureau of Investigation was available for immediate consultation, he slammed the phone down with two words: "Hoover Building." It didn't take a skilled reading of the secretary's tone. The driver flexed his right foot, uncaringly oblivious to the posted speed limits.

By the time he stepped out of his limousine and into the headquarters of the FBI, Harkutlian had coordinated what had to be said to whom by whom. When he was ushered into the office of the director, he found Zarbach on the phone, being briefed about the incident by the attorney general. As soon as he was through with that conversation, Zarbach took the conference call Harkutlian had orchestrated.

"This is an urgent matter, Brent," Harkutlian declared. "Spare no effort on this guy."

The director was about to react when a voice on the speakerphone pre-empted him.

"Brent, he's copied files that *must* be retrieved, *immediately,*" Robert Carlson urged. "We can't overstate the importance of this matter."

"They're right, Brent." Roone Hackelman's voice thundered over the speakerphone. He'd cut short his meeting with the senate foreign affairs committee as soon as he'd heard.

"What's in these files?" Brent Zarbach inquired.

"Let's not waste time with details." It was the speakerphone again, now Lee Trujillo, chairman of the Joint Chiefs of Staff. "Let's find and stop this guy before he starts posting classified Pentagon documents on the damned Internet!"

"What do we know about him?" Zarbach asked. He had a ton of other questions, but they could wait until the wheels of law enforcement had started turning.

Robert Carlson consulted the list of names Wayne Bryant had assembled for him. "His name is Richard Harding. H-A-R-D-I-N-G. He lives in Austin, Texas. He's a freshman at the University of Texas. And I'm faxing over details of Pantheon Telesystems, address, names, etc."

"Good enough for now," Zarbach said. "I'll put our best people on it and get back to you."

With urgent pleas for rapid results, the others hung up. Ed Harkutlian watched as Zarbach stayed on the phone, now on the issuing side of instructions. He noted the director's insistence that Steven Vogel drop everything to oversee the FBI investigation.

"Vogel's our top computer crime expert," Zarbach said when he put the phone down. "He's the agent who nailed Kevin Mitnick last year."

Harkutlian recognized the name. The 1995 capture of Kevin Mitnick, America's most notorious hacker, had received extensive media coverage. If Vogel was the best they had, he was hopefully good enough.

The secretary of state's mind was still whirring when he left the Hoover Building. The ride back to the State Department gave him an opportunity to mull further over the situation. Twice he reached to call the White House, and both times he held back. It was bad form to apprise the President of a problem without having a solution. Chances were the FBI would get the guy, with luck sooner rather than later. At least then they'd know the extent of the problem, and hopefully what it would take to contain it. *Then* he would tell the President. For now, he would take his chances and give Zarbach some time.

"Richard cock-sucker Harding," he growled, his face locked in a scowl. "What slime-infested gutter did your ass crawl out of?"

CHAPTER FOUR

On July 26, 1908, exercising the authority vested in him under Title 28, United States Code, Section 533, then-Attorney General Charles J. Bonaparte appointed a small force of agents to act as the investigative branch of the Department of Justice. The following year, by order of Attorney General George Wickersham, the agent force was named the Bureau of Investigation. In 1935 the word Federal was officially added to the title. From its humble beginnings, the Federal Bureau of Investigation has mushroomed over the years into an investigative juggernaut of 10,500 special agents and 14,000 professional, administrative, technical and clerical support personnel, with an annual budget of almost three billion dollars.

Each of the FBI's nine Headquarters divisions is organized along broad functional lines into sections, which are further divided into smaller, more specialized units. One of the eight sections comprising the Criminal Investigation Division, the Financial Crimes Section, consists of four units: Health Care Fraud, Financial Institution Fraud, Governmental Fraud, and Economic Crimes. Surprisingly enough from the nomenclature, it is the Economic Crimes Unit that has responsibility for investigating, among other matters, crimes involving computer fraud and abuse.

Less than fifteen minutes after Harkutlian left FBI headquarters, the bureau's Economic Crimes Unit chief briefed one of his subordinates, Supervisory Special Agent Steven Vogel, on the situation.

Vogel wasted no time. During the drive from 935 Pennsylvania Avenue to Andrews Air Force base he called the head of the FBI's resident agency in Austin, Supervisory Senior Resident Agent Mitchell Wakeman. The two talked for over ten minutes and local wheels were set in motion.

Upon arrival at Andrews, Vogel was shown aboard the FBI director's Lear C-21 by a stoic, stiff-backed sergeant of the 89th Military Airlift Wing. After the briefest of introductions, a somewhat more amiable pilot asked his passenger to fasten his seatbelt and enjoy the ride.

"How long will it be?" Vogel asked, strapping himself in.

"It depends on the jet stream," the pilot replied. "Figure around noon to twelve-thirty, Central Time."

Vogel nodded and closed his eyes, resigned to the fact that there was no faster way for him to get there. Seventeen minutes after take-off, as the Lear streaked southward at an altitude of 35,000 feet, Steven Vogel resumed working the phones. There was at least two hours of flight time ahead of him, time best spent learning all he could about Pantheon Telesystems and Richard Harding.

✦   ✦   ✦

While resident agencies, of which there are 400 or so, are satellite offices, smaller than the FBI's 56 full-fledged field offices, Austin's resident agency is the nation's largest. Mitch Wakeman commanded two squads comprising a total of 24 special agents, as well as six administrative support personnel. He immediately dispatched two men from his white-collar crime squad, Special Agent Raphael Lopez and Special Agent Steve Chase, to Pantheon Telesystems. After a quick address check with the Texas Department of Public Safety, two other special agents, Juan Camacho and Franklin Stiles, were on their way to Richard Harding's apartment. Wakeman then assigned the agency's principal legal advisor, a special agent who was also an attorney, two tasks. The first was filling in the blanks on a boilerplate Affidavit In Support of Search Warrant form for the two locations. Following that he was to process an arrest warrant for Richard Harding. Having completed the mobilization of his own staff, Wakeman contacted the Austin Police Department's High Tech Unit and initiated the establishment of a multi-agency task force. He completed protocol requirements by reporting to his immediate supervisor, the assistant special agent in charge of the San Antonio field office, and informing him of the situation.

*　　　　*　　　　*

Richard Harding pulled into a visitor parking space in front of the building immediately west of Pantheon's. His view encompassed all of Pantheon's grade-level parking lot, as well as its entrance from the freeway feeder. He killed the engine and rolled down the window. Only the intermittent ticks of metal contracting in the engine bay broke the ambient silence.

Thirty seconds. Maybe forty. Doors, lobby, hallway, doors, cubicle, then back. Forty-five max. It'll be right there in the drawer.

There was no sign of any unusual activity. It stood to reason Neale would keep his trap shut, unless he'd seen KORPEN on the screen. Then he'd panic. For the hundredth time Richard Harding pictured the scuffle with Barry Neale.

Shit. Was that panic or what?

There was no question he'd hurt him. But how bad? Had any of the others seen what had happened? And how would Neale have explained it?

Too fucking risky. Telco repair man after six'll do it. Just me and the cleaners.

He already had everything he needed. A Southwestern Bell technician's shirt, its nametag identifying the wearer as *Greg*; a Builder's Square tool belt, in its pouch a bunch of screwdrivers, Allen keys, wrenches, terminal strips, and a roll of black electrical tape. The cover was simple but effective. On the few occasions he'd used it, he'd easily cajoled unsuspecting clerks into disclosing proprietary passwords or dialups. It was, in hacker vernacular, Social Engineering 101.

Damn it's quiet. Too fucking quiet.

He was just beginning to believe he might be okay, that things might not be as bad as they'd seemed, when his reverie was abruptly shattered. First there was a wailing siren, then flashing lights as a police car lurched off the freeway onto the feeder and careened into Pantheon's parking lot. The fanfare was repeated in short order as two more patrol cars announced their arrival. But it was the car that followed them that sank Harding's heart. An unmarked white Mercury Sable, the driver obviously immune to speed limits, screeched to a halt behind the police cars. Two men in casual civilian clothes jumped out and followed the uniforms into the building. Harding was, as he put it, butt-bare broke, but he would have borrowed to bet they were from the government agency with the motto *Fidelity, Bravery, Integrity.*

Dismay gave way to dread. He cranked the ignition and gingerly backed the car out of the parking space.

Stupid son of a scumbag motherfucker!

His heart pounding, he eased the Volkswagen back onto the feeder. As his eyes flicked back and forth from the road ahead to the rearview mirror, he made a U-turn under the freeway overpass and headed back towards town.

*   *   *

"What's this?" Jim Marshall asked nervously.

"Consent to search," Special Agent Raphael Lopez replied. "You sign it, we'll get to work."

They were standing in the building's lobby, just a corridor and dou-ble doors away from the computer department. Marshall thought about what evidence might be found to point to Harding's real reason for being at Pantheon. "If I don't?" he inquired, trying not to sound con-frontational.

"If you don't, we just wait till the search warrant comes through."

Marshall's better judgement prevailed. As Barry Neale and Bill Davis watched, he signed Lopez's form.

"Where's Harding's computer?" Lopez demanded.

"Over here," Barry Neale said, leading the way. Lopez followed him to Harding's cubicle. Marshall and Davis towed along, followed by Special Agent Steve Chase. Two Austin Police Department officers stayed behind in the lobby, one at the building's front door, the other at the computer department doors, both with instructions to bar any unauthorized entry or exit until Lopez indicated otherwise. Rosie Eisen peeked out at the group from her station.

"Okay," Lopez said, looking around the cubicle. "Nobody touches anything. Nobody goes in here." He turned to the Pantheon men. "Who else here, apart from the three of you, knows about this?"

"My secretary and one of our programmers," Neale replied, gesturing towards Eisen. "They heard the scuffle with Harding, but they don't know what it was about."

"Okay. I need everyone to stay put. We'll take statements in a few minutes." Lopez glanced back into Harding's cubicle. "Is that machine networked?"

"Yes," Neale replied

"Server?"

"Uh...that's in the computer room," Neale said, pointing at the smoked glass partition.

While Steve Chase stayed at Harding's cubicle, Lopez was already on his way. "Show me."

Wishing he were an ostrich near a hole in the ground, Neale led the way into the computer room, followed by Lopez and an increasingly nervous Jim Marshall. Lopez walked around slowly, studying the layout and equipment without expression. "Which server?" he asked.

Neale pointed it out.

Lopez paused in front of the machine and decided it was a good thing Wakeman had called for technical support. "Okay. Nobody touches anything in here either. No one touches any keyboards, no one turns anything on or off, no one changes the status of any of the computers."

Barry Neale swallowed hard. Marshall frowned and dropped his head.

The technical skills required for proper securement and preservation of evidence at a computer crime scene were beyond the expertise of Raphael Lopez and Steve Chase. The FBI men were relieved when, minutes later, two APD High Tech Unit men arrived.

The tekkies looked their age. Mike Munroe was twenty-two, his partner, Clyde Swift twenty-five. They were accompanied by three more APD patrol cars, and officers were immediately posted at all doors leading in to or out of the building. Munroe and Swift took a first, perfunctory look at Harding's cubicle and the computer room, then got to work. Swift laid the bags he was carrying on the floor. He unzipped the smaller of the two, and pulled out a 35mm camera with motor drive and flash attachments, and an 8mm video camera. As Swift set about assembling his gear to videotape and photograph the cubicle and its contents, Munroe started assessing the equipment in the computer room. Moments later, Clyde Swift summoned him back to the cubicle.

"Check it out," Swift said, pointing at the desk's lower drawer. Munroe glanced at the drawer's contents and let out a long whistle. He donned a pair of latex gloves and reached into the drawer. A few seconds later he was following the wires to the crude splices at the windowsill.

"Van Eck?" Swift asked, buoyant with expectation.

"Looks like it," Munroe replied, equally impressed with the discovery.

"No shit!" Swift beckoned the Pantheon trio over. "Whose is this stuff?"

"I've never seen it before," Neale replied sheepishly.

"What is it?" Lopez asked.

Munroe's eyes were on the laptop. "Who uses a great white shark screen saver?"

The lump in Neale's throat grew. He barely got the words out. "I do. Why?"

Munroe shifted the laptop around to show the others the screen. Neale's face registered acute distress.

"Where's your computer?" Swift asked Neale.

"In my office."

"Go type something on it. Anything. Just a couple of keystrokes."

Neale did as he was told. When he rejoined the others, he was alarmed to see what he'd typed on his computer displayed on the laptop.

"What is this?" Marshall asked.

Munroe nodded knowingly. "The state of the art" he murmured.

There was silence all around.

"With this set up," Munroe said, turning to Neale, "Harding could see everything you typed on your computer."

There was an audible gasp as Neale pondered the implications.

"Did you go online with the Pentagon?" Lopez asked.

Neale took a deep breath, exhaled, and nodded.

"He piggy-backed his way in on you," Swift guessed.

Marshall was beside himself. "How?"

Munroe explained. "Computer monitors work like TV's do," he said. "In a TV, a high voltage electron beam is projected onto a the screen from the inside for a few milliseconds at a time. The screen's coated with phosphor, which glows when it's hit by the beam. The picture is created by tracing the beam around the surface of the screen—about sixty times a second—each time either making the phosphor glow or leaving it off, depending on what the picture is supposed to be."

Clyde Swift was the only person in the room familiar with what Munroe was saying. The others, including the FBI men, listened intently.

"It's a freak of nature," Munroe continued, "that any flow of electrons—which is essentially what electrical current is—always radiates an electromagnetic field. That holds true whether the electron flow takes the form of a lightning strike, or, as we have here, the beam inside a computer monitor. In effect the monitor acts like a small radio station, generating a pattern of radio waves. Have you ever leaned towards a monitor while talking on the phone?"

The Pantheon men were statues. Chase and Lopez nodded.

"You know that buzz in the ear piece? That's the monitor's electromagnetic field. The closer you get, the stronger the field, the louder the buzz."

Chase nodded again. Neale shuffled his feet and exchanged an uncomfortable glance with Jim Marshall.

"When people use a computer," Swift added, "they think the information they're typing—or viewing on the screen—is private." He shook his head. "Wrong. Just as a radio receiver reads the signals from a radio station out of thin air, so too will a receiver, if tuned to the correct frequency, pick up the signals from a computer."

Marshall went from glancing at Neale to glaring at him.

"Once it's picked up the signals, it's easy to display them on another screen. The process is called Van Eck monitoring, after the Dutch engineer who first demonstrated it."

"Something like using a sniffer?" Marshall said, his eyes still on Neale.

"Exactly," Munroe replied. "How do you know about sniffers?"

"Oh," Marshall said, turning to Munroe, "someone told me about them."

"So Harding read my keystrokes?" Neale asked, his voice hollow with dread.

"See this wire?" Swift said. "It goes from this box, which is the receiver, to the metal window frame. It's the antenna that picked up the signals. Of course he tuned it to your computer first. This here is a frequency counter that just displays the signal's frequency. And this cable takes the signal from the receiver to the laptop, where it's reproduced in its original form. And judging from the fact there are two receivers and frequency counters,

I'll bet he had one setup tuned to your monitor, the other to your keyboard. That way he could pick up any password that would appear as X's on your screen. The guy knew what he was doing."

"Christ!" Marshall groaned. "Look, we didn't know any of this was going on."

"We'll get to that," Lopez said. He turned to Munroe. "How long do you need?"

"Here, three, maybe four hours. And we'll need to take some of this stuff to the lab."

Marshall wiped a nervous hand across his mouth. "What are you saying?"

"What we're saying," Lopez replied, "is that it's probably going to take a few days to complete our investigation. And some of your equipment will have to be taken away for inspection."

"Wait, wait. We've got a business to run!"

"There's been a violation of federal and state laws here, Mr. Marshall," Lopez noted politely. "I'm afraid your business concerns will have to wait."

Barry Neale was a pathetic sight. His shoulders were slumped, his hands were in his pockets, and he was staring blankly at his shoes.

Marshall's hand flicked across his mouth again. "Well, you didn't tell me that earlier. I want to withdraw my consent until I talk to our attorney."

Lopez knew it would be a matter of thirty minutes to an hour before the search warrant was issued. By now Cooper Seigal would have filled out the affidavit and transmitted it electronically to the chief division counsel at the San Antonio field office. As soon as it was reviewed and Okayed, Seigal would run a hard copy down to the federal courthouse for review and signature by a U.S. magistrate, then personally deliver it to Pantheon. At that point, Marshall's attorney would advise his client to get the hell out of the way.

"That's fine," Lopez replied. "We'll wait for the warrant. In the meantime, nobody touches anything."

          ★   ★   ★

Come on asshole, answer your fucking phone!

Richard Harding hung up, scowling. He was getting the answering machine at Renberg's apartment, and when he paged Renberg, no response. He glanced up at the clock on the dashboard. It was about half an hour since he'd seen the feds at Pantheon. He scowled again as Barry Neale came to mind.

I hope they're frying your balls.

Renberg had to be avoiding him. At this hour, he had to be either at home or on campus. Harding pulled out of the mall parking lot, back into the street.

I hope they break 'em before they fry 'em.

    *   *   *

While Harding's hopes for the fate of Barry Neale's testicles might have been wishful thinking, he was on the mark about Brad Renberg's intentions, if not his whereabouts. The first three times his pager had beeped that morning, Renberg had checked the number, pursed his lips, then turned his attention back to the southbound traffic on I-35. He did wonder about Harding's progress, but not enough so to exit the freeway and find a phone. By the time the fourth page came through he was already pulling into the driveway at his aunt's house in San Marcos. He parked the Jeep and again checked the number. It was as expected. He pulled the pager off his belt, turned it off, and tossed it onto the passenger seat.

"Mutley, stay!"

The German Shepherd stayed in the back of the Jeep with little protest. Renberg had the key ready by the time he reached the front door. He went straight to the smaller of the two bedrooms. After a moment's hesitation at the door, he turned the handle and pushed softly.

The shades were drawn and the room was dark, but he knew where to look and quickly made out her outline. Her breathing was light and regular. For Brad it was a good sign, an indication she was comfortable. There was precious little solace in her waking hours. Ever since the bastards had turned her life into hell…

He stepped gingerly to the bedside, careful not to make a sound. As his eyes adjusted to the darkness he saw she had her back to him. He leaned down and reached out a hand to caress her hair with the lightest of touches. She never stirred when he straightened up and moved away from the bed. He paused at the door. The regular breathing continued unabated.

He stepped out of the room and gently closed the door. As he'd done countless times in his life, he cursed the bastards with a passion.

*　　　　　　　　*　　　　　　　　*

"What's happening?" Vogel's voice was clear and free of static. If he didn't know, Mitch Wakeman would never have guessed Vogel was calling from the skies over Arkansas.

"No sign of Harding. We've secured all the equipment. It's pretty elaborate in the computer room but we've got APD's High Tech boys involved. We couldn't get a consent to search the computer room so we're waiting on a warrant."

"What about Harding's apartment?"

"Our boys are there, ready to go as soon as *that* warrant comes through. It should be anytime now."

"Okay. Let me know if you get him. I'll see you in about an hour."

*　　　　　　　　*　　　　　　　　*

Kelly Calloway was sitting on the sofa in her living room when the movement at Brad Renberg's front door caught her attention. She stepped closer to the window for a better look. Richard Harding had his back to her, but he looked left and right as he knocked and she saw his face.

"You looking for Brad?" She stood in her doorway across the landing.

Harding jumped. "Yeah."

Calloway stepped out onto the landing. "He's not home."

"You know where he is?"

"No. But you're welcome to come in if you want to wait."

"I can't. If you see him, could you tell him to call Richard? It's urgent." He turned and ran down the stairs. Calloway watched him climb into the Golf.

Had he not been so preoccupied, Harding might have noticed that Mutley hadn't barked when he was at the door. Knowing well that Renberg never took Mutley to lectures, he might have surmised that searching for Renberg on campus was going to be a waste of time.

✶   ✶   ✶

As Kelly Calloway stepped back inside her apartment and closed the door, Mutley was in fact barking, but many miles away, in San Marcos. A boy riding by on a bicycle stopped to check out the fat-tired Jeep and got close enough for Mutley to take offense. Brad Renberg ran outside in time to see the alarmed kid back off and jump on his bike.

"Mutley, quiet!" Renberg shouted.

Mutley continued to bark as the boy pedaled off. An elderly neighbor screwing a water sprinkler onto a hose looked up from across the street as Renberg approached the Jeep.

"It's okay boy," Renberg said. "Quiet!"

Mutley responded with a whimper. Inside the house the woman in the bedroom stirred. The barking stopped, but she'd already heard it and was now awake. She sat up, dropped her feet to the shag carpet and reached for the dressing gown at the foot of the bed. She shuffled out of the bedroom.

Renberg was at the side of the Jeep stroking Mutley's mane when the dog looked past him at the house and whimpered again. Renberg looked up.

"Hey!" he beamed, striding back to the front door. "Look at you! You look like a million dollars!"

"Brad!" the woman whispered, a faint smile breaking on her face.

He took her in his arms and hugged her tight.

"Brad!" she said again.

"Hi mom!" He held her head against his shoulder and slid the door shut with his foot. "You're looking well."

"You're just saying that."

"I mean it."

"I've missed you."

"I've missed you too."

"How is school? And what about the new girl?"

"School's fine, and I'll tell you about Kelly in a second. First, let's go do your shot."

Mutley whimpered one more time and sat down as the neighbor across the street turned on the sprinkler.

*   *   *

It was as he was parking the Volkswagen that Harding remembered his sister. He briefly contemplated driving back home to leave the car as promised, then he changed his mind. He touched the disk in his breast pocket. The priority was Renberg.

He punched the numbers on his cellular phone and waited for the answering machine.

"Sade, it's me. I know I promised to have the car back but something's come up and I'm tied up at the Smurf. Uh...if you need it page me...and...uh...shit, just page me."

His first stop was at Taylor Hall. He ran up the stairs to the third floor office Renberg shared with two other teaching assistants. There was no one there. Harding skipped back down the stairs to the first floor computer lab. He wove his way around the terminals, scanning the faces for

Renberg. He tried the lounge near the vending machines in the basement. Then he ran back up to the first floor.

"I'm looking for Brad Renberg," he told the secretary at the
Computer Science department office. "It's urgent. Any way you can
check his schedule for me?"

"I could tell you what classes he's signed up for," she replied, "and you
could look up the course schedule." She pointed to the course schedule
book. "But I suggest you check with his supervising professor."

"Who's that?"

"She referred to a list thumb-tacked to the wall. "Professor Weinstad,
fourth floor, 203."

This time he rode the elevator. The professor's secretary checked and
told him Renberg's time was his own on Tuesdays.

Harding went back downstairs. Renberg sometimes studied at the
Perry-Castaneda library, but it wouldn't be easy to find him if he was
there, and the clock was ticking. He sometimes ate at the Union
Building, which was closer.

Again Harding ran. It was the most exercise he'd done in a year and it
hurt. The union was crowded, and he paced around the food courts and
vendor booths keeping his eyes peeled. Again Renberg was nowhere to
be seen. Harding stood outside the main entrance, watching the flow of
students with fading hopes. He figured it would be futile, but nonetheless
he paged Renberg one last time as he crossed over to the next building
to the east of the Union. As he entered the Peter Flawn Academic Center
he still hadn't heard anything, and no longer expected to. It was only a
matter of time before they'd come looking for him. In the meantime, he
knew exactly what he had to do.

He pushed through the doors and the turnstile at the entrance to the
ground floor library and turned left, weaving his way through anony-
mous bodies as he ran up the stairway to the second floor. He was
breathing hard when he pushed through the double glass doors of the
Student Microcomputer Facility.

                    *   *   *

The Lear touched down at Austin's Robert Mueller Municipal airport at 12:24, having gained an hour crossing from Eastern to Central Standard Time. Six minutes later an increasingly impatient Steven Vogel was hustling into the front passenger seat of Mitch Wakeman's gray Ford Crown Victoria, eager to get down to business.

"It's fifteen minutes to Harding's place," Wakeman said. "Do you want to go there first?"

"We might as well," Vogel said, buckling up. "Still no sign of Harding?"

Wakeman shook his head. "No."

　　　　*　　　　　　　　　*　　　　　　　　　*

Two hours after briefing Brent Zarbach on the Harding affair, Ed Harkutlian hadn't heard back from the FBI director. He succumbed to anxiety and called for an update.

"Vogel mobilized Austin on his way to Andrews," Zarbach said. "He should be on the ground there soon. I'll let you know when I hear from him."

It was less than Harkutlian had hoped to hear and he scowled as he hung up the phone. He dropped his head and scratched his brow. The timing just couldn't be worse. There was less than two months until the election. The Republicans would have a field day.

He picked up the phone and placed a call to the secretary of the treasury. During a terse, three-minute conversation, Edward Harkutlian successfully lit another fire. The treasury secretary passed the information on to his deputy secretary, who in turn informed the undersecretary of the treasury for enforcement.

The undersecretary's direct supervisory authority extended over the department's five enforcement bureaus, the U.S. Customs Service, the Bureau of Alcohol, Tobacco and Firearms, the Federal Law Enforcement Training Center, the Criminal Investigations Division of the Internal Revenue Service, and the oldest of America's law-enforcement agencies, the United States Secret Service. Within minutes, the director of the Secret Service had been apprised of the situation. It was as direct a path as Ed Harkutlian could get. He cared little that the FBI's Brent Zarbach would castigate him for getting the Secret Service involved. Harding had to be hunted down as quickly as humanly possible. As far as Harkutlian was concerned, the more hunters the better, inter-agency rivalries be damned.

Protection Operations—what most Americans associate the United States Secret Service with—is actually one of seven organizational divisions within the agency. Notification of the electronic break-in at the Pentagon was forwarded to another, the Financial Crimes Division.

Ever since 1984 when, after a long bureaucratic tug of war with the FBI, the Secret Service was mandated national investigative responsibility for certain classifications of computer crime, the two agencies have had their share of contentious arguments over turf. As a result, in cases when there is a clear overlap of jurisdiction, the two agencies might share intelligence and pool resources, but the spirit of cooperation can be less than wholehearted.

Having headed the Electronic Crime Branch of the Secret Service's Financial Crimes Division for almost four years, Lawrence Luenberger was acutely sensitized to the nuances of jurisdictional sparring. The information that was passed down to him suggested the break-in at the Pentagon bore the hallmarks of a classic inter-agency squabble. While the FBI normally handled cases involving national security, terrorism and organized crime, an overlap can occur in cases of password or access code theft involving computers used by or for the U.S. government. Until it could be established that no such theft had occurred, Luenberger was free to go for it. In essence, he could safely instigate an investigation to determine whether the Pentagon affair fell within his agency's investigative jurisdiction. Put more bluntly, Luenberger would happily tell his men to stay in the FBI's face as long as they could.

    *   *   *

Compared to the manpower available to his counterpart at the FBI, the resources available to Manny Schweitzer, special agent-in-charge of the Secret Service's Austin field office, were somewhat limited. Apart from his assistant special agent-in-charge and the administrative help, five special agents staffed the office. One was conducting an undercover investigation of a credit card fraud and cellular phone-cloning ring. In consideration of the time already invested in the effort, Schweitzer decided that agent would stay put. He dispatched two others, Special Agents Noel Markovski and Randy Dawson, to investigate the Pantheon affair.

At about the same time as the Lear jet carrying Steven Vogel touched down in Austin, Markovski and Dawson left the Secret Service office on the sixth floor of the Federal Building at 300 East 8th Street. Depending on the traffic, they anticipated a ten to fifteen minute drive, ample time to call ahead from the car and alert the FBI that they were coming.

*   *   *

As soon as the cab reached Whisper Hollow's parking lot off San Marino, Sadie saw the police car. There was only one, but it was pulling up outside Building 12.

"What we got here?" the cabbie murmured through his cigarette.

"Slow down," Sadie said.

As the driver pulled to the right and stopped, Sadie slid into the middle of the back seat, away from the window. There was nothing to suggest the police had anything to do with her, but she couldn't help thinking of the cocaine in her bedroom.

"Let's get out of here."

The driver coughed and pulled the cigarette out of his mouth. "Where to?"

Sadie's eyes were glued to the police car. "I don't know. Just drive. Go around the block."

Moments after the Taxi glided past the patrol car and turned right on Parker, a gray Ford Crown Victoria raced off Woodward onto Parker in the opposite direction. It turned left into the Whisper Hollow Apartments and skidded to an abrupt stop outside Building 12.

*   *   *

The Student Microcomputer Facility at the University of Texas in Austin is a large room with 224 computers—PCs and Macs—arranged in fourteen two-sided rows of sixteen machines each. Rows A through G run down on half of the room, separated by an aisle from rows H through N in the other half. The complete length of one wall, that next to rows A through G, was floor-to-ceiling glass. Richard Harding saw before he entered the room that it was full.

He typed in his account number at one of the two control desk terminals and waited anxiously for a PC. When his turn came six minutes later, he found himself on F5, closer to the glass wall than he would have liked. Records would later show his login time to be 12:43 p.m.

*   *   *

Mitch Wakeman and Steve Vogel arrived to find the Hardings' apartment undergoing a thorough, methodical dismantlement. While the apartment manager waited outside and an APD officer stood guard at the front door, FBI agents and APD High Tech Unit officers sifted through the entire apartment, paying particular attention to the computer, peripherals and accessories in what was obviously Richard Harding's bedroom. Trash receptacles were emptied onto the floor, their contents itemized, tagged and placed into Ziploc plastic bags that were then loaded into cardboard boxes and taken downstairs. Latex-gloved hands leafed through every book, magazine, folder, envelope and note pad. Not even the phone books were spared.

Moments after they got there, Wakeman and Vogel were staring at framed photographs of Richard and Sadie Harding when they were notified that a vial of cocaine had been discovered in the larger bedroom. They went to take a look. While the vial was evidence of a crime, it had been wrapped in pantyhose and hidden under more pantyhose in a far corner of the bottom drawer of a dresser. An attorney for the defense would argue it was inadmissible, having not been obviously in view. The search of a dresser full of female underclothes in a bedroom other than that of the male suspect would likely be deemed to fall outside the scope of the warrant. Wakeman was considering the legalities when he noticed the bedside phone had an integral answering machine with an illuminated message light. He reached down and pushed the playback button.

"Sade, it's me. I know I promised to have the car back but something's come up and I'm tied up at the Smurf. Uh...if you need it page me... and...uh...shit, just page me."

"What the fuck's the Smurf?" Vogel murmured.

Wakeman shrugged his shoulders. "Anyone know what the Smurf is?" he shouted.

Special Agent Franklin Stiles stuck his head into the room. "The Smurf?"

"Yeah."

"This guy's a student at UT, right?"

"Yeah."

"That's what they call the computing center on campus. It's short for the Student Microcomputer Facility."

The color was draining from Vogel's face. "Do you know where it is?"

"Sure. Right there off Guadalupe and-"

Wakeman was already making for the door. "Let's *go!*"

*　　　　　　　*　　　　　　　*

It was on the third time around that Sadie discovered it wasn't about her cocaine stash. A man in jeans and a polo shirt emerged from the apartment carrying Richard's computer. He laid it in the trunk of an unmarked car and went back inside.

Sadie's fear turned into alarm. She found herself wishing it *had* been the cocaine.

"Do you want me to keep going around?" the cabbie asked.

"No," she replied anxiously. "I need to find a payphone."

* * *

Captain Mark McCarron first received word at 12:47. He was in his office at the University Police Building just east of the stadium, washing down a ham and cheese sandwich with a carton of pasteurized orange juice, when the dispatcher informed him Mitch Wakeman was on the line. McCarron suppressed a burp and aborted his next bite. He'd been with the campus police for close to six years, three months of which he'd spent in a training program at the FBI Academy in Quantico, a fact attested to by a plaque on his wall. It was also a fact Wakeman was aware of, which was why he'd called McCarron in the first place.

McCarron slid his feet off the desk, brushed a breadcrumb off his shirt and reached for the phone.

Mitch Wakeman told McCarron he had reason to believe that a student suspected of perpetrating a computer crime was at the student computer facility referred to as the Smurf. "We're on our way," Wakeman said. "How soon can you get there?"

"Three minutes," McCarron replied. "Do you expect trouble?"

"I don't know. There could be. The name's Richard Harding, white male, 20, five-eight, a hundred and forty pounds, brown hair, brown eyes. Take him if he tries to leave, otherwise wait until we get there."

"Got it. It's in the library building just west of the tower. Second floor."

"We know where it is."

"The entrance is off the south mall. I'll wait at the control desk."

* * *

Richard Harding slipped the disk into the PC's external drive and tapped a few keystrokes. When KORPEN appeared on the screen he glanced to his left and right, then started scrolling through the text. The first half was innocent enough, boring even. It was in the second half that things got juicy. At the conclusion of the last paragraph Harding again stole a glance left and right. The students on either side were so close he could stretch out and touch them. But in this setting, no one who read KORPEN would take it seriously. Here it was just the fruit of a freshman student's fertile imagination. Change the context to that of a Pentagon computer, however, and it was a whole different ball game.

Harding accessed the Massachusetts Institute of Technology's Web site and downloaded the program he needed. As expected, it downloaded in a zipped, or compressed format. It was as he was downloading another program to unzip it and make it usable that he first noticed the two men walking across from the stairway to the Smurf. No uniforms, but they clearly weren't students either. His heart skipped a beat and a sense of dread welled up inside him. He ran the unzip program as the men entered the room. One stayed at the doors while the other beckoned to a supervisor at the control desk. He flashed a badge and they talked briefly. Harding's suspicions were confirmed, and he realized he had less time than he'd thought.

The proctor nodded, shrugged his shoulders, and swept his arm in a wide arc, gesturing at the large number of students in the room. When the man turned to survey the faces, Harding edged lower on his chair, hiding his face behind the monitor as his fingers pelted away furiously on the keyboard. The man was still talking to the supervisor behind the control desk, pointing at the computer behind the counter. The proctor was still shrugging his shoulders and shaking his head.

A shrill tone suddenly scared Harding out of his wits. Students all around him looked up from their monitors. His pager was beeping. He silenced it and checked the number. It wasn't one he recognized. Was it

Renberg, at a payphone perhaps? He reached for his phone and dialed the number.

"Brad?" Harding said expectantly when the line was answered.

"It's me, Richard!" Sadie said. "Where are you?"

"Sadie!" He held his head down and whispered. It felt like everyone on the face of the planet was looking at him.

"The apartment was just raided. The cops took your computer. Where are you?"

"I can't talk right now. Where are *you?*"

"I'm going to Michelle's."

"I'll call you. Gotta go!"

He flipped the phone shut. The man was still at the control desk, and the proctor was now at his computer. The man at the door was checking the ID of a student trying to leave. Harding turned back to his monitor, typed an e-mail address, and tapped a few more keys. Three more men appeared at the top of the stairs. Two were in dress slacks and wore ties, the third was in jeans.

Harding's heart was racing. He typed another command and glanced at the floppy disk drive to ensure its little indicator light was on. The men had spread out and were walking down the aisles, scrutinizing the faces around them. Harding flipped open the phone and punched seven buttons. The man walking down the center aisle was now just two rows away. The line connected and Harding dropped his head to his knees. He uttered three short sentences and barely managed to hang up when a hand grabbed his shoulder.

"Richard Harding?"

He looked up at Special Agent Franklin Stiles.

"FBI." Stiles popped his badge out. "You're under arrest."

Bewildered students watched in disbelief as Vogel, Wakeman and McCarron rushed over and surrounded Harding. Stiles slipped handcuffs over Harding's wrists and the phone dropped to the carpet. Mitch Wakeman reached down and picked it up, noted that it was on, and kept it that way. Steve Vogel pressed a button on the PC and retrieved the floppy disk.

Students all around stared in wide-eyed amazement as a pale and somber Richard Harding was escorted out of the room.

CHAPTER FIVE

Edward Harkutlian sat upright in his chair, his right hand cradling the receiver, his left gripping the armrest in tense anticipation. He listened impassively and asked a few questions, nodding almost imperceptibly at the responses. At the end of the conversation he put the receiver down, closed his eyes, and leaned back, relaxing his body. He eased his grip but kept his hand on the armrest, tapping a finger against the leather. The gold Tiffany clock at the edge of his desk read 2:52. It was less than five hours since Vogel had been assigned to the case.

Harkutlian took a small brass key from the center drawer in his desk, and used it to unlock a vertical panel in the antique display cabinet set against the wall to his right. He slid the panel upwards, revealing a variety of rare single-malt scotches and fine cognacs. He ignored the bottles and reached for the humidor. He owned several, but none quite as exquisite as this veritable work of art, handcrafted by Viscount Linley, celebrated cabinetmaker and nephew of the Queen. Harkutlian used both hands to lift the heavy lid, exposing the unvarnished interior. Noting with satisfaction the 70-degree reading on the hygrometer, he selected an aluminum-tubed Romeo Y Julieta Churchill. After unscrewing the lid and removing the cigar, he ran it gently under his nose, savoring the delicate aroma. He held the cigar perpendicular to the scissors and, leaving an eighth of an inch on the cap, snipped the end. He tore a thin strip off the aluminum tube's cedar lining and lit it with a match. Holding the cigar horizontally, he touched the tip to the flame and rotated it, charring the end evenly. With the other end between his lips he held the flame steady half an inch away, drawing slowly while rotating the cigar as it ignited. When the flame died he blew gently on the lit end. The burn was uniform. He completed the routine by removing the distinctive gold band and discarding it in his trashcan.

Back at his desk, the secretary of state buzzed his assistant on the intercom and asked her to get Roone Hackelman on the phone. He swiveled his chair around to gaze out the window while he waited. When Hackelman's raspy voice crackled over the speaker, Harkutlian picked up the receiver. "They got him," he announced.

"I heard, " Hackelman said. "Brent just called."

"Have you told Bob and Lee?"

"Yeah. It's good news, but we'll feel better when we know how much the son of a bitch knows and what he did with the file."

"Right. At least Vogel seems to know what he's doing."

"That *was* fast. But we should still assume the worst and agree on how to react."

"Fair enough."

"Let's say he read the whole thing and...well, say he gives it to a newspaper. Do we deny it, or try to explain and defend the decision?"

"Back up a little. I never saw a copy of Bob's memo. Exactly what did it say?"

"It's all there, Ed. We knew about men being alive out there and we turned our backs on them."

"We decided in the country's best interests."

"Well...that's kind of beside the point," Hackelman argued.

"What do you mean?"

"The liability here is that we've been lying. Just last month I denied— on national TV, no less—that we weren't doing everything we could to account for our MIAs. I emphasized we had no reason to believe that anyone was still alive out there!"

"And that's been the position of successive administrations for years."

"True, but until now nobody ever had any evidence to the contrary!"

"If Bob hadn't written his Goddamned memo…"

"Let's not start pointing fingers, Ed. There's no time for that. We need to contain this. Remember, the memo mentions you, too."

Harkutlian sighed with exasperation. "Alright. What did it say about the President?"

"Nothing. Speaking of the President, have you told him yet?"

"No."

"I think we should tell him."

"I was waiting to learn the extent of it."

"Well, we should know that pretty soon now. Regardless, what do we do if it's all over the news tomorrow?"

"We deny it. The kid made it up. *He* typed the memo. How could it be authenticated?"

"I don't know," Hackelman responded.

"So we deny it. Hell, Roone, we never saw any evidence those guys were alive."

"Evidence was offered. We never checked it out."

"Because it was irrelevant. Even if we'd seen the tape—*if* there really was a tape—our decision would've been the same. Do we risk 37,000 lives for two?"

"We lied about it, Ed."

"*You* lied about it, Roone."

There was a brief moment of silence before Hackelman responded. "I can't believe you said that. It's good to know where you stand."

"Alright. I didn't mean that. I take it back. We're all in this together. Let's just see what happens with Harding. If it hits the fan, I say we deny it. Talk to Bob and Lee. Run that by them and let me know."

"In the meantime…"

"In the meantime, I'll tell the President," Harkutlian grumbled. He set the receiver down and leaned back, deep in thought. The swiftness of Harding's capture had exceeded all expectations. What they needed now was an equally rapid damage assessment. One, Harkutlian hoped, that would render Hackelman's worst-case scenario redundant.

He drew on the cigar and exhaled gently, letting the smoke drift out of his mouth. The rich cocoa bean spiciness tingled his senses before giving way to a complex, lingering aftertaste, but the secretary of state's delectation was less than complete. There was still ample cause for concern.

*   *   *

When he learned that the FBI had arrested Richard Harding, the first words out of Lawrence Luenberger's mouth were not fit for prime time. The chief of the Secret Service's Electronic Crimes branch was still smarting when he got Marty Schweitzer on the phone.

"I dispatched Markovski and Dawson immediately," Schweitzer protested. "By the time they hooked up with the FBI the kid had been arrested."

"Didn't we already have someone investigating a hacker ring down there?" Luenberger asked irately. "I thought we would've had a head start!"

"One of our agents is undercover, on a cloning case," Schweitzer replied. "We're close to cracking that one, and the FBI's also on it, which is why I didn't want to blow our agent's cover. But I don't think that case is related to this Pentagon deal."

Luenberger grunted in consternation.

"*They* had a head start on *us*, Larry," Schweitzer protested. "We can only work with what we know. We're going to win some and lose some."

"It would be nice to win *one*," Luenberger grumbled. "It would be nice to win just *one*."

*   *   *

Richard Harding was surprised. He had expected a building that looked official, if not ominous. Something close to the federal courthouse. Something that *looked* like it housed the FBI. Instead, he was taken to 8200 North Mo-Pac Boulevard, a modest, unremarkable three-story brown brick commercial office building at the corner of Mo-Pac and Steck. Two flags, the Stars and Stripes and the Texas Lone Star, fluttered in the breeze on poles out front. Vogel, Wakeman and Stiles escorted him into the little elevator lobby, one wall of which bore a tenant directory listing suite 310 as the Austin Resident Agency of the Federal Bureau of Investigation. When they stepped out of the elevator on the third floor, the declaration was more prominent, with large letters taking up almost the entire wall to the right. Wakeman's fingers pulsed on a keypad to unlock the front door.

Inside it was more like what Harding had expected. They walked through a metal detector into a small reception area with a couch, a table adorned with law-enforcement magazines, a large plaque with names and photographs of the FBI's Ten Most Wanted, and two framed portraits, one of J. Edgar Hoover, the other of Director Brent Zarbach. Across from the metal detector was a thick glass window—bulletproof, Harding guessed—behind which sat a receptionist. Harding was shown past the window and past another door that looked as hefty as was implied by the keypad recessed in the wall to its right, into an interview room furnished with a desk and three chairs. Another door—this one of standard gauge—led into a smaller room where Harding's mug shots and fingerprints were taken. There was a sink where he washed his hands before being shown back to the interview room.

He was seated in one of the chairs in front of the desk and asked to give a voluntary statement. They had treated him firmly but courteously, and he agreed. Wakeman took the chair behind the desk, and Stiles the one next to Harding. Vogel stood by the door, his arms across his chest. Apart from the sparse furniture and a telephone on the desk, the room was bare.

Wakeman started by making sure Harding understood there was no attorney present.

"I don't need one," Harding said. "I didn't do anything wrong." He was surprised there was no tape recorder, just Special Agent Stiles taking notes.

"Okay, Richard," Wakeman said politely. "Let's start at the end and work backwards. What did you do with the disk?"

"It's the one you found at Taylor. I didn't want any trouble so I wiped it clean."

"What was on it? Why did you think there would be trouble?"

Harding shrugged his shoulders. "None of it meant anything to me."

"So why did you run from Pantheon?"

"Because Neale went berserk."

"Why take the disk with you, Richard?" Vogel asked. "If you were in a hurry to get away from Neale, why take the time to remove the disk first?"

Harding stared impassively at the notebook in front of Stiles. "It was a spur of the moment thing. I panicked. Neale was mad. I took the disk so I could find out why. When I checked it out, nothing made any sense to me. So I erased it. I didn't want any trouble."

Wakeman shook his head. "You ran from Pantheon almost six hours ago. It wouldn't take you that long."

"I told you, I panicked and I was scared," Harding insisted. "It took me a few hours to figure out what to do."

Wakeman exchanged glances with Vogel. "What was on the disk, Richard?"

Again Harding shrugged his shoulders.

Wakeman stared at Harding, who met his gaze for a few seconds, then shifted his eyes back to the notebook.

"You know that was a classified document you copied," Vogel said.

Before Harding could answer there was a knock on the door. Wakeman stepped out into the reception area, where Special Agent Juan Camacho was waiting. The two men conferred briefly, then Wakeman stuck his head around the door and beckoned to Vogel.

"His phone is cloned," Wakeman whispered when Vogel joined them. "And that last number he dialed, the one I got when I hit the SEND key, it checked against one of the cloning ring suspects. Brad Renberg."

"Renberg!" Vogel pursed his lips. "You'd have thought the son of a bitch had learned a lesson!"

"What has it been now?" Wakeman said. "Three years?"

"Something like that," Vogel replied. "He was on probation for two, and that started back in…'93?"

"Yeah." Wakeman turned to Camacho. "Have Cooper get a warrant for Renberg. Get his address from DPS and get a search warrant."

Harding looked up apprehensively when they returned to the interview room.

Vogel held up the list they'd found in Harding's pocket. "Where did you get the dialups Richard?" His tone was less tolerant now.

"I downloaded it off a bulletin board."

"Is this your handwriting?"

Harding stared silently at the notations Renberg had scribbled next to the printed numbers on the list.

"Who's handwriting, Richard?"

Harding sniffled. "That list's been circulated. You know how it is."

Vogel laid the list back on the table. "You're in a bundle of trouble, Richard. For starters, you're using a cloned phone. That's good for a few years at least. You know what kind of shit goes down behind bars?"

Harding swallowed hard and sniffled again. When he looked up, Wakeman thought he saw fear in his eyes.

"We know about Renberg," Wakeman said. "What are you hanging around the likes of him for?"

Harding flinched. Wakeman leaned closer. "We can cut you a deal here, Richard. We can tell the judge you cooperated, maybe he'll go easy on you. But first you have to cooperate."

Vogel sensed Harding was wavering. "Tell the truth, Richard. Tell us about Renberg."

Harding shifted his eyes uncomfortably around the room. "Okay."

Vogel's demeanor was calm but his intensity was palpable.

Harding cleared his throat. "I stole the list from Renberg."

Vogel stared at him hard. "You stole it?"

Harding nodded. "The rest is like I told you before."

Vogel grit his teeth as his patience waned. Wakeman nodded towards the door and the two of them stepped out again.

When he came back into the room a few minutes later, Wakeman leaned over so he was speaking two inches from Harding's ear. "We're going to talk to Renberg, Richard," he said. "We'll be back. In the meantime, you think real good about what's going on here, and who your friends are. Because the sooner you come clean and level with us, the sooner we'll be able to help you."

*   *   *

Leaving her was always bittersweet. He was her only reason for living, literally the only person for whom she smiled. Yet much as he loved her, and good as he felt about the comfort his presence gave her, seeing her inevitably got him down. She was always so depressed. She had her reasons, and he empathized, but it was still tough to deal with.

"Aunt Charlene will be back tomorrow evening," he said, pecking her on the cheek as he prepared to leave. "I'll see you in the morning."

He immediately sensed the familiar withdrawal. It was easier now that he expected it. Who could blame her? Thirty years ago the only man she'd ever loved had gone away, leaving with a promise and taking her soul. Now she handled farewells by "disengaging", as the shrink had put it.

Brad knew she was watching from behind the curtains, but he didn't look back. He walked Mutley down to a hydrant at the corner and let him relieve himself before tethering him back to the jeep's roll bar.

"Let's go home, Mutt."

He backed out of the driveway, honked his horn, waved once, and was off.

*   *   *

"Make a right at 28th," Camacho said. "Two blocks, turn right at Rio Grande. It's the Sandpiper Apartments and it should be on the left." Special Agent Franklin Stiles was driving, with Camacho in the passenger seat next to him. Special Agents Raphael Lopez and Steve Chase were in the back. Wakeman and Vogel followed close behind in Wakeman's car.

The apartment manager had been notified and was waiting. Wakeman held his gun in one hand and knocked on Renberg's door with the other. Stiles stood tensely to his left, away from the window, his gun also out. Steve Vogel crouched at the top of the landing, his outstretched arm keeping the apartment manager two steps down and out of harm's way. Camacho and Lopez were at the bottom of the stairs, and Chase stood guard out at the street.

Wakeman stepped aside and motioned with his head. "Unlock it."

Stiles and Vogel held their positions as the manager slid a key into the lock and turned it. Wakeman turned the door handle and nodded twice. With the third nod he shoved the door and they stormed in.

It took mere seconds to establish there was no one home. Vogel checked in the bedroom, then came back into the living room. Wakeman was studying the photographs on one of the makeshift shelves in what passed as Renberg's entertainment center. There were two of an older lady, and he guessed it was Renberg's mother.

"Is this Renberg?" Lopez asked, pointing to a photograph of a young man in military uniform. The photograph looked old, but Lopez wondered whether that wasn't just the fact it was a black-and-white.

Vogel glanced across. "No. There's a resemblance though. His brother, maybe." He turned his attention to the book titles. They all had to do, in one way or another, with computers. Renberg seemed to own every UNIX manual ever published, and a wide assortment of titles about the Internet. There were a number of academic books that reflected Renberg's major, alongside a smattering of low-circulation cyberspace novels.

Wakeman caught sight of the answering machine on the shelf next to the TV and moved in for a closer look. There was a red *1* in the message indicator display. He reached for the button. He'd already got lucky once with Harding. If this message told them where Renberg was he'd abandon his principles and play the next state lottery.

There was a single elongated tone followed by Richard Harding's voice. "Zube, answer your damned phone. I found what you've been looking for, man! Check your mail and page me."

Wakeman looked up from the machine. Vogel took a deep breath and met his stare.

"What's Zube?" Camacho asked.

"Renberg," Vogel replied. "Zuberman was his handle back in '93. Look at that." He pointed to a framed color drawing of what at first glance looked like a Superman emblem. When he looked closer, Camacho saw it was a *Z* instead of an *S*.

"It doesn't look good from McCarron's side," Frank Stiles interjected, flipping his phone's mouthpiece. "Renberg doesn't have any classes today."

"Shit!" Vogel hissed as Wakeman's phone rang. It was Seigal calling from the office with more bad news.

"Harding split from Pantheon around 8:40 this morning," Seigal reported. "His phone records show that since then, he made fifteen calls. One to his own apartment, which would be that message you heard when you were over there. The other fourteen were split down the middle to two numbers. Renberg's apartment, and another number we're checking on. He always dialed them in pairs, one then the other."

"Hold on," Wakeman said. He told Vogel about Harding's calls. "Do you think this ties in with the cloning ring?"

"I'd be surprised if Renberg is involved in that," Vogel replied pensively. "We never did put our finger on what made him tick, but I'd say he's above that kind of thing. He's in a different league."

"Check if Renberg had a phone on campus," Wakeman said to Seigal. "If so, I'll bet that's what the other number is. Call me back." He snapped the phone shut, grimaced, and rubbed his brow. "You're Harding, and you find something on a Pentagon computer," he said, turning back to Vogel. "Whatever it is, you figure Renberg would want to know. You call him, but you can't reach him. Meanwhile, you're running out of time. What do you do?"

"E-mail," Vogel replied, "and leave him a voice message saying check your mailbox."

"So he did wipe the disk clean. But only after copying it to Renberg's mailbox."

"And to find that mailbox," Vogel said, "we need Renberg."

"Renberg," Wakeman noted, "or anyone else who knows his e-mail address."

"I'll call McCarron," Frank Stiles said. "It's bound to be on a server somewhere at UT."

Vogel shook his head. "You can call him, and he might get us an address, but I guarantee it won't be *the* address. No. Renberg's sure to have more than one, and the one we need will be remote and secure. Web-based, I'll bet, possibly not even on these shores."

"Renberg might be the only person who can tell us where it is," Wakeman said, "but he's not the only person who can tell us *what* it is."

Vogel caught his drift. "Right."

Wakeman was already on his way to the door. "You guys wait here," he said. "We'll go deal with Harding. Take Renberg if he shows."

$*$ $*$ $*$

Kelly Calloway couldn't believe her eyes. She was in her bathrobe, barely out of the shower when she saw them going in.

She tore the robe off as she rushed to the bedroom, her mind whirring. Forgoing underwear, she slipped into jeans, threw on a T-shirt and tugged on a pair of sneakers. She shook the water out and ran her fingers through her hair.

She grabbed the phone, dialed Renberg's pager, and left an urgent message. Five, then ten minutes went by. Two of the men left the apartment and ran downstairs. Another three came out and closed the door. Two of them disappeared downstairs, while the third ran up the steps to the third floor landing. Calloway watched as he crouched behind the railing, leaving only his head visible from below. His eyes were fixed on Renberg's door.

She wondered how many more there were. She walked out and locked the door behind her. The one upstairs would be watching. Keeping her head down, she crossed the landing and took the stairs down to the ground floor. There was no sign of the others, although she hadn't expected them to be out in the open.

Brad had said he'd be back around three. It was 2:50.

✶   ✶   ✶

Special Agent Frank Stiles watched from inside the car across the street as the attractive blonde skipped down the stairs. His colleague Juan Camacho positioned himself in the shadow of a van parked at the corner of Rio Grande and 28th Street. He had a clear view of 28th all the way down to Guadalupe at the edge of the UT campus. Looking north, he could see where Steve Chase was watching Rio Grande's other end, at the T-junction with 29th. If Renberg showed, they'd let him park and walk up the stairs. With Raphael Lopez covering from above and Camacho, Stiles and Chase coming up from behind, they would take him on the landing at his front door.

✶   ✶   ✶

Renberg eased his foot off the gas and pulled onto the 15th Street off-ramp. He stayed on the I-35 northbound feeder to the corner of Oakwood Cemetery, where he turned left onto Martin Luther King Jr. Boulevard. At the edge of the UT campus he slowed down again and turned right, onto Guadalupe. He passed 21st and 22nd. At 24th the light turned red and he slowed to a stop. A stream of people, mostly students, crossed Guadalupe in both directions.

The light turned green and he pulled away. Just past 26th he flicked on the left turn signal, checked his rearview mirror and slid over one lane. Visiting with his mother was always such a downer. It was a relief to get back on his own turf.

The shock came halfway into the turn onto 28th, when someone suddenly jumped out into the street in front of him. He stomped on the brakes and veered sharply right. As he screeched to a stop, a frantic Kelly Calloway clambered into the jeep, yelling at him to get the hell out of there.

CHAPTER SIX

Contrary to what most Americans would think, you do not have to be a U.S. citizen to become an agent of the FBI. You could also qualify by being a citizen of the Northern Mariana Islands, a fact of which Special Agent Juan Camacho was living proof.

Born in 1968 to Roman Catholic parents on the island of Saipan, one of fifteen in Micronesia that make up the Northern Marianas, Camacho was already fluent in three languages—Chamorro, Carolinian and English—by the time he turned ten. Twelve years later, Camacho received a Bachelor's in chemistry from the University of Hawaii at Manoa, and instead of flying back to Oceania in the North Pacific Ocean, he went east, to California. San Francisco was home for two years, until a friend pointed out he qualified, by citizenship at least, to join the FBI. Camacho also met the other requirements. He cleared the minimum age by one year, had a valid driver's license, and had a degree from a four-year resident program at a college accredited by the Commission on Institutions of Higher Education. His vision bettered the minimum required—uncorrected 20/200, corrected 20/20 in one eye and at least 20/40 in the other—and he passed the color vision test. His application was accepted and he moved east again, this time to the FBI Academy in Quantico, Virginia. He endured an intensive fifteen weeks, during which, in addition to the academic and investigative

subjects covered in classroom sessions, the curriculum included training in physical fitness, defensive tactics, practical application exercises,
and the use of firearms. After the two-year official probationary period,
Camacho found himself assigned to the resident agency in Austin.
Those who knew him at Quantico would describe him as a likeable, if
somewhat intense, man. And true to his nature, as he stood at the corner
of Rio Grande and 28th Street on the afternoon of Tuesday, the 3rd of
September, Juan Camacho was watching with hawk-like intensity.

As soon as the Jeep appeared at the corner he snapped the hand-held
wireless to his mouth. The Jeep swerved to avoid hitting a woman, and
came to a stop in the middle of the corner. Camacho watched slack-
jawed as the blonde jumped in. The Jeep sped off northbound on
Guadalupe, forcing an oncoming car into a fire hydrant.

"Frankie, get over here!" Camacho thundered. "He's headed north on
Guadalupe! *Get over here!*"

Stiles cranked the ignition, jerked the shift lever down and floored it.
The tires squealed as he flung the car around and shot down Rio
Grande. He never came to a stop at 28th, but he threw the door open
and slowed down enough in mid-turn for Camacho to scramble into
the passenger seat.

"*Son of a gun! Left at the corner!*"

Raphael Lopez took the steps in threes and fours. When he got to the
street Steve Chase was sprinting towards him down Rio Grande. The
FBI agents realized too late they were powerless to join the chase.
Wakeman and Vogel had taken one car, and Stiles and Camacho were in
the other.

*   *   *

"What's going on?" Renberg shouted in alarm.
"Turn right!" Calloway shouted back.

He swung the Jeep off Rio Grande onto 28th Street. Mutley whined as he slid into the roll bar.

"What the *hell* is going *on?*"

"*You* tell *me*, Brad," Calloway snapped, watching the traffic behind them. "And start with why the FBI's crawling all over your place!"

"*What? Shit!*" He turned right onto Fruth and right again through the stop sign at 29th.

"For Christ's sake, don't get us killed!"

"Are they behind us?" He slowed down and turned left on East Street.

Calloway glanced backwards again. "It doesn't look like it."

He followed East as it bent to the right and his expression turned sullen. "I knew the prick would get in trouble."

"Who?"

He glanced at the mirror and ignored the question.

"I just risked my neck for you, Brad. The least I deserve is an explanation."

"First we need to get out of here," he said grimly, turning right again on West 30th. At Cedar he turned left, away from UT.

"Fine," she said, relieved that at least she had caught him in time. She checked behind them again. "First we get out of here, and then you tell me."

                    *   *   *

When Stiles and Camacho turned left on Guadalupe they could see all the way to 29th Street and there was no sign of the Jeep. Camacho guessed Renberg had turned on Fruth. They honored the stop sign at 29th. Left was back towards Guadalupe and Rio Grande, unlikely. They turned right. They could see a long way down 29th, and there was no Jeep. They made the quick left turn at East and followed it around. A short block later they were at 30th. There was still no sign of the Jeep. Staying consistent in their logic they turned right, away from Guadalupe.

They passed Whitis, Cedar and University before finally conceding they'd lost him.

*   *   *

The afternoon crowd at *Sugars* was typically sparse, a fact that seemed lost on the center-stage performer. Despite the abundance of empty chairs she pranced around to the throbbing reggae as if the house was packed. A lone customer meandered his way to the edge of the stage and commanded her attention. After tantalizing him with a frontal quiver she turned her back and offered a close-up of her rump. By the time she stretched her string Renberg could have sworn the man was dribbling saliva.

"Y'all need some company?"

The offer was apprehensive. It was unusual for a customer to be accompanied by an attractive female. And when it did happen, they rarely wanted a table dance.

Renberg eyed the redhead's bountiful cleavage. Had she consulted him for a stage name, he might have suggested Silicon Valley. "No thanks. But there is something you could help us with." He beckoned her closer. "We're looking for Crystal."

"She's not here. I think she works the night shift."

Renberg slipped her a twenty. "Can you check if someone knows how I can reach her? It's important."

"You could get a lot more for that," Valley said, pushing the bill back at him. "I'll see what I can do."

Calloway waited till they were alone again. "So…Sugars, huh? You come here often? You look entirely comfortable."

He wasn't in the mood and let it show. "You know what they say about necessity."

She let the remark hang. As the reggae faded out the DJ campaigned for a show of appreciation. The brief rustle of applause was drowned out by U2 and Roweena was announced on the stage. Calloway noticed another performer approaching from the bar. Her demeanor was purposeful, and Kelly decided it wasn't about a table dance.

"Are you looking for Crystal?" She stood at the edge of the table, one hand on her hip.

"Yes," Renberg replied. "Do you know where she is?"

"Maybe. Depends on who's looking."

He leaned towards her and she gave him an ear. "Tell Sadie it's Brad. It's about Richard."

The names did the trick. "Okay. I'm Michelle. Wait here."

When she returned a few minutes later Michelle told Renberg to stand by the payphone in the vestibule next to the men's restroom. He was there and waiting when it rang.

"Hello,"

"Brad?"

"Sadie!"

"Where's Dick? What's going on?" She sounded perturbed.

"*I* was going to ask *you*."

"He's not with you?"

"No. Why?"

"Stay there, Brad. Wait for me." The line went dead before he had a chance to respond.

"Shit!"

Kelly and Michelle were both waiting outside the vestibule.

"Where is she?" Brad asked.

Michelle's expression made it clear she wasn't going to say.

"Look, she asked me to wait for her. I'm going to wait, but I just want to know how long."

Sadie had talked to him, and it wouldn't give much away. "Ten minutes."

He nodded in resignation. As he led Kelly back to the table, he continued to deflect her questions.

∗   ∗   ∗

"He got away, Mitch." Camacho's dismay came across loud and clear on the phone. "We would've had him, but he was warned."

"What happened?"

"A woman waved him down at the corner of Guadalupe and 28th. I was at Rio Grande and 28th and I saw it. I didn't see his face but there's no doubt it was a black Jeep. The woman stopped him as he was turning onto 28th and she jumped in and they took off fast down Guadalupe. By the time Frank picked me up they were out of there. We looked for a while but they were gone. And Mitch, just before that, Frank saw the same woman come down the stairs from where Renberg's apartment is."

"She must be a tenant. Check all the apartments with a view of Renberg's."

"Steve's already doing that."

"Okay. Seal off Renberg's place. *Damn!*"

★   ★   ★

At first Kelly Calloway couldn't remember who Sadie Harding reminded her of. But the conversation was only seconds old when she realized it was the Richard who'd come knocking on Renberg's door.

"The cops raided our apartment." Sadie said, dropping into the chair across from Renberg.

"When?" he asked.

"This afternoon. I got there as it was happening."

"Where was Richard?"

"I don't know. He borrowed my car this morning and was supposed to bring it back at noon, but you know him. I got home in a taxi and found cops all over the place. My car wasn't there, so I paged Richard. When he answered he thought it was you that had paged him. I told him about the cops and he said he couldn't talk. He said he'd call me back."

"And?"

"He hung up. I told him I'd be at Michelle's and I went to wait for his call."

"He never called back?"

"No. I tried him again and someone did answer, but it wasn't him."

"He came over to your place earlier in the afternoon," Calloway said to Renberg. "I told him you weren't there and he said to tell you to call him. He said it was urgent."

"Shit. Why didn't you tell me?"

"Because," Calloway snapped, "I was too busy trying to get you away from the FBI!"

"You too?" Sadie asked, her eyes widening with surprise. "What the hell are you guys up to?"

"It's Richard, not me," Renberg said defensively. "Sadie, this is Kelly, a friend of mine."

The two exchanged nods.

"What did he do?" Calloway said.

"I'm not sure."

"When I paged him and he thought it was you, I tried calling you," Sadie said. "You weren't at home, and I didn't have your cell phone number."

"I don't have a cell phone," Renberg said. "I have a pager."

"Well you weren't responding to your pager," Calloway pointed out. "*I* paged you when I saw them inside your apartment."

Renberg suddenly remembered. "Shit! I turned it off earlier and forgot to turn it back on."

"Why carry a pager if you're going to turn it off?"

For the first time since they'd met, Renberg felt Kelly Calloway was encroaching. But considering what she'd done for him that afternoon, he let it slide. His pager had been off since San Marcos. And Harding had paged him several times while he was on the way.

"I'll be right back." With Kelly in tow he went back to the payphone in the vestibule. He deposited a quarter and dialed seven digits. A few seconds later, under Kelly's watchful eye, he dialed another four digits.

As Kelly committed the number to memory, a recorded voice told Renberg he had two voice messages. He shifted the handset from his left hand to his right.

"Zube, answer your damned phone. I found what you've been looking for, man! Check your mail and call me."

He blinked twice and swallowed. A muscle twitched in his left eyelid. The recorded voice announced the second message.

"Brad, it's Kelly. For God's sake, wherever you are, stop and call me, now! I'm at home. Whatever you do don't come here! Call me!"

He dialed 11 to replay the messages. He heard the first one over and hung up. He stood motionless in front of the phone as the adrenaline flooded his body.

I found what you've been looking for!

"What?" Kelly demanded.

He turned slowly and leaned his back against the wall.

"What is it?" she insisted.

He looked up listlessly. She could see he was there in body only. His mind was miles away. For the second time in two days she saw a different Brad Renberg. It was the same detached look she'd seen when the Pentagon spokesman was on Headline News the night before. And just as before, she knew that right then she had no chance of reaching him.

He brushed past her and she followed him back to the table. Just as they got there Michelle ran over and grabbed Sadie's arm.

"Greg says there's a story about Richard on the TV!"

In a flash Sadie was out of the chair and running past the bar. Brad, Kelly and Michelle followed her through a door marked *EMPLOYEES ONLY*, down a short corridor and through another marked *PRIVATE*. The manager's protests subsided when Sadie told him the new faces were friends.

It was a local station, broadcasting live from the south mall outside the Peter Flawn Academic Center at the University of Texas. The anchor was describing the extraordinary scenes of earlier that afternoon, when campus security and agents of the FBI had apprehended Richard Harding, a UT freshman, and led him away in handcuffs. No word was out yet on why the arrest was made, but it was noteworthy that Harding had offered no resistance. According to eyewitness reports, he hadn't even seemed surprised. It was almost like he'd expected them, one of the witnesses said.

Sadie Harding's hand shot to her mouth.

"We've just learned," the anchor continued, "that the FBI, APD and campus security are searching for another suspect, Brad Renberg, also a student at UT, believed to be hiding somewhere in the Greater Austin area."

A photograph of Brad Renberg's face appeared on the screen, followed by a telephone number to be called by anyone with information as to his whereabouts.

They were all mesmerized by the news flash. It was only when Kelly Calloway turned back to glance at him that she realized Renberg wasn't there. He'd been standing behind them all, next to the door, and now he was gone.

In near panic, Calloway scrambled out of the office and back into the club. She strained her eyes against the dim light and ran straight to the front door. She pushed through it just in time to see Renberg's Jeep screech its way out of the parking lot.

*   *   *

Vogel mulled over his strategy. It was either come down hard, try to intimidate Harding, put the fear of God in him and hope he'd squeal, or be the nice guy, the only friend in the world he could trust to get him out of the mess he was in. In his experience, strong-arming hackers was rarely necessary. They typically weren't hardened criminals, and in Harding's mold, they tended to act out of a belief that information was

the right of all who could access it. In their eyes they weren't doing anything wrong.

He decided to lay things on the line.

"Neale captured all your keystrokes, Richard. We know about KOR-
PEN. Along with your fingerprints on the keyboard, that's all the evidence we need. It doesn't matter who you were working for, your ass is
going to burn. Now, you can play dumb, but I guarantee you'll have
plenty of time to reflect on that, and regret it. We're talking years in the
slammer, Richard. On the other hand, you can do yourself a favor and
cooperate. It's your decision, buddy."

Harding stared at the tape recorder. "I told you what I know."

"Not everything, Richard. I need it all. Renberg's the one who put
you onto this, and he's the one who needs to pay for it."

Harding nibbled on his lower lip.

"Tell me about the e-mail, Richard. Tell me about KORPEN and the
e-mail."

Harding's eyelids fluttered and he moistened his lips. He clasped his
hands on the table and hung his head.

"Richard, listen to me. Renberg doesn't care about what happens to
you. Don't be stupid now. Think of yourself first. Take care of yourself."

Harding was wilting, Vogel could swear it. The kid was nervous. He
was in trouble big time, and he had to know it. He opened his mouth to
say something, then changed his mind. He folded his arms and rocked
back and forth.

Mitch Wakeman sighed and took a step closer to the table. "We don't
have much time, Richard."

The rocking continued for a few seconds, then it stopped. Vogel was
sure they had him. They were so close he could touch it.

Harding sniffled and ran a finger across his nose. "I want to talk to an
attorney."

        ★   ★   ★

Austin had changed. His first memory of UT was a football game his mother took him to when he was eight. Back then the clock tower was easily the city's tallest structure. Now here he was in a parking lot surrounded by office buildings as tall. The fancy office towers detracted from Austin's quaintness. They'd started building them in the boom of the late seventies, and they hadn't stopped until the bust, half a decade later. That was when it had all started to unravel.

He'd never forgiven the bastards. How could he? No, he'd sworn instead to get back at them. He'd breathed, eaten, schemed, dreamed, sweated and strained, just to get back at them. Driven by the memory, and motivated by his anguish, he'd tried, single-mindedly, tirelessly, and incessantly.

Then he had put it all behind him. Or so he'd thought.

I've found what you've been looking for!

He got out of the Jeep, walked to the edge of the structure and peered down to the street below. Eight stories up, and this was just the parking garage. The office tower itself was forty!

He'd tried to get to his office at Taylor to check his e-mail. He had a computer there, the only one they allowed him now. But the place was crawling with cops. So he'd taken refuge in a parking garage just south of the campus.

So much had changed, yet nothing had.

There was still time. He could call and tell them Harding had stolen the list. They couldn't pin a thing on him. Nothing new, at least.

He stole it, and he's a liar if he tells you otherwise. Come on, guys, that shit's all in the past for me. I've come clean, for Christ's sake!

That would be the smartest thing to do. After all, he'd been in San Marcos all morning. He had an alibi. They could check with his mother.

Ha! That'd go down nicely with Mom! Hi Mom—these here men are from the government. They want to ask you some questions about me. Yyyuh!

He leaned over further as a siren sped by on the street below. It was an ambulance, not a cop. Was he going to live in fear of sirens? For how long?

The easiest thing to do, the best thing, was to call them. Let the chips fall where they may.

He took the elevator down to the fourth floor and crossed the covered bridge into the lobby. An escalator took him down to the ground floor and another to the basement. There were two payphones across from the Federal Express booth, next to the frozen yogurt stand. He drifted over and ordered a large vanilla/chocolate twist.

"Cup or cone?" the attendant asked.

I've found what you've been looking for!

"Will that be in a cup or a cone, sir?"

It was a momentous decision. There'd be no turning back.

"Yes."

"Sir? Which one?"

He turned away, his brain numb to external stimuli. He paused at the end of the counter as a painful image flashed through his mind. There was just a slight tremor in his hand when he reached for the phone.

*　　　　　*　　　　　*

Fidelity, Bravery, Integrity.

Steve Vogel was itching to cut loose. At times like this, third world justice oozed merit. The greasy punk was lying through his teeth. All it would take was two minutes. A couple of slaps around the head, the threat of a couple of teeth on the table, and the mere mention of a penis probe. The truth would gush so fast they wouldn't know what to do with it. Fuck due process and legal recourse.

Fear, Blood and Intimidation was more like it. Vogel watched with unbridled disgust as Richard Harding exercised a basic constitutional right.

"Where are you?" Sadie demanded. "What have you done?"

"I'm at the FBI office. They're just asking me some questions."

"Why were you arrested?"

He was aware how close Vogel was. "It's someone else's fault. But anyway, I need an attorney. Can you call Glanzer?"

"Jesus, Richard. We don't need this right now!"

"Sadie, I can't stay on the phone long."

"Damn it, Richard…"

"Sadie…"

"Okay, okay. I'll call David. Where's the FBI? You have an address?"

"Mo-Pac and Steck."

"Okay. Just…sit tight."

Avoiding eye contact, Harding hung up and sat tight.

"Stupid." Vogel said it softly, but there was no masking his disdain. He'd given the sleaze-bag too much credit. It wouldn't even take two minutes.

✳   ✳   ✳

The Texas State Capitol is a large domed structure, second in size only to the U.S. Capitol in Washington, D.C. Lyndon Terrel guided his APD patrol car north around the brown facade onto Congress Avenue. He was just a quarter of a mile south of the UT campus. From the sounds of it, they'd missed out on some good action that afternoon. The chief wouldn't be happy. FBI and campus police, but no credit for APD. They'd been called on to provide backup and support at Pantheon and Barcelona, but when it came time to make the arrest, everyone had a role except APD.

It was a sign of the times that so much fuss was made over a couple of kids with computers. No guns, no weapons, no drugs, no physical harm. Just computers.

He turned left at Martin Luther King Jr. Boulevard, went three blocks, then turned left again on Guadalupe Street. He was going to have to get one. He'd resisted for a long time, but they weren't going away. Just like with the Motorola in the patrol car, it might be intimidating at first, but once you learned how it was easy. He'd get him one of those state of the art machines with an Internet connection. A Dell, probably, to support the local economy. Hell, he'd even get e-mail and check out the dirty pics on the Internet. He just had to figure out how to pay for it.

A block up ahead on his right, a gleaming white Range Rover came down 17th Street, slowed down at the intersection, and turned right onto Guadaloupe. It was one of them fancy-ass high-dollar luxury import SUVs. Hell, it could've been a magic carpet as far as Terrel was concerned. That didn't give 'em the right to ignore a stop sign.

He switched the lights on, gassed the engine, planted himself at the Range Rover's tail and sounded a couple of bwurps. The right turn signal flashed and the 4.0 pulled towards the curb. Terrel pulled up behind it and came to a stop on the far side of the parking structure's exit ramp. He got out of his patrol car and checked his rear. He was blocking part of the exit ramp, but not enough to prevent cars from getting out. He sauntered over to his prey.

The driver's license and insurance card were in order. Against the protests of the driver, who swore she'd really meant to stop and had actually almost stopped, Terrel wrote the ticket. The diamond on the lady's finger was the size of a golf ball, so she could afford the fine. And the bump in her insurance premium wouldn't dent her checkbook.

After she signed the ticket, Terrel handed back her license and, smiling through his Ray-Bans, wished her a good day. As he walked back to the patrol car a black Jeep drove out of the parking garage and stopped at the cashier's booth on the exit ramp. While the driver paid his fee, Terrel slipped the ticket book back into place in the driver door side pocket and turned off the lights. He radioed in his notification that the traffic violation stop was complete and prepared to pull away. A glance at his side view mirror showed the Jeep was now coming up alongside him so he waited and let it pass. Once the traffic lane cleared, Terrel shifted into drive and rejoined the flow. He'd take a decked-out

Suburban over them Rovers any day. Hell, the Suburbans were bigger, that was for sure.

The light at 15th turned red and he pulled up alongside the Jeep. At green the Jeep turned right onto 15th, and Terrel proceeded down Guadaloupe. As he approached 14th an audible tone drew his attention to the Motorola data terminal in his patrol car. An All-Points Bulletin was being transmitted over TLETS, the Texas Law Enforcement Telecommunications System. Within seconds the screen displayed the information:

```
HIGH PRIORITY LAW ENFORCEMENT REQUEST:
   FBI requests immediate assistance. All agencies
Central Texas region to be on the lookout for sus-
pect  name  Bradley  Renberg,  white  male,  age:  29,
height:  6-1  Weight:  185#  Hair:  Black  Eyes:  Blue.
Suspect  was  last  seen  driving  a  black  '88  Jeep
Wrangler license WJN 633. Suspect is not known to be
armed but should be approached with caution.
```

Lyndon Terrel frowned. He checked his mirrors, then turned his head and checked both sides of the street around him. He looked in his rearview mirror again and came to a stop. The street was clear behind him. He reversed a few feet and turned right on 14th, murmuring Brad Renberg's license plate number. At the next intersection he slowed down and checked both sides of San Antonio Street. He turned right, towards 15th. One block later he made a left turn and scanned the street ahead. He was just about to radio for support when he glimpsed it. The black Jeep was two blocks away, heading west on 15th.

Terrel had to get closer. He drove down 15th, passing cars as he went. By the time he crossed Shoal Creek and the Lamar Boulevard overpass he'd made up a lot of ground but he still couldn't read the plate. The Jeep passed Parkway and maintained its westerly heading on Enfield Road. It was cruising within the speed limit, no hint of anything suspicious. Terrel continued to narrow the gap while reciting Renberg's plate number like a mantra. At Marshall Lane he got within range.

"Well looky here," Terrel crooned. There was just a motorcycle between them, and the Jeep was three car lengths away. It sported a bumper sticker that read *IT TAKES AN AGGIE TO BE PROUD OF BEING ONE*, but that wasn't what put a smug smile on Terrel's face. The Jeep's license plate, now clearly legible, was WJN 633.

CHAPTER SEVEN

"It looks like this thing is far from over, Ed."

When his assistant had said Brent Zarbach was on the line, Ed Harkutlian figured they either knew what Harding had done with the file he'd copied, or...

He'd have bet on the *or*. "Why?" he asked the FBI director.

"There's someone else involved. His name is Brad Renberg, and he's got a history. Have you heard of Triple D?"

"No. What's Triple D?"

"It was a loosely-knit hacker gang in the eighties. Demons of the Digital Domain, they called themselves. They used to mess with the phone system in a big way. They manipulated network switches to do all sorts of stuff. They could tap lines, call forward calls, and disconnect service to anyone they wanted. This Renberg fellow was one of the quieter members until he got caught busting into a Pentagon computer a few years ago. He supposedly reformed after that. Now it looks like he's back to his old ways."

Knots formed in Harkutlian's stomach. "Do we know where he is?"

"He lives in Austin. He's a graduate student at the University of Texas. Our people down there are searching for him."

Harkutlian furrowed his brow. It figured. Harding's capture was too easy.

"This isn't your typical kid pulling a prank, Ed," Zarbach warned. "Renberg's thirty. And whatever it is Harding copied, it looks like he e-mailed Renberg a copy."

The knots tightened. "Brent, the truth is, we don't know exactly what they've got."

"That's all I have right now."

"Thanks, Brent. Please keep me updated." The secretary of state set the receiver down and rubbed the back of his neck. It was amazing what stress did to the body. It clogged the brain and tensed up muscles all over. An hour ago there had been reason for optimism. Now the situation threatened to spiral downwards. And the election was only eight weeks away.

Suddenly the knots weren't just in his stomach, they were every-where. Harkutlian poked the intercom key on his handset. "I need to speak to the President," he demanded.

A brief moment later he was told the call was going through. He grabbed the receiver a few seconds before Stan Daulton's greeting came across the line. The usual pleasantries were exchanged, and Harkutlian got to the point. "Do you remember who Douglas Strams and William Pickard are?" he asked.

They were familiar names, but the President couldn't quite place them. "Remind me," he replied.

"The two POWs in North Korea. Back in April. Remember?"

Stan Daulton remembered. "Yeah," he replied, his mood suddenly sobering. "What about them?"

"You remember that deal? The defector and the videotape?"

"I remember, I remember. What about them?"

"You remember how Roone was having surgery about that time?"

"Sure."

"Well, Bob Carlson wrote him a juicy little memo, to apprise him of that situation."

Daulton smelled trouble. He held his silence in anticipation of more.

"That was back in April," Harkutlian continued. "Earlier today, a hacker copied that memo off a computer at the Pentagon."

The President frowned as he digested the news.

"The FBI picked the guy up a few hours ago, only to discover he'd already e-mailed a copy to another hacker."

"What was in the memo?" Daulton asked warily.

"Enough. It's all laid out."

"Everything?"

"Pretty much."

"Names?"

"Mine and Lee's. And Roone and Bob, of course."

The President didn't say anything.

"According to Roone," Harkutlian went on, "there was no mention of you."

A faint sigh of relief came through from the other end of the line. "What's the current status?" the President asked.

"They're looking for the second guy. Until he's caught, we don't know."

"This could get ugly," Daulton stated dryly.

"Nobody other than you, Roone, Bob, Lee and I knows about the memo."

"And them hackers…"

"Well, yes, of course, them too. I meant no one else on this side of the fence. I got Brent to put his best people on it. The Secret Service is also involved. Considering that the perpetrator has already been caught, I'd say they've done well so far. Hopefully it's one down and just one to go."

"That's still two too many."

"That's what we're dealing with. If the media get a hold of this, I say we flatly deny it. There are no signatures or fingerprints—nothing to prove the memo is for real."

Stan Daulton hung his head in dismay. "Jesus, Ed. We don't need this right smack in the middle of the campaign!"

"I know. What can I say? Murphy strikes again. But I think we can contain it. With a little luck, there may not even be anything *to* contain."

The President shook his head, then nodded. "I can only hope you're right." He sighed with trepidation. "Okay. Let me chew on this for a while. We'll talk about it some more when you come over tomorrow."

"Right. I'll see you then."

*   *   *

"It was wrong for us not to at least check it out," Lee Trujillo said dejectedly.

"Don't be so pessimistic," Robert Carlson argued. "Look how fast Harding was caught. Chances are they'll get Renberg too." Carlson had personally brought the news to the chairman of the Joint Chiefs of Staff as soon as he'd heard from Brent Zarbach.

"Even if Renberg's caught, copies of the memo are probably all over the Internet by now."

"We don't know that," Carlson countered. "But even if it is, Ed's right. How could anyone prove it's for real? Anyone can type a memo on a computer!"

Trujillo rose from his couch and put on his jacket. He scooped a folder off his desk and placed it in his briefcase, then snapped the case shut and lifted it off the credenza. There was an aura of despondency about him that Carlson had never seen before.

"We can control it," Carlson insisted.

Trujillo nodded lamely. He stood at the door to his office. "I'm going home," he said somberly.

Carlson stared blankly for a few seconds, then walked out ahead of him.

*   *   *

"There was someone else involved," Lawrence Luenberger said.

"Yeah, we heard about Renberg," Schweitzer replied. "Markovski and Dawson are on their way back to the FBI office."

"Good. I'm sending an EC with the details I've gleaned up here."

Fifteen minutes later the Electronic Communication from Luenberger was on Marty Schweitzer's desk. It spelled out all the Secret Service knew about Brad Renberg, and noted in no uncertain terms the major points the agency could score by beating the FBI to him.

✴   ✴   ✴

Lyndon Terrel was excited. Advancement came with achievement and achievement needed opportunity and hell if that wasn't what this was. If he, Lyndon Terrel, could lead the task force to the suspect, there was no knowing how far his stock would rise. Damn, if *that* wasn't something to toot your horn about!

At Pease Road a *RIGHT LANE CLOSED AHEAD* sign forced the traffic to merge into the left lane and Terrel ended up seven cars back from the Jeep. It lasted for one block, and when both lanes reopened he closed to within three cars. They passed Hatford and Wethersfield, at which point the Jeep's right turn indicator flashed. After passing Newfield it turned onto the Mo-Pac northbound onramp. Terrel followed it and again slipped back a few car lengths.

He was tingling, thinking of maximum impact, maximum exposure and maximum gain. The question was how. He had to decide in a hurry, before another cop spotted Renberg and shared the glory.

The Jeep signaled it was exiting at Northland. Terrel followed as it turned left, crossed under Mo-Pac and hung a right onto Bull Creek Road. The surprise came less than a mile later when it turned right again onto Mesa Drive and headed up towards the affluence of Austin's Northwest Hills. Now the homes were getting bigger and pricier with the view. The traffic also disappeared, and Terrel was clearly in the Jeep's rearview mirror. He couldn't drop back for fear of losing him in the winding roads, so it was decision time. The jeep turned left onto Cat Mountain Drive and continued climbing. A *NO OUTLET* sign at the intersection told Terrel he had him. He radioed in his position, declared he had cornered the suspect, and requested immediate backup. Just as his message was ten-foured the Jeep abruptly disappeared into a driveway. Terrel pulled up in time to catch a glimpse of its rear fender behind a closing garage door at 7603.

Terrel parked his patrol car on the street in front of the three-car garage, wondering what the hell the suspect did for a living to afford a place like this. His radio advised him other APD units and the FBI were on their way. He got out of the car and walked around the side of the multi-tiered residence. The view on the other side was to the west, a sweeping vista of Lakewood Village, North Mesa and Lake Austin. Renberg was either well to do, or he had well-heeled friends.

Terrel couldn't cover both sides of the house at once. If he stayed with the car, Renberg could escape on foot down the mountain to the north or west. And if he covered the mountainside, Renberg could leave the way he arrived. He went back to the car.

It was three interminable minutes before the first backup unit arrived, followed in close order by another. The instructions from HQ were to secure the area and wait for the FBI. Terrel took control, fanning his colleagues around the residence to cover all the angles.

As the crow flies it was less than three miles from 8200 Mo-Pac to Cat Mountain Drive. Driving distance was closer to six. Steve Vogel rode with Special Agent Juan Camacho and they were now accompanied by one of the Secret Service agents, Noel Markovski. They arrived to find the three patrol cars blocking the exits from 7603's three-car garage. Lyndon Terrel briefed them on the pursuit and learned that this was not Renberg's residence. He accompanied the federal men to the front door.

They only had to ring once. The tall, lanky young man who opened the door was genuinely surprised to see the badges, patrol cars and uniform.

"We're looking for Brad Renberg," Steve Vogel said as he displayed his badge.

The young man's surprise turned to amazement. "You won't find him here!"

"His Jeep's in the garage."

"I swapped Jeeps with him twenty minutes ago. He asked to borrow mine for the afternoon so he could check out some upgrades I've made."

Of the hearts that sank at the news, none sank deeper than Lyndon Terrel's.

*   *   *

Brad Renberg decided against I-35 and US-290. He didn't have much time before they caught on, and back roads felt safer than the freeways. He took Manchaca Road south out of Austin to Manchaca, then crossed into Hays County on FM1626.

He drove at the speed limit and Peirce's Jeep ran beautifully. Renberg had planned to one day modify his own along the same lines. A 305cu-in. V-8 for the juice, a four-inch suspension lift to improve axle articulation and accommodate the 32-inch BF Goodrich All-Terrain tires, ARB differential lockers front and rear, and an ARB snorkel that lifted the air intake to the top of the windshield, giving the jeep extreme wading capabilities. Complementing the setup was a 9,000-lb bumper-mounted electric winch that could pull the jeep up and out of virtually any terrain it couldn't conquer under its own power. It was one of the reasons he'd called Pierce and not someone else. If he were to be chased, there were few places off-road he couldn't go. Chances were he could lose anyone within minutes.

His pager beeped repeatedly, and it displayed Kelly calloway's number every time. But he wasn't about to stop and call her. She'd saved his neck earlier, and leaving her like that at *Sugars* wasn't exactly fair, but he couldn't afford to have her around. It was even less fair to drag her any deeper into this. Besides, she would weigh him down and get in the way. He glanced behind him at Mutley. Even Mutley might prove to be a burden.

FM1626 continued to wind into the hill country, and he pushed on through the town of Hays down to Mountain City. A few miles later he turned towards the sunset on FM 150.

Greg Pierce wasn't going to be happy either. There was no way he could have told him. What was he going to say?

Hey, Greg, I need to switch Jeeps with you 'cause every cop in the county's looking for mine.

And there was still Pendergraft up ahead. Hopefully when they found out they'd all understand.

At Hays City his luck was still holding out. The radar detector had buzzed a few times, but it was always X-, not K-band, and he hadn't even seen a police car, let alone tried to outrun one. It was almost forty minutes since he'd switched jeeps with Pierce. He continued on towards the southwest on FM3237. As the roll of the hills became more pronounced the sun dipped below the horizon, taking the shadows with it.

He approached Wimberley in the cover of darkness, just another set of lights on the road. About one mile before the town square he turned left onto Flite Acres Road. Another two miles brought him to Hidden Valley Road. One more turn, to the right, down and across the low-water bridge, and he was there.

It was a single-story structure with an attached one-car garage and a front porch overlooking the Blanco River. Mutley recognized the house and barked, tipping off Chris Pendergraft. By the time Renberg parked the Jeep, Pendergraft was on the porch.

"New Jeep?" he said as Mutley ran towards him.

"Nah. Borrowed a friend's."

Pendergraft patted Mutley and shook Renberg's hand. "What the hell's going on, man?" He opened the door and Renberg stepped inside. "You're all over the news."

"I need to use your computer to check my mail and I'll be gone."

Pendergraft studied Renberg's face. They'd known each other for six years, two of which they'd spent as partners in crime, though they never viewed their activities as criminal. Crusaders was more like it, warriors for information freedom, but not criminals. In Renberg's case, the law had seen it differently. In the face of Renberg's insistence that his 1994 expedition into the Pentagon was a solo effort, the public prosecutor had repeatedly tried to get him to incriminate his cohorts in Triple D. He'd held out, a position which those cohorts, chief among whom was Chris Pendergraft, would never forget.

"Tell you what," Pendergraft said. "I'll go to Terri's. I've got some business in San Antonio tomorrow anyway. When you got here, I was already gone. You've got your own key to my place, and you just let yourself in. I'll be back late tomorrow. I'll find the place as I left it and never even know you were here."

It was vintage Pendergraft. If the roles were reversed, Renberg would have done the same.

"Thanks," Renberg said. "I won't forget this."

"I'll be out of here in five."

Renberg stepped out onto the porch and called for Mutley. Pendergraft put an overnight bag together and called his girlfriend in San Antonio. When he backed his car out of the garage, Renberg was waiting to pull the Jeep in.

"The key's in the bike, if you need it," Pendergraft said. It was an older Suzuki GS750 that he loved tinkering with and kept clean. "The helmet's on the peg by the door."

Renberg closed the garage door as Pendergraft drove off.

The connecting door led straight into the main room, a living room-come-den, one corner of which held the dining table across from the open kitchen to the right. The bedroom and bathroom were on the same side of the house, across the living room from the kitchen. On the near side, adjacent to the garage, was a little room set up as an office.

Pendergraft had been legitimate for almost two years and now made decent money freelancing his programming skills to software developers. His computer was a late model Sun workstation that packed way more punch than he needed. As Mutley re-acquainted himself with the house, Renberg reached for the keyboard.

His primary mailbox was at Netmail.com, a Web-based e-mail service founded and owned by another ex-Triple D member. For Brad Renberg, the service offered unsurpassed security. Because of the Triple D connection, Renberg was allowed to program his own access barriers to secure his mailbox from even the service operators. There was literally no one else in the universe who could read his e-mail.

His world slowed down as he typed: *www.netmail.com*. When the connection was made he typed his user name, which was also his e-mail address, Brad@netmail.com, then his password. The latter consisted of an eight-digit number that depended on a mathematical function relating three variables: the number of days that had passed since the day he was born, the hour of the day it was in military time, and the number of leap years remaining before the year 3000. Renberg made daily mental adjustments to the first and calculated the function manually using the second as appropriate for any given hour of the day. When he entered the result as his password, it was compared to the result as calculated by his password protector program at Netmail. Only if the two numbers matched could his mail be accessed.

The service listed three unseen messages. He highlighted the one originating at Harding's UT address and hit the ENTER key.

```
Brad@netmail.com-> korpen.pgp
Pretty Good Privacy(tm) 2.6.1—Public-key encryp-
tion for the masses.
     (c)1990-1996 Philip Zimmermann, Phil's Pretty Good
Software. 29August 94
     Distributed by the Massachusetts Institute of
Technology. Uses RSAREF.
     Export of this software may be restricted by the
U.S. government.
     Current time: 1996/09/03 02:17 GMT
     File is conventionally encrypted.
     You need a pass phrase to decrypt this file.
     Enter pass phrase:
```

It hadn't occurred to him Harding's message might be encrypted, but there it was. Harding had used PGP, which stands for Pretty Good Privacy, a popular encryption program widely touted as "encryption for the masses" and available for free on the Internet. Renberg used it extensively. So extensively that when his hard disk was analyzed by the FBI's Computer Analysis and Response Team in 1994, the only files they could read were clean files that contained nothing of interest to them. Which made them most interested in the files they couldn't read, those encrypted with PGP. As part of the plea bargain negotiated by Renberg's attorney, two of the conditions Renberg had to meet to escape doing time in prison had to do with PGP. First, he had to provide the CART team with his pass phrase, the key to decrypting his files. Second, while he was allowed to engage his passion for computers legitimately by pursuing a doctorate in computer Science at UT, Renberg was prohibited from using PGP or any other encryption program for the duration of his probation.

Broadly speaking, PGP can be used for two types of cryptography: Asymmetric, or Public Key, and Conventional, or private key cryptography. The latter is the simpler of the two. Text is encrypted and decrypted using the same password. In contrast, Public Key encryption uses two keys: one to encrypt the message, the other to decrypt it. The fact that Renberg's probation terms precluded his using encryption meant he couldn't have a public key, a fact well-known to his friends and associates, Richard Harding included. It explained why Harding's message was *conventionally* encrypted. To decrypt it, Renberg would need the password or pass phrase Harding used to encrypt it, which in turn explained the *"…Check your mail and call me…"* part of Harding's voice message. All of which posed a major problem: He had to talk to Harding.

Mutley made known his displeasure at being left behind, but for Renberg it was a no-brainer. By now they'd be on the lookout for Pierce's Jeep, and even though it was dark outside, he could still be spotted. Besides, the helmet's full facial visor would hide his face.

With Mutley safely in the house and the Jeep stowed out of view in the garage, Renberg obliged the Suzuki's four large cylinders with a quick flick of his wrist and let out the clutch. The motorcycle pulled away willingly, the raspy growl of its seventeen-year-old engine a testament to Pendergraft's mechanical acumen.

He avoided crossing the low-water bridge on the bike, opting instead to drive towards Wimberley's town square before heading south on FM12. The increasing gradient was an opportunity to flex the bike's muscle, and within minutes he was at the T-junction with FM32. He stayed on 12, turning left for the ten-minute run into San Marcos.

It was a warm night, the southeasterly wind carrying temperate moisture off the Gulf of Mexico as it blew across the coast into Texas.

I've found what you've been looking for.

12 brought him in to San Marcos from the west, and the first pay-phone he saw was at the Exxon station at Bishop Street. He called Austin directory assistance, then *Sugars*. The female that answered heard his request but couldn't help him. Neither Sadie Harding nor Michelle were there. Michelle had worked the afternoon shift and left at seven. And if Sadie was working the night shift, she hadn't shown up yet. And no, she couldn't give him Michelle's phone number, or tell him what Michelle's last name was.

He tried Harding's apartment and got the recorder. He hadn't expected her to be there anyway. There was one more possibility. He checked his pager's memory and dialed a number.

Kelly Calloway answered on the second ring. "Where are you?" she demanded angrily.

"I don't want you involved in this any more than you have to be, Kelly."

"Damn you, Brad! I'm already involved! If it wasn't for me where would you be right now?"

"I don't want you getting in trouble."

"Where are you?"

"Never mind. I need you to do something for me."

"I want to know where you are!"

"Listen to me Kelly. I need to talk to Sadie. She's at Michelle's place, but I don't know her last name and I don't have her number."

"I have it. Sadie and I exchanged numbers after you disappeared on us."

"What is it?"

"Tell me where you are."

"Give me the number, Kelly."

"I want to be with you."

"No, Kelly. Give me the number."

"I need to be with you, Brad."

"Give me the number, Kelly!" he shouted, startling her.

There was silence for a moment, then she gave it to him. He immediately hung up and dialed Michelle's number.

"Hello,"

"Michelle?"

"Yes."

"I need to speak to Sadie."

She recognized his voice and handed the phone over.

"Hello?"

"Sadie, it's Brad."

"Where are you?"

"Have you heard anything from Richard?"

"Yes. He's with the FBI."

"Can you see him?"

"I'm going to see him in the morning with an attorney."

"What time?"

"Nine."

"I need you to ask him something."

"What?"

"Ask him for the key."

"What key?"

"Just ask him for the key. He'll know what you're talking about. Page me and leave a message on my voice mail. Tell me what he says. Will you do that?"

"What's going on, Brad?"

"Richard will tell you tomorrow. Can I count on you?"

She paused for a moment. "Yeah."

"I'll wait for your page." He hung up, glanced around, and hastily put the helmet back on. The Suzuki roared to life at a touch of the ignition. In the pensive, wary solitude that marked his mood, he headed back to Wimberley.

            *   *   *

Later that evening CNN's Nightly News co-anchor informed her viewers that the next story was a sign of the times: Brad Renberg, a graduate student at the University of Texas, had just earned the dubious distinction of becoming the first computer hacker to make the FBI's Ten Most Wanted Fugitives list.

CHAPTER EIGHT

What little sleep he got overnight was fitful. Three times he awoke in a cold sweat, his mind churning. The third time was just after six and he got up off the sofa. He opened the door and let Mutley out, then put a kettle on the burner. As he waited for the water to boil he yawned and stretched and thought ahead a few hours.

It was the uncertainty that was so unsettling. Would Sadie be allowed to see Richard? If she talked to him, would he tell her? And the bigger question, what the hell had Richard found? If that turned out to be bogus, it was the end of the road. They'd never trust him again. For all the talk about rehabilitation and reform, it had taken just a few words to send him reeling back like a junkie.

He poured the water over the tea bag and stirred in two teaspoons of sugar. Everything hinged on Richard.

He was on the front porch, watching the river and drinking the last of the tea when a pickup slowed as it drove past the house. Mutley barked and charged as the driver threw out the morning paper. Renberg called out to Mutley and stepped off the porch. He walked around the side of the house and picked up the paper. It was the September 4th edition of The *Austin American Statesman*. Renberg slipped it out of the protective plastic wrapper and his heart stopped. His picture was splashed across the front page. Two pictures, in fact, the front and side mug shots from

1993. He hadn't changed much, the hair was still worn in a ponytail and he still sported his signature goatee. He stared at the paper and turned hollow with fear. The Ten Most Wanted?

He went inside, thinking back to the day, sixteen years ago, when he'd first met his father. They'd talked about the love of family, the love of country, and the love of God. They'd talked about courage, and fear. Courage, his father had said, was not acting without fear. It was acting *despite* it. It was staring fear in the face, and not letting it stop you.

The Ten Most Wanted Fugitives? That was for serial killers and people who bombed federal buildings.

"...suspected of complicity in computer fraud and computer trespass...the illegal breach and transfer of classified Department of Defense documents...has a prior record of violating Pentagon computers...should be considered a threat to national security."

For Christ's sake!

They'd gone way overboard, but what else was new? Ironically, the article gave him heart as much as it scared him. If nothing else, it suggested the bounty was for real.

Renberg tossed the paper and called Mutley in. "Let's find you something to eat, boy," he said, surveying mostly empty shelves in the refrigerator. Mutley had been raised on a strict diet of Purina Puppy Chow for the first two years, and Purina Dog Chow thereafter. Beer, chips and salsa dip wasn't going to cut it.

He didn't expect to hear from Sadie before mid- to late-morning at the earliest, so he figured he had about three hours. He started in the bathroom. He spread part of the newspaper on the floor around the sink and laid one page flat on the sink itself. First to go was the goatee. He'd worn it for six years but this was no time for sentimentality. Scissors shortened it enough for a razor to erase it. The hair went next. Again he started with the scissors and snipped with abandon. When he'd cropped it short he lathered shaving cream into the remainder and had at it with the razor. An electric machine might have helped but he couldn't find one. He ended up shaving his scalp by feel in a steaming shower.

Mutley tilted his head when he saw him.

"It's okay, boy," Renberg said. "It'll all grow back."

The helmet already covered his head when the electric opener raised the garage door. He let the engine warm up for a few seconds as the door came down, then he slipped the remote into his pocket and drove off. The dips, bumps and occasional pothole forced him to keep his speed down as Spoke Hollow twisted and snaked its way for two and a half miles to the junction with FM12. A right turn on 12 took him over the Blanco River Bridge and straight into the center of Wimberley. He turned right at the far side of the little town square and crossed a smaller bridge over Cypress Creek. A quarter of a mile later he pulled up outside the Brookshire Bros. grocery store. After a six-minute wait for the 7:00 a.m. opening he was the first customer of the day through the door. He found a 4.4-lb. bag of Purina Dog Chow on aisle 8a and felt a pang of dread as he realized money would be a problem. He doled out $3.82 and was left with thirty-two dollars and change. He picked up the bag of dog food and stepped back outside. The clerk at the checkout register thought nothing of the quick-stop biker who hadn't bothered to take off his helmet.

It was 7:28 when he got back to Pendergraft's house. He left Mutley munching in the kitchen and retreated to the den, where he turned on the TV and tuned in the weather channel. The local forecast was dismal. A front was expected to blow through before the day was over, bringing with it several inches of rain. He hoped he'd have enough time before it arrived. He checked the bookshelves in the study and quickly found what he was looking for, a *Texas Atlas & Gazetteer* with an ample map of the surrounding roads and towns. He studied the map, then tore it out, folded it, and slipped it into his pocket. His pager beeped at 7:57, then again five minutes later. Both times it was Kelly's number on the display, but calling her from Pendergraft's place was out of the question. He gave Mutley his usual after-meal water splurge, checked that all the doors were locked, and headed out again.

It was a strange feeling knowing what he wanted, but not where he was going. There was only one way to find out, so he drove back into Wimberley. This time when he crossed Cypress Creek he passed Brookshire Bros. and turned left on 2325. He drove past the Wimberley High School and turned right into the Woodcreek subdivision. He took the first right at El Camino Real and again at La Toya Trail. Less than half a mile later he parked the bike on the side of the road and climbed the stone steps—over two hundred in all—to the top of Old Baldy.

He'd been there once before with Pendergraft, who often used the lookout as a spot to clear his head. One could see for miles in all directions from the top of the hill, which made it a great vantage point. It was only when he got to the top and was sure he was alone that Renberg took the helmet off. He took the map out and got his bearings. For ten minutes he scoped out the surroundings, sure there must be something he could think of up here. He went back and forth from the map to the surrounding countryside, following roads, staring hard at the school grounds, considering Woodcreek, and thinking back to the town center. Nothing gelled. Old Baldy wasn't such a hot idea after all. Besides, it was in Wimberley.

The way down took less effort. He drove through Woodcreek and came out on the other side, on FM12. He turned left and headed north. According to the map it was about fifteen miles to Dripping Springs. The road was near-deserted and he covered the distance in eighteen minutes. On the way he noticed what looked like a telecommunications post on a prominent hill to his right. There was a small brick hut, several satellite dishes and an antenna tower. Because of its height, the hill looked like it had potential, but the only way he could see to get up it was through a locked gate. He committed the hill to memory and followed his instincts north. The terrain flattened out some, and Renberg wondered if that would work to his advantage or against him. He stopped at the intersection with FM150, which, according to the map, ran southeastward for maybe five miles to Driftwood. He decided to check it out on the way back, and pushed on for two more minutes until he hit Dripping Springs and Highway 290.

He turned right at the T-junction, towards Austin. It immediately felt wrong, but he stuck with it for half a mile before making a U-turn. He passed the junction with 12 and kept going west on 290. Less than half a mile later he pulled into a Chevron station on his left. It was part of a small shopping center and, since nothing else had looked remotely suitable, it was worth considering. The gas pumps were outside the *Trailhead Country Store*, and Renberg pulled up in front of the two payphones facing the road. He left the bike running and lifted the receiver off each phone in turn, but was disappointed. Neither had a number in the number slot. He was lifting a leg over the bike when something else occurred to him. Some one hundred or so yards back towards the east was the *Sidesaddle Bakehouse*, a freestanding structure with a wooden deck. He cruised over, parked the bike and walked in. Sitting at a table was out of the question—he would have to remove the helmet—so he ordered two donuts to go. As he paid for them he asked the young lady at the counter for the telephone number. She seemed surprised by the request and asked him to wait. She stepped back into the food service area and disappeared through a door, only to reappear a few seconds later and hand him a card. It was one less thing to remember. He thanked her and walked out onto the deck.

The donuts were excellent. And the combination of *Sidesaddle Bakehouse* and *Trailhead Country Store* wasn't bad either. Renberg looked up and down 290 and decided it would work. Not perfect, but he was definitely in business. When he got back on the bike and left the parking lot, both his stomach and his spirits were replenished.

He went back to the phones at the *Trailhead Country Store* and called Kelly.

"Thank God!" she exclaimed at the sound of his voice. "I've been grinding myself into the ground worrying about you."

"Don't, Kelly. I'm alright."

"Two FBI agents came by here last night."

"What?"

"They asked me about yesterday. They saw me stop you and get into the Jeep with you."

"Shit. I'm sorry Kel-"

"It's okay. I told them I was late for a class and caught a ride with you."

"They'll check that out today. They'll be back."

"I know. I won't be here."

"What are you going to do?"

"I want to be with you."

"When this is over, Kelly. I promise."

"Where are you?"

"I'm safe."

"Where?"

"I have to go. Where will you be if I need to reach you?"

She sighed despondently. "I can stay with friends. I'll page you with a number."

"Use my voice mail so I know it's you."

"I wish you'd let me be with you."

"I don't want you involved. Just let me know where I can reach you."

"Brad…"

"I've got to hang up. Bye, Kelly."

"I just-"

He hung the receiver on the hook and looked over at the *Sidesaddle Bakehouse*. When it was all over he was going to make a life with Kelly Calloway.

He retraced his route back towards Wimberley on 12, and stopped again at the intersection with 150. The map indicated he could take 150 to Driftwood—about five miles, then get back to 12 on another road, unnumbered on the map, that met 12 a few miles south of where he was. He checked his watch. It was 8:15. He turned on 150.

Driftwood was aptly named for there wasn't much there. The landmark Renberg needed took the form of the *Old Driftwood Country Store*. It stood at the corner of Driftwood and Elderhill Road, which, from the signage, appeared to be the road back to 12 that he'd seen on the map. Now was the time to find out, so he took it and emerged back on 12 five minutes later. It would definitely work, and Driftwood was good because at another intersection near the country store, 150 continued on towards Kyle, and 1826 ran off to the northeast towards Austin. Several escape routes, should he need one.

He headed back towards Wimberley. Dripping Springs and Driftwood were in. Now it was up to Richard to speak, Sadie to deliver, and the weather to hold.

                    *   *   *

If Brad Renberg had suffered an uncomfortable night, Richard Harding had endured a sleepless one. After calling his sister from the FBI's resident agency on Tuesday afternoon, he'd been handcuffed and driven by special agents Juan Camacho and Frank Stiles to the Austin Police Department headquarters at 715 East 8th Street. Stiles had duly filled out the Travis County central booking form and transferred custody of Harding over to a County Corrections officer. He had been relieved of his watch, his belt, and the contents of his pockets, before being escorted to his accommodations for the night, a 90-square foot cell that would have been at best adequate for him alone. As it was he shared it with two other inmates, neither of who expressed the slightest pleasure at making his acquaintance.

A little after nine on Wednesday morning, Stiles and Camacho took Harding to the Federal Courthouse at 200 West 8th Street. His initial appearance before the U.S. magistrate lasted under ten minutes. In the presence of the two FBI men, two U.S. marshals and an assistant U.S. attorney, Harding was informed of the charges he faced and advised of his right to an attorney. The magistrate summarily denied bail. At 9:37 a scared and dejected Richard Harding was led out of the courtroom by the two U.S. marshals. Seconds later a David Glanzer pushed through the main doors to the courtroom, looking for his client. Sadie Harding trailed close behind.

As soon as he was brought up to speed on the morning's proceedings, Glanzer requested a separate hearing on the bond issue and asked to speak to Richard. He conferred briefly with the magistrate, then informed Sadie that he was going to see Richard right away, but that she would have to wait until 11:00 a.m. for the first visiting hour. When she stepped out of the courtroom into the hallway, Juan Camacho made his move.

"Miss Harding?" he said from behind her right shoulder.

She turned to face him. "Yes?"

"Juan Camacho." He held up his badge. "Special Agent, FBI. May I have a word with you about your brother, ma'am?"

"What about him?"

"Would you care to have a seat?" He gestured towards a bench. They walked over and sat down.

"Richard's in a lot of trouble," Camacho said. "He gained unauthorized access to a Pentagon computer yesterday, and copied some classified files."

She closed her eyes and shook her head.

"The evidence against him is solid. His fingerprints are all over the computer that was used. Actually, he hasn't denied doing it."

She opened her eyes slowly. "What's going to happen to him?"

"The magistrate has denied bail. Richard will be tried, and if convicted, we're talking a few years in jail at least."

She took a deep breath.

"He's also been using a cloned cell phone. That's not going to help."

Tears were welling in her eyes and her lower lip began to quiver. "He's a good kid."

"That may well be. But it looks like he mixed with the wrong crowd."

A tear broke loose and streaked down her cheek. She wiped it with the palm of her hand.

"Do you know Brad Renberg?" Camacho ventured.

She glanced at him and nodded.

"We believe he's the one who is behind this. Richard was just tagging along for the ride."

There was no reaction.

"Did you know Renberg hacked into a Pentagon computer a few years ago?"

She shook her head.

"And got caught doing it. Got a one year suspended sentence and three years probation. But Richard's not likely to get off so easy. See, back then Renberg never copied anything. But now Richard, he copied stuff he shouldn't have even been reading. What's worse, before we arrested him, he e-mailed it all to Renberg."

She wiped her eyes. "I knew they were friends. I met Brad a couple of times. And I knew they were into their computers. But I had no idea…"

"Well it's not the kind of thing they'd advertise."

She nodded and wiped her hand on her jeans.

"When are they going to let you see him?" he asked.

"Eleven."

"Are you going to wait around here or you want to go get a coffee or something?"

"I'll wait. I brought an attorney. He's with Richard now."

"I hope he's good. For Richard's sake."

"Where will they take him?"

"Travis or Bastrop County jail. They use both."

There was an awkward silence. Thirty seconds. Forty seconds.

"You could help Richard out as much as that attorney, uh…what's your name?"

"Sadie."

"Sadie."

So it wasn't just friendly concern. "What do you mean?"

"Well, if he listens to you, you could convince him it's in his best interests to cooperate with us."

"By…?"

"We need to talk to Renberg, you know? Make sure he doesn't do anything stupid."

"You think Richard knows where he is?"

"He might."

She thought about it for a moment. "What if he doesn't?"

"He could still tell us what he copied, and where he e-mailed it."

She thought some more.

"Sadie, Renberg's our man here. Not Richard. I guarantee you it's Renberg who set him up to this. And now Richard's the fall guy. Now, if he cooperates with us, the judge will hear about it. That kind of thing has an effect, you know?"

She was quiet, pensive.

"Talk to him, Sadie." Camacho stood up and handed her his card. "By helping us he'll be helping himself."

She looked at the card. There was a gold seal in the top left-hand corner and the words *Federal Bureau of Investigation* in capitals to its right.

"You've got my office number and my pager number. Call me anytime."

"I'm going to see him at eleven," she said. "I'll talk to him."

"Good. And you won't have to wait until eleven. I can arrange for you to see him right away. There's just one thing, Sadie. You need to make sure he understands we don't have much time. Tomorrow won't do us any good. If he's going to get smart and cooperate, it's going to have to be real soon. Like this morning, now. Before Renberg does something stupid and it's too late."

"When can I see him?"

"Wait here."

Camacho walked down the hallway and disappeared around a corner. Moments later he returned with a marshal who took Sadie to join her brother and David Glanzer. Camacho watched them go, then dialed the office on his cell phone. Mitch Wakeman was waiting and took the call immediately.

"Big sister's on board," Camacho said. "She's on her way to see him."

*   *   *

"Jesus, Ed," the President fumed. "We can deny it till we're blue in the face, the Republicans will still have a field day!" It was just the two of them within the corner-less walls of the Office.

"I'm not so sure," Harkutlian demurred. "I still say we deny the whole thing. But if there is a smoking gun we don't know about, and the Republicans try to score some points off it, we can dig up documents from administrations past—Republican administrations—to neutralize their play. If one party's guilty here, both are."

"If?" the President said. "The election is in two months! The names on that document belong to four high-ranking members of this administration. *Presidential appointees!* So much for our standing in the polls!"

"Our position is consistent with that of every administration since Eisenhower's, and I'm saying we can prove that."

"What good could possibly come from that? You know what that would do to the public's faith in the institution of government?"

"People will get over it. It's a matter of saving lives."

The President shook his head. "We need to make sure it doesn't get to that."

Harkutlian maintained his stoic composure. "Agreed. Our best bet is to quash it. But there is one potential complication."

"What's that?"

"The videotape. Assuming it really exists."

Stan Daulton stared at his secretary of state. "What do you propose we do about it?"

Harkutlian shrugged a shoulder. "Let the North Koreans take care of it. For one thing, if it's for real, it's probably hidden somewhere in Pyongyang. Plus, it would be just as embarrassing for them as it would for us."

The President's expression indicated he hadn't fully caught Harkutlian's drift.

"All you'd have to do," Harkutlian suggested, "is get the CIA to drop a word to the North Koreans about Kwang Soo. They'd shut him up *real* quick."

Continuing to stare, Stan Daulton nodded a few times. "Yeah. We can do that."

"That would take care of the only thing standing between us and a rock-solid denial. No videotape, no proof. There's no other way for any-one to authenticate that memo."

The President ran his hand along his desk. The Resolute Desk, so named because it was made from the dismantled oak timbers of the *HMS Resolute*. Queen Victoria had presented it to President Rutherford B. Hayes back in 1880, and it had been the desk of every president from Hayes to Eisenhower. John Kennedy had used it. Jimmy Carter had pulled it out of the Smithsonian and put it back into service. Ronald Reagan had used it, as had George Bush, if only for a while. It was over one hundred years old. The President wanted it for another four.

"For all our sakes," he said, turning his eyes to his secretary of state, "I sincerely hope you're right."

                ★   ★   ★

Sadie was careful to pick her moment. She waited until Richard's attention was on Glanzer. "Brad called me last night," she said, watching for his reaction.

He stopped in mid-sentence and turned to look at her, his eyes wide with surprise. "What?"

"He wanted to know if I was going to see you."

Richard forgot about Glanzer. "What did he say?"

"He told me to ask you for the key."

"Where is he?"

"He didn't say. But I got the impression you'd know."

Richard stared at his sister. "Why? What did he say?"

"He just asked where you were and if I could see you. When I told him, he said to ask you for the key."

"When are you going to see him?"

"I don't know. If you don't know where he is I have to wait for him to call me."

"I don't know where he is."

"Great. So what's this key business? What the hell are you guys doing messing with Pentagon computers?"

Richard had side-stepped the question when Glanzer had asked a few minutes earlier.

"Page him. I'll give you the number."

"What did you copy Richard?"

"Who told you I copied anything?"

"The FBI guy. Camacho. He said you cracked a Pentagon computer and copied classified information and e-mailed it to Renberg."

"What else did he say?"

"He said Renberg set you up to this. He said Renberg's the one they're really after. He said if you tell them where Renberg is, they'll tell the judge you cooperated."

"I don't know where he is."

"For God's sake, Richard," Sadie said angrily, "you're in enough-"

"I said I don't know where the fuck he is, okay?" Richard snapped.

"Okay, settle down you guys," Glanzer interjected. "No need to start jumping on each other now."

"I don't know where he is, Sadie. And if I did, I wouldn't tell them."

"Oh that's good, Richard," she retorted. "That's great. Well, let me tell you something. We know where *you* are, and it doesn't look pretty."

"Brad will get me out."

Glanzer and Sadie looked at him like he'd lost his mind. "If that isn't the dumbest thing I've ever heard," Sadie said with a smirk. "What's he going to do? Crack another computer and arrange for the charges to be dropped?"

"Okay," Glanzer said, pushing his chair back as he stood up. "I'll go see if the judge won't set bail. I'll be back and we can go over what happened. I'm going to need the truth, Richard."

Richard's reaction was muted. Sadie waited until Glanzer had left the room before asking: "What do I tell Brad?"

Richard glanced at the marshall at the door, then he leaned over and whispered in her ear.

"What?" she asked.

"That's what you tell him."

"That's the key?"

"That's it." He leaned over and whispered it again.

"And what is that? What have you found? What's he been looking for?"

"Just tell him. And don't worry about me."

She leaned over and kissed him on the forehead. "What am I going to do with you?"

He pecked her on the cheek and pushed her away. "Go!"

                     *   *   *

Camacho intercepted her when she stepped off the elevator. "How did it go?" he asked.

"He wants to cooperate," she said. "But he doesn't know where Brad is."

"You believe that?"

"Yes."

"That doesn't do us any good."

"I know. But he suggested I page Brad and tell him I have a message for him. One that Richard said I should only give him face to face. Not over the phone. Brad should agree to meet me."

"That's good," Camacho said.

"Just a couple of conditions," Sadie said, "other than the good word you're going to plant in the judge's ear about Richard."

Camacho eyed her warily. "What?"

"I don't want to be there when Brad's arrested. I don't want him to know."

"I can appreciate that." Camacho replied. "That's fair. We'll set you up with an electronic tracking device that'll put out a signal that we can monitor from a distance. He'll never know we're there. After you leave we'll wait a while before picking him up. What else?"

"Richard was driving my car yesterday. Before he was arrested he parked it at a meter on campus. I'm going to need it back."

"No problem. I can take care of that."

"And the apartment."

"That too."

"Okay."

"Just out of curiosity, what's the message from Richard going to be?"

"I'll think of something. Maybe…that he wants to know if he got the e-mail and if he has any questions."

Camacho nodded. "What's the pager number?"

"Why do you need to know?"

"Is it a 553 number?"

She didn't respond.

"Before he was arrested Richard made several calls to two numbers. One was Renberg's apartment. We thought the other might have been Renberg's office on campus but it wasn't. It was his pager, wasn't it?"

They would find out anyway. She nodded. "553-1597." There was no harm in building their confidence in her. "Do I page him now?"

Camacho thought about it. Realistically it would take two or three hours to process an order for the tracking device and get a judge to approve it. In the meantime they could get her car released by campus police. He checked his watch.

"That's fine. Tell him you can meet him at…say one or one-thirty. Tell him you've got to get your car back first. And the part about Richard giving you a message for him is good. Stress the face-to-face part."

Sadie's mind was whirring. She wanted to help Richard. That was the only thing she was sure of.

"Deal," she said anxiously.

"Deal," Camacho responded, looking her straight in the eye and hoping he could believe her.

*   *   *

"Where are you?" Renberg asked when he answered the page.

"At a payphone."

"Where?"

"In the federal building."

He was taken aback. "Call me from somewhere else."

Before she could react the line went dead. At Camacho's urging she left the federal building alone, on foot, and tried again from a convenience store a few blocks away. This time Renberg stayed on the line.

"Did you see Richard?"

"Yes. We need to meet."

"Did he tell you?"

"Yes. But he said not to talk on the phone. Where are you?"

It made sense. It was what Richard *would* have said. "San Marcos."

"Where do you want to meet?"

"You know where Blanco is?"

"I'll find it."

"Take 290 west. It ends at 281 and you'll turn left and it's eight miles to Blanco."

"Got it. What do I do when I get there?"

"On 290 you'll pass through Dipping Springs. There's an Exxon station at an intersection with a traffic light. It's the only Exxon station in Dripping Springs. About a quarter of a mile past it on the left there's a place called the Sidesaddle Bakehouse. Go inside and order something. There'll be instructions for you."

Sadie bit her lip. He was going to cover his bases.

"Can you leave now?" he asked.

"No. Richard was using my car yesterday and he left it on campus. I need to go get it back."

"Shit. All right. Page me again when you've got the car. I'll be waiting."

She walked back to the federal building and reported to Juan Camacho. After consulting on the phone with Mitch Wakeman, Camacho instructed Sadie to take a cab to the campus police building on Manor Road and ask for Captain Mark McCarron.

"Wait for me there," Camacho said. "We'll get your car, and get you set up with the tracking device.

"How big is it?"

"It's dressed to look like a pager. You just leave it in his car. If he finds it, he'll think you dropped your pager."

*   *   *

It was almost 1:30 when she set off. Some five miles ahead of her on 290, Steve Vogel monitored her progress from the passenger seat of Mitch Wakeman's car. She was a red blip on the screen of an IBM Thinkpad, superimposed on a detailed road map, the scale of which could be varied as necessary. Juan Camacho was armed with an identical setup in a Jeep Cherokee driven by the Secret Service's Noel Markovski, five miles behind her. The similarly equipped third two-man team of FBI agents Franklin Stiles and Raphael Lopez was already in position outside Blanco.

The tracking device clipped to Sadie Harding's belt operated on the global positioning system satellite network. The pulsating signal it emitted was read by three satellites which pinpointed its position to within one hundred yards and fed the information to receivers connected to auxiliary ports on the Thinkpads.

Wakeman and Vogel passed the *Sidesaddle Bakehouse* a quarter of a mile beyond the Exxon station in Dripping Springs. They noted there was no sign of Pierce's Jeep, and maintained a steady speed heading west on 290. Six minutes later the signal on the screen stopped moving. They continued west, but slowed down. Ten miles to the east, Camacho confirmed the signal had stopped on his screen too, and he told Markovski to slow down.

Sadie parked her car and entered the *Sidesaddle Bakehouse*. There was a little vestibule at the entrance, then the main dining area with the service counter to her right. There were people eating at two tables on the inside and the exterior deck was clear. She ordered a glass of lemonade and sat down.

Renberg waited a full five minutes. He had watched her pull up and go in alone and he'd seen nothing suspicious. He left the Suzuki running outside the *Trailhead Country Store* when he made the call.

"Ma'am," one of the girls behind the counter called out, "I believe there's a call for you."

Sadie stepped behind the counter and was led through the prep area to a phone in the office.

"Hello?"

"Go back to the Exxon station and turn right on 12. In a couple of miles there's a fork to the left. It's the first fork you'll come to. The sign says Driftwood and Kyle. Take that road. Driftwood is four or five miles. Park at the Old Driftwood Country Store and get out of the car."

"What about-"

The line went dead. He was back on the bike by the time she walked out. He watched her get into the Golf and drive back towards 12 on 290. No other cars followed her. No one made a sudden U-turn on 290.

It was about a minute after she turned right on 12 that she was passed by the motorcyclist. She was concentrating on not missing the sign for Driftwood, and paid no attention when he overtook her. The motorcycle had disappeared when she saw the sign up ahead, just past a cemetery to the right. She slowed down, gave an oncoming car the right of way, then turned left on FM150. Two minutes later, satisfied that nobody had followed her, Renberg eased the Suzuki out from behind an oak tree in the cemetery and took 150 towards Driftwood.

*   *   *

Vogel had magnified the scale and immediately saw she'd turned back. He called Camacho, who'd seen it too.

"That could be him," Vogel said. "He could have met her at Sidesaddle. Blanco may have been a smokescreen."

"Yeah," Camacho agreed. "If so, we should hear from her real soon. Wait…I'm showing the signal's going south on 12."

"I see it," Vogel said.

"She must have planted it," Camacho said. "She was going to head straight back to Austin. She wouldn't take 12."

"Not unless he told her to."

"We're westbound on 290. If she's on her way back we'll see her."

*   *   *

Sadie couldn't miss the *Old Driftwood Country Store* because there was nothing else. She parked in front of the store and got out of the car. Dark clouds were building to the north. She hoped she wouldn't have to wait long.

*   *   *

"It looks like it's going to piss down," Wakeman said as they approached the Sidesaddle Bakehouse.

Vogel's eyes were on the screen. "It's stopped again. In Driftwood."

Wakeman slowed down. "I don't see her car."

Vogel shook his head. They pressed on towards 12 and moments later saw the Exxon station.

"There's Juan and Markovski," Wakeman said.

The Cherokee had pulled into the station. Wakeman came in from the opposite direction and pulled up alongside it. "She isn't going back to Austin," he said, "and she's not at the Sidesaddle."

"That must be her in Driftwood," Camacho said. "He's moving her around."

Vogel was studying his screen. "If he's going to San Marcos, the closest way is 150 to Kyle then 35 or backroads. Looks like Blanco was a decoy."

"Let's get Franklin and Raphael to San Marcos on 32," Wakeman said. "You take 12 through Wimberley and we'll follow him down 150."

While Wakeman and Camacho rolled up their windows, Markovski told Stiles what was happening. Steve Vogel's eyes stayed glued to the stationary blip.

*   *   *

Sadie was leaning against her car when the motorcycle appeared. She was taken by surprise when it stopped, even more so when he slid the visor up and told her to get on. As she wrapped her arms around his waist and held on against the force of the sudden acceleration, her mind was on planting the tracking device. They hadn't expected a motorcycle.

He sped down Elderhill Road, his eyes darting back and forth from the road ahead to the rearview mirrors. It was all clear in both directions when he slowed down and pulled to the side of the road. She eased her hold on him and he turned around. He left the engine running and again pushed the visor up.

"What did he say?"

"He said to tell you I found what you've been looking for."

He glanced down the road in both directions and met her eyes again. "When you asked for the key, exactly what did he say?"

She didn't flinch, and was careful with the answer. "I found what you've been looking for."

"That's it?"

"Yes."

He smiled to himself and nodded. "Hold on."

She did so with her left arm only when he revved the engine and turned the bike around. Again he accelerated hard, now back towards Driftwood.

Sadie's right hand was on the tracking device clipped to her belt. There was a leather strap under her groin, splitting the seat into driver and passenger halves. It wrapped downwards around the sides of the seat under her legs. She pulled the tracking device off her belt and clipped it to the strap on the right side. It stuck out under her thigh, but unless he sat way back when she got off, it wouldn't touch him. If he looked he would see it, but there was nowhere else. Besides, she was out of time. She could see the Old Driftwood Country Store about two hundred yards up ahead when Renberg slowed to a stop and told her to get off. She did and he turned the bike around. Without a word he sped off, leaving her standing at the side of the road. She watched him go, then started walking. When a clap of thunder followed the first lightning strike, her walk turned into a run.

          *   *   *

Markovski and Camacho had just passed the Elderhill intersection on 12 when the blip started drifting across the screen again, this time west, away from Driftwood, towards 12. Wakeman and Vogel had already turned onto 150.

"It's off 150," Vogel said, "heading back to 12 on Elderhill. It'll hit 12 in a few minutes. Juan and Markovski should be right there."

Wakeman slowed down and called Camacho. "She's coming back towards you."

"I know. We've passed that intersection."

"If he's taking her to San Marcos they'll head south behind you. We'll turn back to 12 and stay behind him."

"It's stopped again," Vogel said.

"Wait a second," Wakeman said. "She's stopped again."

"I see it," Camacho replied.

Wakeman considered the next move. "We're not turning around yet," he said. "Let's see what happens."

They didn't have to wait long. Seconds later the blip started back towards Driftwood.

"Son of a bitch is playing games," Camacho said.

"Turn around," Wakeman said to Camacho. "I'll bet they go south from Driftwood on 150."

"I bet you're right," Camacho agreed.

A few moments later they discovered they were both wrong. "It's going back towards 12," Vogel announced.

"It's headed back towards us," Camacho agreed.

"Okay," Wakeman replied, his mind racing. "We'll be in Driftwood in a couple of minutes. You drive up Elderhill and see what's going on."

With the first rumble of thunder, Wakeman drove past the *Old Driftwood Country Store* just in time to see Sadie Harding turn her Volkswagen Golf onto FM 1826, towards Austin. He turned onto Elderhill and called Camacho. "We just saw Harding, alone in her car. It looked like she was headed home. That must be Renberg on 12. Pass him and meet up with-"

"Hold on!" Camacho yelled. "I think he just passed us! He's on a motorcycle! The son of a bitch is on a *motorcycle!*"

CHAPTER NINE

CIA Director Wilson Dale listened attentively as the President laid it out. He asked several questions, got answers to some, and respectfully resisted the urge to persist on those Stan Daulton skirted. Daulton concluded the conversation by asserting he would sign a Presidential Finding as soon as the document was prepared. He instructed Dale not to let the formality delay implementation of his order, and demanded immediate action. Dale's response was as could be expected. As soon as he hung up the telephone, he summoned the agency's Far East Division chief to his office. Jamie Blair was ushered in moments later.

"We've got a situation in Korea," Dale said gruffly, his frown accentuating the lines on his brow. "One of the North's bigwigs wants to come over."

Blair's own forehead creased as his eyebrows shot up. "Who?"

"Kim Kwang Soo."

"Whoa!" Blair said, recoiling at the name.

"What do we know about him?"

Blair took a few seconds to steady himself. "Well, he *is* a bigwig, that's for sure. He's a member of the Central Committee of the ruling Worker's Party, and one of the oldest at that."

Dale was all ears.

"He was once the personal tutor of Kim Jong Il," Blair added. "He helped create the regime. But he's best known as the author of the 'juche'—the North's isolationist code of self-reliance. They don't come much bigger than that!"

"Hmmm," Dale toned, the frown still set on his face.

"He would give us unprecedented insight into the inner workings of the ruling elite," Blair continued. "It would be a diplomatic coup of major-"

"We're not taking him," Dale said bluntly.

Blair wasn't sure he'd heard right. "*What?*"

"In fact, we need him stopped."

Blair stared incredulously. "I don't understand."

Dale chose his words carefully. "We need to leak word of his intended defection to the authorities in Pyongyang."

Blair was stunned. "Leak word?"

"Before it happens."

Shock waves reverberated around Blair. "But they'll kill him!" he protested redundantly.

Wilson Dale's gaze was steady as he nodded. "Exactly."

*   *   *

Brad Renberg's heart told him to race, but his head prevailed and he stuck to the speed limit. He was too close now to let something as petty as a traffic violation stop him.

I've found what you've been looking for.

So simple, yet virtually impossible to guess. He'd heard Harding say it, and he'd replayed it in his head over and over, but he'd never have thought to try it.

The first loud thunderclap rocked him. A sudden gust of side wind pushed the bike left. He leaned right to counter it and immediately dropped his speed, scared by how close he had come to losing control. He was ten, maybe fifteen minutes from Wimberley. He braced himself and prayed he would make it before the downpour.

*   *   *

Three miles west of Renberg on Elderhill Road, with Markovski and Camacho now in his rearview mirror, Mitch Wakeman was also concerned about the weather. "What do you think?" he asked Vogel. "Do we take him now or wait for Stiles and Lopez?"

"I wonder where she put the tracking device," Vogel replied. "I'd love to know how secure it is."

Wakeman speed-dialed Stiles' number on the cell phone. "Where are you?"

"We just passed Fischer on 32. I'm guessing about ten minutes before we hit 12. It looks like we'll be ahead of him if he takes 12 into San Marcos."

"We're behind him and Markovski is behind us. Let's track him into San Marcos and see where he's going."

"That lightning's beginning to put on a hell of a show behind you guys."

"If the rain comes and he stops, we move in."

       *   *   *

The lightning and thunder had intensified when Renberg crossed the Cypress Creek bridge in Wimberley. His speed was down in the thirties, and even that was pushing it in the swirling gusts. But there was still no rain, and thankfully no slick pavement to contend with. The closer he got, the greater was his urge to speed. Once he turned off 12 onto Spoke Hollow he was less likely to run into a cop, but he was restrained by other inherent dangers. There were sudden dips and turns, potholes, and an occasional blind corner, none of which encouraged haste on a motorcycle.

It was a big relief to finally pull up at the house. He stopped the bike and reached into his breast pocket for the remote, glancing around as the garage door went up. It looked like he was the only person foolish enough to venture out as the front moved in. As soon as he drove in he closed the door, removed the helmet, and hurried into the house.

The barking was frantic, as was always the case during thunder-storms. To Mutley it was doomsday and his mission was to warn the world. Renberg quieted him down some, but he couldn't check the dog's restlessness.

In the garage, heat was dissipating from the Suzuki's engine, slowly cooling it down. Still securely clipped to the strap on the saddle, the transponder planted by Sadie Harding continued to bounce its signal off the satellites.

*   *   *

"He's turned off 12," Stiles said.

"He might just be taking back roads," Lopez replied. "Check with Wakeman."

Wakeman beat him to it. Stiles set his laptop aside when the phone rang.

"He's turned," Stiles said, pre-empting his boss.

"We show him on 217," Wakeman said. "Maybe he just wants off the main roads. He'll still have to come out on 12 again, but there are two places, looks like about two and four miles from San Marcos. Where are you?"

"I see those intersections," Stiles replied, his eyes on the screen. "We're about three miles from the first."

"You're still ahead of him, so keep going and wait in San Marcos. Did Juan tell you Renberg's on a bike?"

"Yes."

"Call me when you reach San Marcos."

It was six minutes later when Stiles called, and he hadn't reached San Marcos. "It looks like he's stopped again."

"Yes," Vogel said. "We're on Spoke Hollow, two miles away."

While Vogel kept the line open with Stiles, Wakeman slowed down and used a hand-held wireless CB transceiver to communicate with

Camacho, who was still right behind them. "Let's be careful here," he said. "This could be a momentary thing or a mechanical problem."

"I've already passed him once," Camacho noted. "If he sees me again it might register."

"Right. Stop when we're half a mile from him, if he isn't moving by then. I'll drive past him and see what the deal is."

"What do we do if he's broken down? If he hitches a ride, we're screwed trying to track him."

"If he's stuck we take him."

"He'll know it was Sadie."

"Tough."

Camacho knew better than to argue.

Vogel could tell from the map on his screen that they were very close to the Blanco River. They turned one corner and realized from the row of houses on the left that they were now running parallel to it. Two hundred yards later they passed the blip on the screen.

"No mechanical breakdown," he murmured to Wakeman. "We've passed him." He looked behind them. "He must be in one of those last two or three houses before the river crossing back there."

"Are you sure?" Wakeman asked.

"Uh huh."

Wakeman spoke to Camacho again. "Okay, he's not at the side of the road. It looks like he's pulled into a house here, and we've narrowed it down to one of about three. I'm turning around. I'll drive past again to get the numbers."

"What if he's watching?"

"We need to know which house."

"That river crossing goes to Flite Acres," Vogel said. He brought the phone back to his ear. "Are you there?"

"Here," Stiles replied.

"Do you see Flite Acres on the map?"

"Just a second...yes."

"See the river crossing between Spoke Hollow and Flite Acres?"

"I see several."

"The first one. To the west. Hidden Valley."

"Got it."

"Get there. Renberg's in one of the houses on the south bank. There's three ways out. Spoke Hollow in two directions, and across the river to Flite Acres. We'll take care of Spoke Hollow. You cover the bridge."

"We're on our way."

Wakeman had turned the car around and they were gliding past the houses. He and Vogel both read the numbers. "2411, 2301 and...2200."

Thirty seconds later they met up with Markovski and Camacho. Wakeman was on the phone with the Texas Department of Public Safety. He asked to hold while the addresses were checked against the DPS database. He U-turned again while he waited. "2200 is Arnold Pugh," he said, as Vogel scribbled the name down, "2301 is Elizabeth Mays, 2411, Christopher Pendergraft."

Vogel stopped writing. "Pendergraft was one of Triple D."

"Triple D?"

"The gang of hackers Renberg belonged to."

Wakeman took to the CB. "We've got him. He's in 2411. It's the last house before the road to the bridge. We can expect there'll be at least one more person in there. They've got three ways out, two directions on Spoke Hollow, and across the bridge to Flite Acres. Between us we'll watch Spoke Hollow. We'll wait for Frankie and Raphael to get to the bridge and make our move. You go on up ahead and look at the numbers so you see which house it is. 2411. Pass it and keep going straight on Spoke Hollow. Park as far as you can where you can still see it. You shouldn't be more than a hundred yards. Turn the car around and watch. We'll stay on this side. He can't cross the river without one of us seeing him."

Markovski pulled away. Moments later he and Camacho got a good look at 2411. They drove past, turned around, and pulled over to the side of the road. The early afternoon had turned menacingly dark under the thick cloud cover, but Pendergraft's house, the garage door, and the low water bridge across the Blanco were all clearly in view.

✶   ✶   ✶

Brad Renberg wasted no time. Thunderstorms meant lightning strikes and lightning strikes meant power outages and a power outage meant no computer. He quickly accessed Netmail, calculated his password, and downloaded the e-mail from Harding. The same message he'd seen the first time appeared, the only difference being the entry for current time.

```
Brad@netmail.com—> korpen.pgp
Pretty Good Privacy(tm) 2.6.1—Public-key encryp-
tion for the masses.
(c)1990-1996 Philip Zimmermann, Phil's Pretty Good
Software. 29August 94
Distributed by the Massachusetts Institute of
Technology. Uses RSAREF.
Export of this software may be restricted by the
U.S. government.
Current time: 1996/09/04 03:04   GMT
File is conventionally encrypted.
You need a pass phrase to decrypt this file.
Enter pass phrase:
```

Beside himself with anticipation, Renberg responded to the prompt by typing:

```
I've found what you've been looking for.
```

The screen filled with garbage:

Δ✶⌊M≡Ψ≥A ç'#∝E∉©ΣΩΨτ,πX •92⎰#>Φ"O ⇔ℵH37λΘ

"Come *on!*" Harding shouted in dismay. The unintelligible rubbish meant he'd entered the wrong key. A sudden lightning bolt was quickly followed by a blast of thunder, briefly diverting his attention. Mutley started barking again.

"Shut up, Mutley," Renberg ordered, venting frustration. "It's only thunder, now shut up!"

Renberg scowled at the dog and turned back to the screen. It could be one of a multitude of details. Finding out what could conceivably take hours, but that was the nature of the beast. Short of talking to Harding or getting it in writing, there was nothing else to do but run variations. With an angry grimace, he started with:

```
I've found what you've been looking for
```

Omitting the period didn't help. The result was different but the same. Different characters and symbols, but garbage nonetheless. He tried again:

```
i've found what you've been looking for
```

Still rubbish. On the next attempt he typed so fast he made a spelling error:

```
I've fund what you have been looking for
```

When he saw what he'd done he went back and corrected the spelling. The result was no better than before.

"Jesus, Richard, don't do this to me."

The next explosion of thunder was so loud he jumped. Mutley sprang out from the corner.

"It's okay, boy," Renberg said reassuringly, now himself shaken. "That was a loud one, huh?"

Mutley kept his tail down and barked.

"It's *okay!*" Renberg petted him around the neck for a few seconds then pushed him away. It still wasn't raining but the lightning strikes were more frequent now. Renberg was aware that any one could cause a momentary outage that would necessitate re-booting the computer, wasting precious time. He was also at the point where he needed to start keeping track of the key variations he'd used, so as not to repeat failures. He took a sheet of paper out of the printer tray and wrote down his previous attempts. Then he tried:

```
i've found what you have been looking for
```

The phrase ended up being another entry on the list. He willed himself to stay calm and composed. He could succeed on the next attempt, or it might take hours. The most important thing now was patience and persistence.

*   *   *

The first raindrops that spattered down on the windscreen were big and clumsy, as if in warning of the torrent about to be unleashed. Seconds after turning off Flite Acres and descending on Hidden Valley, Franklin Stiles slammed on the brakes at the sight of the river crossing. It was his first encounter with a low water bridge, and he was taken by surprise.

"It's almost under water!" he exclaimed.

"It's driveable," Lopez replied.

As Stiles inched the car across he noticed the gate. "Is that for when the water's too high?"

Lopez nodded and brought the CB radio to his mouth. "We're coming across the bridge. I see a computer screen in the center bay window. There's someone at a desk."

"Let's go!" Vogel urged.

"All right," Wakeman said to Stiles. "Park on this side and block the bridge. How many doors do you see on the river side?"

"Several. The whole siding is floor-to-ceiling glass. Bay windows, and it looks like at least three sliding glass doors."

"Okay. We have the front door, and the garage on this side. Juan?"

"Here." Camacho was in the car with Markovski, listening to the conversation.

"Pull up to the intersection. Noel goes riverside with Franklin and Raphael, you come with us and cover the front."

It was about fifty yards from the river to the house. Stiles pulled the car off the bridge and shifted the gear into neutral. By the time he engaged the parking brake Lopez had already jumped out. Markovski pulled his car into the intersection thirty yards ahead.

"One of you needs to come around the far side," Stiles said into his radio. "If one of us crosses over he'd see us through the window."

"Okay," Wakeman responded. "Noel's coming around."

As Stiles crept up to the house, Wakeman pointed Juan Camacho to the garage door. A dog started barking as Markovski snuk around the far side. Stiles and Lopez were crouched at the corner closest to the bridge. Between the six of them, Wakeman, Vogel and Camacho up front, and Markovski, Stiles and Lopez on the river side, they had the house surrounded. All had their guns out. Another flash of lightning produced a booming roll of thunder, and the rain came down in earnest. The barking became louder and deeper.

Wakeman and Vogel glanced at each other and exchanged nods. Wakeman released the safety catch on his gun and made for the door.

        *   *   *

Brad Renberg cursed out loud as another random stream of symbols filled the screen. He resisted the urge to smash his fist into the monitor and typed in the next iteration.

      I'VE FOUND WHAT YOU'VE BEEN LOOKING FOR.

He started adding to his handwritten list when Mutley growled and ran to the front door.

"Settle down, Mutt," Renberg hissed. Mutley paid no attention and ran across the den towards the kitchen, still growling as he went. He growled at the sliding glass door for a few seconds, then suddenly went wild. The hair on his back sprang up and he started barking again, only now more viciously than before.

"Shut up, Mutley!" Renberg shouted angrily.

The dog responded by running to Renberg, then to the front door, then back to the kitchen, all the time barking furiously. Renberg sensed the change and followed Mutley into the kitchen. "What is it, boy?"

Mutley's barks increased in pitch. Renberg saw the upright hair on his dog's back and recognized the urgency. This wasn't just about the weather. There was a message here, one Renberg had seen before, one he understood. Mutley was warning of danger.

Renberg peered out of the kitchen window towards the river and saw the car blocking the bridge. The rain was falling steadily now, but he could see there was nobody in the car. He ran to the guest bathroom and checked the other side of the house. There was another car at the intersection of Spoke Hollow and Hidden Valley. This one, too, had no one in it. He'd seen enough. Two empty cars and Mutley in hysterics added up to trouble. He switched the lights off in the den and the kitchen. It was now as dark inside the house as it was outside. Calming Mutley down was out of the question. Despite all the barking and the sound of the rain and thunder, Renberg still jumped at the banging on the door.

"*Open up!*" Wakeman hollered. "*FBI!*"

Everything happened very quickly. From where he stood Renberg could see two men run from the corners of the house to the porch door. Mutley raced over, barking hysterically. Renberg had left and returned through the garage, and he knew both front and back doors were locked.

"*Open up! You're surrounded!*"

They were now trying to force the front door, and it sounded like they were on the verge of busting through. A flash of lightning showed another man running to the sliding door at the kitchen. They had him cornered. Renberg dashed to the garage, thinking about an escape in the Jeep. His heart sank when he realized it faced inwards and he'd have to back out. They'd shoot the tires out in a second. And the motorcycle would be a deathtrap in the rain. There was the sound of shattering glass as a window was smashed. Renberg ran back into the den and saw it was the vertical strip of glass next to the front door. Too narrow for an adult human to fit through, but an arm reached in to fumble with the lock. Mutley charged and the arm disappeared.

"Mutley, come!" Renberg shrieked, slipping back into the garage. When Mutley followed him, Renberg darted back into the house and slammed the door, locking it from the den side. He pulled the garage door remote out of his pocket, pushed the activator, then let it fall from his hand as he rushed into the bedroom.

Alone in the garage, and unable now to protect his master, the German shepherd went berserk. When the garage door suddenly opened, Mutley charged.

Mitch Wakeman had his arm through the broken pane and was trying to unlock the front door. Steve Vogel was next to him, anxious to get through. Juan Camacho was alone, three feet from the garage door when it opened. As the white blur knocked him down the gun fell from his hand. From the corner of his eye Vogel sensed the movement and spun around to see the big dog attacking Camacho. Vogel brought his gun around and fired. Camacho's instincts also kicked in. He lashed out with his bare hands at the dog's head and tried to get up off the ground. Sharp teeth ripped the flesh in his left hand, mangling tendons and crushing bones. As he made a desperate effort to spring up, the bullet hit his back, shattering the vertebrae at the base of his spine.

At the sound of the shot Mutley left his first victim on the ground and rushed the men at the front door. Wakeman turned around as the second shot ran out. Mutley was hit in the chest and landed just short of Vogel's feet, yelping in pain. Vogel loosed a third bullet into the dog's head and the yelping stopped, leaving only the sound of Camacho's moans through the rain.

When they heard the shots, Markovski, Stiles and Lopez abandoned their efforts to break through doors on the river side and raced around to the front of the house to where the action was. They arrived in time to see Steve Vogel running into the garage and Mitch Wakeman dropping to one knee beside a delirious Juan Camacho.

From where he stood in the bedroom, Brad Renberg knew well that if he stayed in the house it was all over. He unlatched the lock and slid the glass door open. He ducked low and sprinted out onto the porch, over the railing, and onto the slick grass. The rain pelted him hard as he ran to his left, towards the house next door, away from the car blocking the bridge.

With both hands grasping his gun Vogel first checked the Jeep. He tried the door that led into the house and found it locked. He swung around, saw the others congregated outside the garage, and realized what had happened.

He tore around the side to the back, screaming that Renberg would get away. Markovski and Lopez followed him as Wakeman and Stiles urged Juan Camacho to stay lucid. Vogel jumped on the porch, ran across the back of the house, and found the open door.

"*Over here!*" he yelled as he jumped over the railing. He ran down to the river, scanning the water in both directions. Lopez and Markovski followed him down and spread out along the riverbank, Lopez left and Markovski right, towards the bridge. Vogel peered frantically in all directions as another flash of lightning lit up the sky. He could see a hundred yards downstream beyond the bridge, and about fifty upstream to the point where the river curved to the left and disappeared from view. He craned his neck and brought a hand to his forehead to shield his eyes from the rain. Lopez and Markovski were running back and forth and doing three-sixties.

Frenetic as their search was, there was no sign of Brad Renberg.

CHAPTER TEN

At full sprint, it took Renberg six seconds to reach the house next door. He held his head down and kept running, across the back of 2301 and on around to the far side of 2200 Spoke Hollow. By the time he reached the bend in the river he was soaked to the skin and amazed he hadn't been shot at. He ran twenty more yards up the riverbank to where he could no longer see Pendergraft's house. He paused for a few seconds, hoping Mutley would come, but not daring to call. Another lightning flash spurred him to move on and he dived into the river.

It was no less than twenty yards wide and about four feet deep. He thrust his arms and kicked for all he was worth, figuring it was faster than wading across. When he reached the other side and tried to get out, he twice slipped and fell back in the water. He made it on the third attempt and ran up the soggy bank, past the nearest house to Flite Acres Road.

His mind was spinning as he considered what to do. Aunt Charlene's in San Marcos? The thought jarred his senses as he realized he'd completely forgotten about his mother's insulin shot that morning. With all that was happening, it had slipped his mind. And it was major wishful thinking to hope she'd taken care of it herself.

There were two cars in the first driveway, both unlocked, but neither with keys in the ignition. Running left would take him upstream, towards

3237. Downstream felt safer. He knew the Blanco wound its way from Wimberley to San Marcos and he was clutching at straws. He'd never been farther along Flite Acres than Hidden Valley, and he needed to hurry before they came across the low-water bridge. He turned right and ran, going from one driveway to the next in the hope of giving himself somewhere to hide if a car appeared on the road. Within a few minutes he saw the Hidden Valley turn. He slipped over to the next lot and paused behind a Suburban parked in the driveway. He crept across to the side of the house and peered across the river at Pendergraft's place. There was one man running up the bank to the porch, and another walking upstream along the water's edge. The car blocking the bridge was still there, still unattended. Renberg felt a pang of remorse. There was no sign of Mutley. More significantly, there was no *sound* of Mutley.

He retraced his steps back to the driveway and tried the Suburban's doors. The driver's door was open, but there were no keys inside. Renberg was an ace with computers, but he knew precious little about hot-wiring cars. He was sure it was a simple matter of connecting two wires, but which two and where? Resolving to learn if he survived, he moved on to the next house, at the corner of Flite Acres and Hidden Valley. He was sure the car blocking the bridge would be unlocked, and he'd bet the key was in the ignition, but it was too risky. He'd have to cross the river again, and whether he went in the water or across the bridge, he'd be too exposed. Besides, even if he succeeded, they'd know which car to look for.

Hidden Valley snaked its way down to the river from Flite Acres. He could run across it without being seen from Pendergraft's house. Once across Hidden Valley he'd be downstream of them, and at least by way of the river, heading towards San Marcos. With luck, he might even find a car to use. He hesitated momentarily, then sprinted across Hidden Valley.

★   ★   ★

It was immediately clear that Juan Camacho's injury was serious. He was on his side, having taken a bullet in the small of his back.

"Don't move him!" Wakeman warned. "Call for help!"

While Wakeman stayed at Camacho's side, Franklin Stiles ran to the car. He was one of two agents at the Bureau's Austin Agency who worked road trips, handling FBI business outside of Austin, and dealing with local law enforcement agencies in remote counties around the state capitol. After consulting a list of numbers from an inside pocket in his daily planner, he called the Hays County Sheriff's office in San Marcos on his cell phone.

"An officer is down and needs emergency assistance!" he reported once he had identified himself. "There's been a shooting, and a suspect is at large. We're in Wimberley, at 2411 Spoke Hollow, where Spoke Hollow intersects Hidden Valley, south side of the river."

Of the emergencies encountered by law enforcement personnel, none precipitates as galvanized a response as that of a fallen officer. When the Hays County Sheriff's office dispatcher aired the request for assistance, units from several different agencies reacted immediately. As it usually is, the Sheriff's transmission was being monitored by the dispatcher at Wimberley EMS Systems, Inc., a five-man outfit equipped with two fully stocked ambulances, both with Advanced Life Support capability. The three paramedics on duty instantly went on alert, pulled an ambulance out of its shelter onto the tarmac, and waited. The tone-out came moments later, two tones heard only by Wimberley EMS, followed by a description of the injury as a gunshot wound, and details of the location. Seconds later, upon receiving confirmation that the scene was secure, the paramedics were on their way. After checking en route and being advised the low water bridges were passable, they elected to take what would be the shortest route: 3237, then Flight Acres to Hidden Valley.

They were the first of the field units to arrive at the scene. They found Juan Camacho barely clinging to life, in deep shock, and losing blood at a critical rate. Franklin Stiles told them he had already checked into Starflight, the helicopter emergency medical service out of Austin's Brackenridge hospital. As luck would have it, the chopper was temporarily grounded by the inclement weather. The paramedics did what they could to stabilize Camacho's condition before loading him into the ambulance. The initial assessment was he might not make it to Brackenridge, and the only viable alternative was the Central Texas Medical Center in San Marcos. Stiles had worked with Camacho for two years, and needed no prodding by Mitch Wakeman. When the ambulance raced off, he was in it, right at Camacho's side.

Over the course of the next twenty minutes, seven units from three different agencies descended on 2411 Spoke Hollow. Two were state troopers, four were Hays county sheriffs, and one, a dark blue Chevy Blazer, bore the insignia of the Texas Department of Parks and Wildlife.

"He has about a thirty-minute lead on us," Steve Vogel snarled. "I need whoever of you is most familiar with this territory to advise us on how best to establish a containment perimeter." Aware that Mitch Wakeman was glaring at him, Vogel limited eye contact to the new faces.

"If he's on foot, and sticking to the roads, He won't have got too far." It was one of the county sheriffs. "If we put a vehicle at the intersection of 12 and Spoke Hollow, and one at Flite Acres and 3237, there's a good chance he hasn't reached either of those points yet."

"Just in case, another two cars can patrol 12 and 3237," another of the sheriffs said. "We have enough vehicles."

"What about downstream?" Vogel asked, still avoiding Wakeman's eyes.

"You got Spoke Hollow for four, maybe five miles along the river. On the other side, Flite Acres goes a bit further."

"Let's get a couple of cars going downstream, one each side of the river. Get to the end and work back. You all know what Renberg looks like. Consider him armed and dangerous. And he's a devious bastard. He'll be using his head. Shoot if you have to."

"What about a house-to-house?" a trooper asked.

"There are a lot of houses around here that aren't lived in full-time," one of the sheriffs said. "It would be easy for him to break into one."

"Okay," Vogel said. "Let's get the troopers on 12 and…what's the other one?"

"3237"

"Yeah. Four sheriffs cover the roads along the river. That leaves game warden and four FBI. One of us needs to stay here in case he comes back, that leaves four, one in each direction on the roads along the river. Knock on every door, check every house, alert the residents, have them check their cars, bikes, boats. Make sure everything's accounted for." He turned to Wakeman for the first time since shooting Camacho. "Mitch, you want to add anything?"

"Just one thing," Wakeman said dryly. "You all need to be aware that it wasn't Renberg who shot Agent Camacho. Devious, he may be. But I, for one, don't know that he's armed or dangerous."

"Whoa, whoa," Vogel said. "All right. Let's get it all out on the table. The bullet that hit Camacho came from my gun. It was an accident. I was trying to shoot the dog before it could maul Camacho. But it was Renberg who let the dog loose on us. I stress—he's to be regarded a threat to national security. And while we don't know he's got a gun, he's shown he'll use whatever means are at his disposal to resist arrest, and that makes him dangerous."

After going over details regarding communications and protocol, they started to move out. Only Mitch Wakeman stayed behind, waiting for the group to disperse.

"There was no need for that, Mitch," Vogel said preemptively. "I understand how you feel, but you saw what happened. It was an accident. You *know* that."

Wakeman pursed his lips. "We can't have one of these guys catch up to Renberg thinking he shot Camacho. *You* know *that*."

"Granted. But you know what I'm talking about. There's an attitude here, like I meant to shoot your man or something. Get over it."

Again Wakeman pursed his lips, but this time declined to respond. He stared briefly at Vogel, then turned and walked away.

Vogel watched him go. "I'll stay here," he shouted after Wakeman. "I need to check that computer."

With his back to Vogel, Wakeman nodded once and got into his car.

*   *   *

Renberg could move fastest by running on the road but that would also leave him most exposed. The top priority was evading capture, so he stayed on the river side of the houses.

He was aghast at the thought Mutley hadn't survived. He'd intended for Mutley to charge out of the garage to surprise and distract them. The ploy had worked, but had Mutley been the price of his escape? He was sure he'd heard more than one shot. He thought two, but he couldn't be sure if there was a third. Had one of the bastards shot Mutley? One more thing for which he would make the bastards pay.

While the cloud cover made the afternoon darker than usual, it wasn't nighttime-dark yet so he had to avoid open spaces. He was running hard and he tired quickly, but he couldn't stop. When the houses started thinning out, the riverbank terrain became rougher and he moved closer to the water. He could still make out more houses downstream, but they were now fewer and farther in between. He had to dodge bushes and trees, cedars, cypresses and oaks, some with large roots that were like silent traps, waiting for him to put a foot wrong and twist an ankle or snap a bone.

It didn't take long for the first mishap. He was still running, parallel to and some ten feet from the water, slowed now by the increasing sogginess underfoot, when he glanced behind him to check if anyone was there. Suddenly it felt like he'd run into a curtain of nails. He collapsed in a heap on the ground. When he tried to pick himself up, the pain kept him down. It took him a few seconds to realize he hadn't been shot or run into a hunter's snare. He had just run headlong into a large thorn bush. The thorns were nasty, some an inch or more long, and many had torn his skin. The slightest movement was now excruciating, but he had to tend to the punctures. He stayed on the ground, grunting with each breath as he painstakingly picked thorns out of his arms, legs and torso. Some had broken, leaving their tips embedded in his skin. But the shock eventually gave way to relief. There were no debilitating gashes or broken bones, so he wasn't down for the count. He actually took comfort in the rain, letting it soothe his jangled nerves as he caught his breath. He willed himself up off the ground. They would be gaining on him and he couldn't afford to be still. There were more of the same thorn bushes up ahead, so running along the river would be treacherous, and walking was too slow. He turned away from the river, back towards the road.

*   *   *

One by one, the two state troopers, four county sheriffs, and the game warden scouting the roads in their vehicles reported their progress, or lack thereof. They had covered the roads leading from 2411 Spoke Hollow to the edge of the containment perimeter once, and there was no sign of the suspect anywhere. Steve Vogel worried about the diminishing light as afternoon turned to late afternoon and beckoned the evening. When he called the Texas Department of Public Safety in Austin and requested a helicopter with Forward Looking Infrared Radar and night vision capability, he was informed it would be at his disposal as soon as the weather permitted.

*   *   *

Renberg ran one third of a mile past the thorn bush before he had to stop. He was at the side of the road and could quickly disappear in the trees and shrubbery between the road and the river. Every muscle ached and his lungs felt like they were on fire. There was no way he could go on without resting. He staggered around a grassy mound and collapsed. He could see a good fifty yards of the road in both directions, so if anyone approached, he'd see them before they saw him. He first let his head drop back and closed his eyes, but breathing was too difficult with the rain in his face, so he sat up again and leaned forward.

It had to be Sadie. It was hard to believe she would sell him out, but how else to explain it? They had approached her and she'd done a deal.

He thought about the Greek soldier, way back when, who'd run a zillion miles to deliver news of a victory to his superiors, unwittingly giving birth to the modern-day marathon. Renberg wasn't about to duplicate the feat, and decided to take a couple more minutes before pushing on.

He heard the truck before he saw it. It hadn't come around the corner yet when it backfired under deceleration, and there was a loud grating noise as the driver shifted down. When it appeared, Renberg pushed himself up and ran towards the road. It was an old pickup, a late fifties model he guessed. Very old, too old to be FBI. The truck was laboring towards him some twenty yards up the road when Renberg waved it down.

The driver, wearing a Texas Rangers baseball cap and a jaded T-shirt under denim overalls, looked to be about the same age as his pickup.

"Get you in out of the rain, son," he drawled when Renberg opened the door. "What the *hell* happened to you?"

Renberg heaved himself into the passenger seat and closed the door. He could just imagine what a sight he was. "I was hiking along the river," he panted. "When the rain came I started running, and ran right into a thorn bush. It's all superficial."

"You picked a fine time to go hiking!"

"Yeah. It was clear when I started. How far are you going?"

"About another couple of miles here to the camping ground on the other side."

"Great! It's where I was headed by way of the river. I'm meeting someone at the campground. I appreciate you stopping."

"Well, it's a pleasure to help. George D. Wilhite." He thrust a hand out at Renberg.

"Good to meet you," Renberg said, obliging him. "Sam...Sam Carter."

Wilhite pushed the clutch and tried to engage the gear. The shift lever resisted until he released the clutch, revved the engine and tried again. This time he went from neutral to second before finding first. He let out the clutch and the pickup responded.

"Neat truck," Renberg said, giving himself a pretext to look around and check the road behind them. It was clear, and he noticed the shot-gun on the rack behind his head.

"Fifty-seven Ford F100," Wilhite said proudly. "Only vehicle I've ever owned. It belonged to my dad before me."

"You don't see many like this on the road much anymore."

"No, but it'll get you there." He guffawed out loud and reached for a tin of chewing tobacco on the seat next to him. Renberg watched Wilhite spit into a Michelob bottle and replenish the stash in his gum.

He looked behind them again. The road was clear. They were doing about thirty now, and it was a relief to be off his feet. The rain was still incessant and the terrain around the river looked rough. Not impassable by a long shot, but his progress would have been slow. George D. Wilhite was nothing short of a Godsend.

The road twisted and meandered its way for what Renberg estimated was a couple of miles before Wilhite took a right turn and crossed over another low-water bridge, at the far end of which was the entrance to a campground.

"Did you say your buddy's out here?"

"Yeah," Renberg replied. "I'm not sure where. You just go on wher-ever you're set up and I'll take it from there."

"Are you sure?"

"Oh yeah. I don't mind the rain. It was getting here that was going to be a trick, and I appreciate the ride."

It was clear the campground was on the verge of becoming one large mud pit, and the old Ford did well to make it to Wilhite's tent.

"I've got some cold beer in the tent," Wilhite offered. "Be sure to come back now if you don't find your buddy."

"Thanks, I will," Renberg said as he stepped out of the pickup. He waved to Wilhite and took off in the direction of another tent that was farther downstream. He gave it about thirty seconds before looking back. Wilhite had disappeared—to the shelter of his tent and the comfort of a beer, no doubt. Renberg couldn't stop himself from going back. It was a lousy thing to do and he hated doing it but he was desperate. He wiped the rain off the truck's passenger side window—it was the one farthest from the tent—and found his hunch was good. Wilhite's keys were in the ignition. He wasn't sure he could start the engine and get the clunker in gear before Wilhite came out, but it was a chance he was going to have to take. He didn't know how far past the campground Flite Acres went, and four wheels was his best bet to find out.

Just as Renberg swung the passenger door open and slid in, George D. Wilhite realized he'd left his chewing tobacco in the pickup. He emerged from the tent and pulled open the driver-side door to find an alarmed Renberg reaching for the steering wheel.

"What the hell are you doing, boy?" Wilhite thundered.

Renberg's face turned crimson. "I...uh...was just...looking for my wallet," he stammered

"Looking for your wallet?" Wilhite echoed mockingly.

"I lost it...either here, or somewhere back there by the river."

Wilhite grunted and reached into the pickup. He pulled the shotgun off the rack, his eyes never leaving Renberg's. "Well, is it here?"

"It doesn't look like it," Renberg said meekly, glancing under the seat.

"Then you'll be gone?" Wilhite suggested as he pulled the key out of the ignition.

"Yes," Renberg said. He stepped out and closed the door on his side.

As Renberg walked off, he could hear Wilhite grunting behind him. This time, feeling Wilhite's eyes piercing his back, he kept going. He walked towards the other tent, pitched under a large oak tree farther inside the campground. When he was within a few feet of it he stopped and looked back. Wilhite had gotten out of the rain, no doubt taking his keys and shotgun with him. There'd been just a fleeting second there, as Wilhite reached for his shotgun, when Renberg had feared it was over. Despite all that was happening, he still felt lucky. By all counts he should have been arrested or, worse yet, shot by now.

He turned and considered the tent. It was pitched about forty yards from the river, and there wasn't a vehicle nearby. It could be that the camper, just like Wilhite, had gone somewhere and would soon return. As he looked around the answer suddenly caught his eye. There was no vehicle because this camper hadn't come on the road. Right there, sitting on muddy soil close to the water's edge, was a canoe. Renberg's pulse, already rapid, quickened. There was no sound coming from inside the tent, at least as far as he could hear through the beating rain. A canoe could get him downstream on the water faster than he could go on foot. He thought about his mother, and wondered how long she could go without the insulin before something happened. He wondered how bad that something might be.

It was a red canoe and it looked old but it was wooden, which was good. An aluminum hull would likely be noisier to push into the water. It was on its side, resting on the grip of a paddle, the tip of which was wedged against a rock. Renberg grabbed the gunwale and tried to lift. It was heavy, well over fifty pounds, but it lay only a couple of feet from the water, and he decided to drag and push rather than carry it. The slick mud made it easy, as the canoe slid readily over the bank. He grabbed the wooden paddle and waded in.

*   *   *

Considering it was a workday afternoon, Secret Service Special Agent Noel Markovski wasn't surprised to find no cars in the driveway and no one home at the first two houses upstream from Hidden Valley on Flite Acres. When he knocked on the front door at the third house, the retired couple who invited him in out of the rain reacted with intrigue to his badge, and tempered alarm at the notion of a fugitive in their midst.

"I told you they were gunshots I heard," the woman said indignantly to her husband. She turned to Markovski. "He said it was just the thunder. He never listens to me."

"Is that car in the driveway the only one you have?" Markovski inquired politely.

"Yes."

"I'm going to ask you to keep it locked and stay vigilant. The man we're looking for wears his hair in a ponytail and has a goatee. If you see a stranger who fits that description please call 911 immediately."

He turned down the lady's offer of an umbrella, urged them to lock the door behind him, and moved on. He drove thirty yards to the next house, noted there was a car in the driveway, and resolved that the next time he was offered any protection from the rain, he would take it.

The rain was no less a hindrance to Texas Department of Parks and Wildlife game warden Shirley Mathis. She, too, was going house to house, but in the other direction, east on Flite Acres. There was someone home at three of the first four houses she stopped at. No one was missing a car, bicycle, boat, or anything else that could be used for transportation. And the only glimpse anyone had caught of Brad Renberg was either in the paper or on the TV news reports.

*   *   *

Desperate though his situation was, there was at least one thing working in Renberg's favor. The river, at least the section of it that wound through the campground, was calm. There were no rocks or falls, and while the current was building with the rain, it was still relatively light.

The canoe was a two-seater, sixteen feet in length, and a yard wide amidships. Renberg was no expert, but he'd paddled before and he knew enough of the fundamentals to get under way. Within two minutes of clambering aboard he had steered the canoe a hundred yards down the river. Twenty minutes and two dunkings later, he'd covered a full mile.

He crossed two low-water bridges without incident. Both times he got out of the canoe and walked it across the bridge by letting it float over the two inches of water covering the concrete. Half way across he picked the stern up and flipped the hull over to drain it of rainwater.

The temperature was dropping fast, and at this rate it would soon be cold. But as long as there was enough light he had to keep going. It was almost five o'clock, and he estimated there was still a good three hours before sundown.

The rain was still steady but the lightning and thunder had eased. He still wasn't sure where he was going, but his priorities hadn't changed. His mother's insulin was an immediate worry, but that aside, everything depended on Harding's e-mail.

He was deep in thought as he approached a bend, and he promptly got a firsthand lesson in the perils of taking his concentration off the river. The bend was to the right, and he noticed too late the overhanging branch on the left bank in the middle of the turn. He approached the bend down the center of the river, where the water flowed fastest and the canoe felt most stable. What he didn't know was that when a river turns, the faster water is pushed to the outside of the bend. That, coupled with the classic novice canoeist's mistake of concentrating on the obstacle as opposed to how to avoid it, sent him careening helplessly towards the branch. His only recourse was to take a spill. He leaned over and dumped himself in the water just a yard from the branch. He held on to the paddle, and the canoe plowed under the branch into the bank,

coming to rest with its bow wedged in an exposed section of the tree's
roots. He pulled it loose and guided it back to the center of the river
before plopping himself back in. Now his concentration was strictly on
the river, on staying in the center, and on reacting early to obstacles. It
was a timely lesson, as beyond the bend the river suddenly became more
challenging.

The International Scale of River Difficulty is a rating system used to
classify rivers worldwide. The American version is a codification of six
class ratings by the American Whitewater Affiliation, an organization
dedicated to promoting whitewater adventure. Class I is the easiest, des-
ignating rivers with little by way of obstructions, having slow water, and
small waves, if any. At the other end of the scale is Class VI, representing
extreme difficulty and danger. The section of the Blanco that Renberg
encountered after the near incident with the overhanging branch was a
150-yard Class II run, a category with small rocks and small waves,
requiring modest maneuvering skills, and easily manageable by trained
paddlers. But for a fatigued novice like Brad Renberg, it was rife with
pitfalls.

While the turbulence normally associated with fast water produces
instability in a canoe, fast water on its own does not. The instability in
fast water results from changes in current speed or direction, as happens
when water flows around obstructions, or even when fast water meets
slow. Renberg first sensed he was in trouble when small rocks on either
side left a clear passage of about twenty feet down the center of the river.
His speed was the same as that of the water, and by defensive instinct he
tried to slow down. He dug the paddle into the water and locked his
arms in a fixed position. The effort only succeeded in changing the
canoe's direction, not its speed. In a split second he was careening side-
ways towards two rocks fifteen feet away, downstream and to his right.
There was no time for a correction and he intuitively leaned away from
the imminent collision. It was a cardinal error. By leaning upstream,
Renberg dipped the left gunwale under the water, allowing the river to

dump its force into the canoe, filling it with water and smashing its bottom against the rocks. A Kevlar composite hull might have survived the collision, but the old wood shattered upon impact. Renberg was thrown into the water and lost his grip on the paddle. The water flow pinned him against the canoe, which was wedged between the rocks. He pushed himself away and let the river carry him around to the calmer water of the eddies on the downstream side of the rocks. He finally found his feet and waded out towards the bank. When he pulled himself out of the river he trudged ten yards back upstream to where he could see the canoe on the rocks. It was half-submerged on its side. He couldn't see the damage to the hull, but he'd heard the wood splintering. He'd also lost the paddle, so the canoeing trip was history. It was just as well, because downstream of where he stood was more of the same. Not exactly whitewater, but enough rocks and turbulence to intimidate any sane novice. His hand brushed against his pager, still clipped onto his belt. He pulled it off and checked it. It was, as he expected, dead, and he tossed it into the water. He looked back at the canoe. Recognizing that his head, like the hull, wasn't made of Kevlar, he once again considered himself lucky.

He could see the outline of a house off to his left, and another further away in the other direction, downstream of where he stood. He went left and picked his way through the trees, bushes and shrubs, towards the nearer of the two houses.

There were no cars in sight and the house was dark. A Honeywell sticker on the front door warned that the house was wired with an intrusion alarm system. Renberg peered through several windows. The house appeared sparsely furnished, more like a weekend retreat by the river than a permanent residence. There would probably be dry clothes inside, but if he broke in the alarm would trip and give away his location. A long stretch of caliche gravel road led away from the house. Renberg figured Flite Acres at this point was farther from the river than it was upstream. He couldn't even see Flite Acres from where he stood.

Staying off the road was probably safer anyway. The next house downstream wasn't far away. He headed back towards the water.

      *   *   *

Mitch Wakeman drove as fast as he could without being reckless. He
slowed down when there were other cars around, and floored it when
the road cleared. There were enough units establishing the containment
perimeter without him, and they were doing what they could to flush
Renberg out. In the meantime, he needed an effective command post,
and the combination of physical location and centralized communications facilities made the Hays County Sheriff's office the logical choice.
Wakeman heard from Franklin Stiles as he pulled into San Marcos.
Initial X-rays at the Central Texas Medical Center indicated that the
bullet in Juan Camacho's back was lodged perilously close to his spinal
cord. He was already in an operating room, being readied for emergency
surgery, but realistically, the severe loss of blood he'd suffered made his
chances for recovery very slim. Wakeman cursed out loud and banged a
clenched fist against the steering wheel. The fact that Camacho was single
and had no kids was no consolation.
Special Agent Deborah Burke was at her station in the Austin Resident
Agency when Wakeman called. She had never heard him sound so
anguished. "I want a vertical on Brad Renberg," he demanded, his voice
cracking with emotion. "I want anything you get when you get it. I'll be at
the Hays County Sheriff's in San Marcos."
Deborah Burke sprang into action. "Vertical" was Wakeman vernacular for a background investigation of the subject and immediate family
members. Burke immediately summoned the agency's investigative
assistant, and together the two started to dig.

      *   *   *

3400 Flite Acres was a two-story log home, and as Renberg approached it up the grassy bank, he could see there were lights on inside. There was a large porch facing the river, backed by expansive glass doors and towering windows. He crept around the side to the front. There was a two-car garage adjoining the house on the far side of the gravel driveway. Through the window to his right Renberg saw a great room, beautifully furnished in rustic Southwest-style decor. There was a cozy-looking sunken sitting area around a huge brick fireplace set at right angles to the porch, so as not to break the view of the river. But his attention zeroed in on a little area leading away from the great room to the right of the fireplace. From where he stood he couldn't see enough to be sure, but it looked like there was a desk and hutch set back against a wall. He skipped across the front of the house to the window next to the garage. This one showed him a gourmet kitchen, separated by a counter from the dining area beyond. Renberg almost cheered out loud. What he'd seen behind the fireplace was indeed a desk and a hutch, perched in the center of which was a personal computer. He pulled back from the kitchen window, his mind whirring. He couldn't exactly walk in with a "Hi, don't mind me, I just want to use your computer." The people who lived here obviously got around. Would they recognize him? Would they let him in? And how could he stay long enough, *if* they had Internet access, to accomplish what he needed to do?

It could have overwhelmed him, but Brad Renberg believed in fate. Growing up had been tough, and there were questions that could only be answered by chalking circumstances down to fate. Bad as it had been, he'd lost hope in redemption. But this was different. By all rights they should have nailed him back at Pendergraft's house. And it could just as easily have been his head instead of the canoe getting smashed on the rocks. Yet here he was, and if ever there was time to believe someone up there was watching over him, it was now. Lots of "ifs", but only one way to go.

It was when he walked back to the front door that he first saw the words etched into the glass. He couldn't keep the thrill from spreading a weary smile on his face. So it was one down and a ton to go, but at least some of the "ifs" were answered. He turned the handle, opened the door, and walked in.

CHAPTER ELEVEN

Steven Vogel's conscience was clear. Wakeman's reaction was understandable, but they still had a job to do. There was nothing he could do for Camacho now. Hopefully the medical professionals would do their job, and Camacho would be okay. In the meantime, Renberg was still out there and Washington was clamoring for his scalp.

Vogel slid into the chair in front of Pendergraft's computer. He first pondered the top of the screen. www.netmail.com.login. The name implied a Web-based e-mail service. It appeared Renberg had been trying to decrypt a PGP-encrypted message. He reached for the mouse and clicked on BACK. After reading the screen he clicked on BACK again, several times. It was apparent Renberg had made over a dozen attempts to decrypt something called KORPEN.

It was huge. Now he knew where Harding had sent the e-mail. Just as important, he knew Renberg hadn't read it yet. And if he could delete it from the mailbox, Renberg wouldn't be able to retrieve it.

Since it was PGP-encrypted, Vogel knew he had virtually no chance of reading KORPEN. Considering what Harding and Renberg did for entertainment, the password or pass phrase would be impossible to crack. His best bet was to delete it from the mailbox. If nothing else, that would at least ease the time pressure in the hunt for Renberg. Vogel clicked on BACK and found himself staring at a Netmail.com page that told him Renberg had one message in his box. He clicked on the DELETE MESSAGE button and got an instant reminder of what caliber of computer geek he was dealing with. The screen prompted him for a password. He took a deep breath and exhaled hard in frustration. Renberg was as calculating as they came. Everyone used a password to access their mailbox. And the fact that Harding's message was encrypted was no surprise. But to have to input a password in order to *delete* mail, that was a new one. The son of a bitch pulled no punches when it came to his own security.

Vogel snapped the cell phone out of the pouch on his belt and punched in a number. The woman who answered was with CART, the FBI's Computer Analysis and Response Team at the Bureau's Washington, DC headquarters.

"Angie, it's Steve. I need you to do something for me."

"Hey, Steve. Shoot."

"Check out dub dub dub dot Netmail dot com. I need to know where it's incorporated and where the registered office is. Headquarters too."

"Got it. What else?"

"That's it. I'll hold."

He could hear her clicking on a keyboard. She had the answer in less than a minute. "Colorado Springs. Do you want a number?"

"Yes."

He repeated it out loud as he scribbled it down, adding: "I need the number of the Denver field office, and the name of the SAC."

"Just a sec …" More clicks, then the number and a name.

He hung up and dialed Denver. When a receptionist at the field office answered, Vogel asked for Special Agent-in-Charge Matt Jordan. After a quick introduction and a brief case background, Vogel got to the point. "I need someone to contact Netmail and solicit their cooperation in deleting Renberg's mail. We might want to block his access altogether."

"We'll get on it right away," Jordan said.

"His user name is Brad at Netmail dot com."

"Got it. Where do we reach you?"

Vogel gave him his mobile number and explained it was a cell phone. "If for any reason you can't get through, leave me a message at the Austin office. 512-345-1111."

With a firm assurance he'd keep Vogel apprised of their progress, Matt Jordan hung up the phone.

*   *   *

There are no hotels in Wimberley, and most of the town's residents would like to keep it that way. Not that visitors are not welcome—the truth is the contrary—but hotels connote commercial-looking, multi-story buildings with large parking lots, an image at odds with Wimberley's laid back charm. Overnight accommodations for out-of-towners abound, but in forms more congruous to the landscape—ranches, inns, cottages, cabins, lodges, resorts and bed-and-breakfasts, of which there are no less than forty.

Of the lodges, none was finer than River Oaks, but that was of little consequence to Brad Renberg. A lodge was a lodge, and the word *Welcome* was etched under the name in the glass pane on the front door.

He closed the door behind him and stood in the foyer, dripping water onto the Mexican tile.

"Hello?" he shouted over the din of the rain.

There was a log staircase to his left, beyond which he'd seen the kitchen. The living room was directly ahead, its sunken seating area cozily wrapped around a towering brick fireplace. In contrast to their natural, round appearance on the outside, the logs had been hewn on the interior, giving the walls a smooth, flat finish.

"Hello?"

"Coming." It was a female voice that preceded the sound of footsteps on the staircase. She looked to be in her sixties, a petite lady with white hair and a ready smile. Her bright blue bespectacled eyes illuminated a pleasant, comforting face. When she came around the stairs and took a look at him she was clearly taken aback. "Good lord!" she exclaimed. "What happened to you?"

He could imagine how unsightly he looked with his shaved head, soaked to the skin, splattered with mud, and scratched all over.

"I was canoeing on the river when the storm hit. I hit a rock and lost the canoe and everything in it. All my camping gear."

"Goodness! Are you all right?"

"I'm fine. Just soaked. I ran into a thorn bush as I was scrambling out of the river."

Her eyes dropped to the widening puddle at his feet. "We'd better get you dry."

"I didn't mean to drip all over your floor."

"Go into the garage. I'll open it for you."

So far, there had been no indication she recognized him. He went back outside as she made for the kitchen. The garage door opened and he stepped in from under the rain.

"I'll get a towel," she said, lifting the cover on a washing machine. "Take you clothes off and throw them in here. I'll get you something to wear."

She closed the garage door and went inside, leaving him standing next to a Cadillac Seville. So there was a computer *and* a car. With luck, she'd have Internet access, he'd be able to decrypt Harding's message, then use the car to get to his mother in San Marcos.

He started with his shoes and socks, then took off his jacket and shirt. He kept his jeans on until she returned.

"Here," she said, handing him a towel, a T-shirt and denim overalls. "You'll have to adjust the straps. I'm afraid it's the best I can do."

"This is fine."

"Dry yourself and change and come on inside."

"Thank you."

When she went back into the kitchen, he slipped off his jeans and boxers and rubbed himself dry with the towel. The overalls were short, but welcome.

"That's better," she said, looking him over in the kitchen. "I made some coffee."

"Wonderful."

She went back into the garage.

"I really do appreciate this," he said, standing at the door. The washer and dryer were in a corner, next to a wall-mounted rack holding an assortment of gardening tools. She reached for a box of detergent on a shelf above the washing machine and sprinkled in a measured amount of the blue powder. After turning two control dials she put the lid down and brushed past him back into the kitchen.

"How do you like it?"

"Black, please. No sugar." He hadn't heard another sound from upstairs and wondered if they were alone.

"Welcome to River Oaks," she said, handing him the mug. "I'm Connie Kinser."

"This is a neat house, Connie."

"We built it seven years ago. We were living in Houston at the time. My husband worked for Gulf Oil, and this was to be our retirement home. I moved here permanently three years ago, after Bobby passed away."

"And you've turned it into a lodge."

"It keeps me busy."

"It's very nice."

"Thank you. I enjoy it."

"I've never been in a log home before."

"With the exception of the spruce beams supporting the roof," she said proudly, "these are all cedar logs. And what about you? Are you from around here?"

"Austin." He was going to have to give her a name. "Can I use a restroom?"

"Of course. This way." She led him back to the foyer and showed him a guest bathroom.

"I'll take care of that in a second," he said, pointing to the wet tile where he'd stood. He closed the door, set the mug down on the counter, and faced himself in the mirror. She appeared to genuinely not know who he was. If her computer had Internet access, this was where he needed to be. But to rent a room for the night would require payment. He didn't have enough cash, and to use a credit card, he'd have to give her his real name.

She was mopping up the wet spot in the foyer when he emerged from the restroom. "Please, let me…" he said, reaching for the mop.

"It's nothing," she insisted, surprising him with how firm her grip was on the handle. "I'm almost done."

He drained his mug and followed her back into the kitchen. "How much do your rooms go for?"

"There are two guest rooms. The larger one is upstairs, it has a balcony overlooking the river and a queen-size bed. And one down here, next to the restroom, with a single bed and private access to the porch, also with a river view. Upstairs is $155, and downstairs $95 a night. Would you like to see the rooms?"

"That won't be necessary. If I stay it will be downstairs. My name is Kyle, by the way. Kyle Jackson."

"It's a pleasure to meet you, Kyle."

"You too."

Again there was the warm, confident smile. "What do you do?"

"I'm a computer programmer."

"Ah! So is my daughter! She works for a company called Datasource. In Austin. Where do you work?"

"I freelance. I'm in between jobs right now. Uh…may I look around?"

"Of course. I'll give you the tour."

She led him out of the kitchen and back to the foyer. "You've seen the bathroom, this is the downstairs bedroom." She pushed the door open.

It was small, but with the expansive windows, airy. "This was originally Bobby's study, but I converted it into a bedroom two years ago. Both guest bedrooms have cable TV, and this one has its own door to the porch."

"Very nice," he said, stepping back into the foyer. He led the way into the living room. "This is a great room."

"It's where most of my guests like to sit."

"That's quite a fireplace. And having the seating area sunken makes it very inviting." He stepped forward to where the desk in the walkway to the right of the fireplace was clearly visible. "Who works on the computer?"

"Sara—my daughter—set it up for me. I do my accounts on it."

"What software do you use?"

"Quicken."

He smiled and nodded. "That's a good program. What about e-mail?"

"That, too."

"What's your e-mail address?"

"R oaks at AOL dot com." She walked past the desk. "And this, needless to say, is the dining room. The overnight stay includes breakfast, which is served here, or in the bedroom."

"I'll take the ground floor guest room for the night, while the storm blows over."

"Don't you want to see upstairs? There's a loft…"

"That's all right. And I'd like to pay for whatever cost is involved in the laundry."

"Don't worry about that."

"Speaking of payment-" He was suddenly interrupted by the sound of a baby crying in the kitchen. Connie Kinser saw the surprise on his face and smiled.

"That's my granddaughter," she explained. "She's upstairs. There's a monitor in the kitchen for when I'm down here. You were saying?"

"I was going to say…I've lost my wallet, probably when I fell into the river. But I can access my credit card information on the Internet using AOL. Do you mind?"

"That would be fine."

"I'll need you to log in for me…"

"Let me just check the baby." She left him in the dining room and went upstairs. He heard her on the monitor, talking softly to the baby. He was itching to turn on the computer, but he waited. Connie Kinser had been accommodating thus far, and he didn't want to push his luck.

She returned a few minutes later with a folded diaper that she sealed in a plastic bag and threw into the trash. She washed her hands and came back to the desk.

"How old is your granddaughter?"

"Five months. She was born in April." She pulled the center drawer out, revealing a keyboard and mouse.

"What does your son-in-law do?"

"He's a geologist." She switched the computer on. "He's in Siberia for a few weeks, mapping oilfields."

"Your daughter lives with you?"

"Oh no. Sara's way too independent. I just look after Laura during the day while Sara's at work."

"Do they live in Wimberley too?"

"Yes."

"That must be nice for you. Do you have any other children?"

"I have two sons in Houston."

The Windows 95 desktop appeared on the screen, and Connie clicked on the AOL icon. Renberg watched her highlight the ROAKS user name, but she typed too fast for him to catch her password.

"Do you mind how long I stay online if I pay the AOL charges?"

"Fine."

"That'll keep me out of your way for the evening."

"Let me know when you have your credit card information. I'll be upstairs in the loft."

"It shouldn't take more than a few minutes."

Renberg watched her walk up the stairs then turned to the computer. From AOL's channels menu he clicked on the Internet Connection box and waited while AOL's home page downloaded. In the GO TO box he typed: *www.netmail.com.* When Netmail's home page appeared, he typed in his user I.D., calculated and entered his password, and downloaded Harding's message. The list of pass phrase variations he'd already tried was at Pendergraft's house, so it was back to square one. But there was something he needed to take care of first.

He took the steps in twos. The loft was surrounded by log pillars and trusses that gave it a sheltered tree house feel. She was reading in an oversize rocking chair. The baby was a few feet away, on her back in a portable cot.

"Look at that," he said, taking a closer look. "What's her name?"

"Laura."

"She's precious."

"Thank you."

"Connie, I couldn't access my records," he said apologetically. "I'll understand if you prefer that I leave. Or I can give you my watch as security."

She studied his face and considered the offer. "That won't be necessary," she decided.

He noted the television in the corner. It was off, but a ticking time bomb. "Thank you," he said. "You're…you're a good person. If it's okay with you, I'll go ahead and put my clothes in the dryer."

She started to get up. "I'll…"

"No," he said firmly. "You've done enough. I know how to operate a dryer." He skipped back down the stairs.

The washer was in a spin cycle. There was an umbrella hanging from a hook next to the door, and at least one garden tool that would work. He went back inside and ran upstairs again. "The washer's not done yet. I'm going to retrace my steps to the river to see if maybe I dropped my wallet along the way."

"Why don't you wait until the rain stops?"

"I'm anxious to see if I can find it. Can I use your umbrella?"

"There's one hanging in the garage."

"I saw it."

"Are you sure you don't want to wait?"

He couldn't risk waiting. "I'm anxious to find out."

She shrugged her shoulders. "Suit yourself."

He skipped back down to the garage and took a flower pruner off the garden tools rack. Then he saw the hedge shears, and took them instead. He opened the umbrella while waiting for the garage door. The rain had eased considerably, and he didn't have to go far to find what he was looking for. The utility drop to the house was where he'd expected to find it, on the back of the garage. The power cables went through a weatherhead to a meter box before elbowing through the wall to a breaker panel inside the garage. But it was the television cable he was interested in, and that came off the pole separately, closer to the telephone wire. It terminated in a weatherproof plastic junction box mounted on the outside wall, adjacent to the electric meter. Renberg set the umbrella down long enough to snap the TV cable with the shears, the size of which provided him with ample leverage. Moments later he was back in the garage, returning the shears and umbrella to their hooks.

"I decided to heed your advice and wait!" he shouted when he got back to the desk. "I don't need to get drenched again."

"I would have thought so," she replied from the loft.

"My wallet's probably in the river anyway."

He dropped into the chair and considered other potential sources of trouble. It was a few minutes after five. The phone line was a sacred link to the Internet and not to be touched. He could only hope Connie Kinser wasn't a fan of radio news.

It had been a harrowing couple of hours since the FBI had surprised him at Pendergraft's house. He still wanted to know how they'd found him, but that could wait. He hoped the same was true of his mother. He leaned back against the cushion in the chair, pulled the keyboard out of the drawer onto his lap, and propped it up against the edge of the drawer. His face was taut with anxiety as he resumed the tussle between the PGP prompt and the pass phrase.

*   *   *

It had started during the sixth month of her pregnancy. The seat belt never actually became painful, but wearing it caused Sara Kinser enough discomfort that by the seventh month she'd stopped using it altogether. And she'd made no effort to get back into the routine after having Laura. She felt strongly that the government had no more business forcing people to wear seatbelts than it did making bikers wear helmets. Yes it was the law, but this was one that infringed on personal freedom. If she were ever stopped, she'd simply slip the belt on before the cop came to the car.

As she did every weekday after work, Sara Kinser took I-35 south to San Marcos, then 12 into Wimberley. It was about a forty-minute drive, and, thanks to National Public Radio's *All Things Considered*, not one she minded. It was the one time of day when she could catch up on what was going on in the world, and she enjoyed the format of quick headlines followed by in-depth analysis of a couple of the stories. But it was an item from the local news segment that most piqued her interest as she drove home that Wednesday. A fugitive on the FBI's Ten Most Wanted list was on the loose in the area. She'd seen his picture in the paper at the office, but hadn't had a chance to read the article. What she knew was from tidbits she'd caught of a conversation around the microwave at lunchtime. A couple of UT students had bust into a Pentagon computer and copied classified information. One had been arrested on campus by the FBI on Tuesday, but they didn't know where the other was. And the latest on the story was that he was believed him to be hiding in Wimberley! It was real-life drama the likes of which the area was unaccustomed to.

The Pentagon story was still on Sara Kinser's mind when she saw the flashing lights of a county sheriff's patrol car at the intersection of 3237 and Flite Acres. He got out of his car when she approached and motioned to her to stop. She slowed and pulled over and rolled the window down a few inches.

"Evening, ma'am," he said. He wore a bright yellow plastic longcoat and his wide-brimmed hat was covered with a protective sheet of transparent plastic. "I want to advise you to keep an eye open for a suspect that was last seen in the area."

"Is it that UT guy? The hacker?"

"Yes ma'am. Brad Renberg. You know what he looks like?"

"Yes. I saw his picture in the paper."

"Please call 911 immediately if you see anything suspicious."

"I sure will."

She started to roll the window up when he put his hand on it. "One more thing."

"Yes?"

"Please wear your seatbelt. It's for your own safety."

She reached behind her and pulled the belt over her shoulder. "Thank you. I usually do."

She rolled the window up and pulled away, thinking he was what all cops should be like. A ticket for such a petty infraction would have only added to her resentment of the law. She unbuckled the belt and proceeded down Flite Acres towards River Oaks, anxious to tell her mother about Brad Renberg.

CHAPTER TWELVE

Twenty minutes after fielding Steven Vogel's call, the special agent-in-charge of the FBI's Denver field office called him back. The news was not good.

"We contacted Netmail, but they won't cooperate," Matt Jordan said. "They gave us the song and dance about their customers' privacy."

"Get a court order," Vogel quipped.

"CDC's already on it. I'll let you know."

Matt Jordan prided himself on staying ahead of the game. He was the FBI's youngest SAC, testimony to the fact that his aptitude hadn't gone unnoticed. Even while directing one of his agents to contact Netmail, he'd anticipated the company's response and instructed his Chief Division Counsel to draft a court order. Then he'd gone one step further, locating the whereabouts of the US district court judge whose signature would make the order official. She was teeing off on the second hole of the back nine when word came through that an agent was on his way with the document. She reluctantly agreed to be ferried back to the clubhouse to review an advance facsimile, all to the end of minimizing any delay in getting the original signed. Jordan reported to a suitably impressed Vogel that the process—one that could easily have taken several hours—was expected to be completed in less than one.

*   *   *

The first new tidbit of information Mitch Wakeman received on Brad Renberg came from Austin FBI Special Agent Deborah Burke.

"We've got a rarity here," she said. "Right off the bat our check of birth records at Vital Statistics shows that Renberg is his mother's last name. There's no father listed on the birth certificate."

Wakeman moved the receiver from one ear to the other as he swiveled the chair around. "How can that be?"

"Well, he was born in Fort Worth. There's no state law mandating a father's name on birth certificates in Texas."

"What about educational records? He goes to UT."

"Angela's on her way to the Department of Education. I'll check with the UT registrar's office."

"What else?"

"I ran a check on his mother, Mary Renberg. Both her parents are dead. The only surviving sibling is a younger sister, Charlene. DPS doesn't have a current address for Mary, but Charlene lives in San Marcos."

Wakeman jumped. "Where?" He reached for a notepad and scribbled down the address. "What else?"

"That's it for now. You said you wanted it piecemeal."

"Yes. Call me the minute you get any more." He tore the sheet out of the note pad and ran out of the door.

                    ✶   ✶   ·   ✶

It was a Compaq Presario, and in terms of bells and whistles, it featured the state of the art in home computing. The monitor boasted a 17-inch screen, a pair of stereophonic speakers and a built in microphone. 16 Megabytes of random access memory and a 1.6 gigabyte hard drive complemented a 133 MHz Pentium processor. And there was one particular feature Renberg was unaccustomed to that surprised him. He was trying variations on the key for nearly twenty minutes when, concurrent with the ringing of a telephone, a screen identified as the

Compaq Phone Center popped up, automatically disconnecting America Online. It was a few seconds before he realized what had happened, but it became clear when he heard Connie Kinser's voice on the speakers. The caller identified herself as Valerie at Hill Country Accommodations, and wanted to know if the two rooms at River Oaks were available for rent the first weekend of October. Connie said she thought one was already booked and asked Valerie to hold for a moment. She carried a cordless phone down the steps and over to the desk, and after consulting a yearly planner, confirmed to Valerie that it was indeed so. Renberg took in the Phone Center screen while they spoke. There were several features, including fax capability, a calendar, a message center, call logging, an address book and speed dial. The screen remained in place when Connie hung up.

"That's a neat feature," Renberg said.

"Except when it disconnects AOL," she replied. "I need to install a separate phone line for the computer because more and more of my guests use AOL. Here, let me close down the phone center and log in again."

She clicked on the X at the upper right-hand corner of the Phone Center screen and a prompt asked if she was sure she wanted to exit the Phone Center and stop taking messages. She clicked on YES. There was an *EXITING PHONE CENTER—PLEASE WAIT* message, then the AOL welcome window. She entered her password again. This time Renberg kept his eyes on her right hand and caught an "L" and a "U". He immediately guessed LAURA. It was so typical. People tended to use passwords they could easily remember, and names of parents, spouses, children, grandchildren and pets headed the list. She waited while the modem was initialized and the local access number was dialed. Only after the connection was made did she take the cordless phone and go back upstairs.

With the discovery of Connie Kinser's password, Renberg's comfort level increased dramatically. Getting disconnected from AOL was now a small price to pay for listening in every time she received or made a phone call. He clicked on the Windows 95 START button. Of the options that appeared in the menu, he highlighted the top one, COMMUNICATIONS. The sub-menu included COMPAQ PHONE CENTER. Two more clicks produced the message he sought:

`INITIALIZING COMPAQ PHONE CENTER–PLEASE WAIT.`

Within twenty seconds the phone center was back on the screen. He entered 555-1212 and clicked on DIAL NUMBER. The speakers emitted a dial tone, and he adjusted the volume down using the knob on the monitor. When he heard the tones that indicated the number was being dialed, the DIAL NUMBER button disappeared and was replaced by a HANG UP button. As expected, clicking it killed the call. He minimized the screen down to a button on the taskbar, re-established the connection with Netmail, and went back to jostling with KORPEN.PGP

✳   ✳   ✳

Few people in Texas appreciate the latitude that Department of Parks and Wildlife game wardens have when it comes to law enforcement. The fact is that in addition to the State Parks and Wildlife Code, game wardens are also empowered to enforce the State Penal Code and the State Code of Criminal Procedure. To prepare them for the demands of their position as certified peace officers, the requirements they must meet to qualify—and the training they receive—give little quarter to their counterparts at the FBI.

At 37 years of age, Sergeant Game Warden Shirley Mathis was a veteran of sixteen years at the department, having applied as soon as she'd earned her degree in criminology and reached the minimum required age of 21. She'd breezed through the physical, emotional and psychological examinations, and had graduated from the 35 weeks at the Austin academy third in her class. But more than any coursework, instruction or training she'd received, it was personal character traits that best served Shirley Mathis in the discharge of her professional duties. Most notable was her quiet persistence, throughout the course of an investigation, to leave no stone unturned. Not long after she joined the manhunt for Brad Renberg, that very same persistence was put to the test.

Were her Chevy Blazer not equipped with four-wheel drive and a locking center differential, Shirley Mathis might have waited for the rain to stop before venturing into the mud pit at the entrance to the campground. But equipped it was and venture she did and the first tent she encountered was George D. Wilhite's. Mathis honked her horn once, which was all it took for Wilhite's head to appear. Mathis applied the parking brake and stepped out of the Blazer.

"Good afternoon," she said, approaching the tent.

"We've seen prettier," Wilhite replied.

"I apologize for the intrusion here, we're alerting everyone to be on the lookout for a suspect that's loose in the area. White male, twenty-nine years, six-one, one-eighty-five pounds, black hair, blue eyes, last seen a few miles down the road earlier this afternoon. We just ask if you see anyone fitting that description to please call 911 and-"

"I don't know about the black hair, but some feller hitched a ride with me back there a while back."

"What fella? When?"

"Oh, about an hour back, maybe a little more. His head was shaved and all, mind you. All cut up, he was. He said he'd been hiking and run into a thorn bush."

Mathis got real interested. "Where did you take him?"

"Right here where you're standing. He said he was catching up with a buddy of his right here in the campground."

"Did you see where he went?"

"And there *was* something suspicious about the sumbitch. I come out of the tent here just a few minutes after he's supposably gone, the sumbitch is messing around in my truck. Said he was looking for his wallet."

"Did you see where he went?"

Wilhite glanced to his right. "Last I seen he was headed towards that there tent."

Mathis turned and saw the tent he was pointing to.

"Do you think that's your man?"

"He could be," she replied. "He could be. Your name is…?"

"Wilhite. George D. Wilhite, from-"

"Thank you Mr. Wilhite. I'd appreciate it if you'd stay put. We may need to ask you some more questions."

"I've got my gun with me here. If I see the sumbitch again I can make him freeze and all."

Mathis was already in the driver's seat and slamming the door. "You just stay right here and keep your eyes open."

George D. Wilhite was oblivious to the rain as he watched the Blazer's B.F. Goodrich All-Terrain tires dig into the mud and find traction.

*   *   *

Renberg was forewarned by the baby's crankiness, and he had ample time to minimize the Netmail screen before Connie came down from the loft. This time she went straight to the kitchen.

"They sure let you know when they're unhappy," he said.

"That they do," Connie replied. "She's just hungry. Sara's normally back by now. I guess the weather held her up."

It was past six. He'd been at it for over an hour, typing a seemingly endless stream of variations on the key, none of which had decrypted KORPEN. He'd thrown in spelling errors, messed with the apostrophes, italicized, and ventured combinations of upper- and lower-case letters. And he was prepared to keep trying, all night if necessary, which made Sara a potential glitch on the not-so-distant horizon. What were the odds that someone who worked with computers in Austin hadn't heard the news, seen the paper, or been told by a colleague?

He stood at the door between the kitchen and dining room, watching as Connie Kinser readied a bottle for her grandchild. She emptied two scoops of powdered infant formula into a measured amount of filtered water, screwed on a nipple that she took out of a home-style autoclave, then vigorously shook the bottle.

"Does your daughter typically just pick the baby up and go home?"

"Oh she'll stay and cook and eat dinner with me sometimes. It depends."

He nodded and walked past her towards the garage. "I'll go check on the dryer. It should be done by now."

It was, and he changed back into his jeans and denim shirt in the first floor bedroom. The rain had tapered off to a mere drizzle, and as he walked back to the desk he heard the car. He scooted back into the bedroom, left the door ajar and stood behind it with an ear at the crack.

A hearty "Hi!" accompanied Sara's entrance. Connie returned the greeting as Sara bounded up the stairs. For the first few minutes Sara's attention was all on her baby. She told her how pretty she looked and how much she'd missed her. Connie assured Sara that Laura had eaten right and napped right and generally been a delight. It sounded like Sara took over the feeding chore, and she made a comment about Laura's appetite. Then Connie announced she was going to make them some coffee.

"Oh, and when you're done," she added nonchalantly, "come downstairs and meet Kyle Jackson."

"Who's Kyle Jackson?" Sara asked.

"A nice young man who was canoeing down the river," her mother replied from the staircase landing. "He's spending the night."

"Canoeing in this weather?"

Sara didn't wait for Laura to finish the bottle. As Connie Kinser entered the kitchen, Renberg heard the sound of her daughter's footsteps coming down the stairs.

*   *   *

When Hays County Sheriff's Deputy Hale Martin approached Charlene Renberg's door, he did so with an erect posture and a stern, unsmiling face. He rapped bare knuckles against the door and removed his Ray-Bans. Through the corner of his eye he caught a glimpse of the hand that creased the drawn shades aside in the window to his right. He was surprised when a minute went by and no one opened the door. He knocked again, impatiently now, and louder than before. He stared at the door for a few seconds, then walked around to the back of the house. The garden gate at the back was locked. Martin turned back to his car. He got on the radio and reported that somebody was home and had seen him, but wouldn't open the door.

Inside the house, Mary Renberg retreated away from the menace at the front door to the sanctity of her bed. She was confused and disoriented. She felt warm, her skin was dry, and it was getting harder to breathe. She felt a simultaneous urge to urinate and drink, but she stayed doubled up on the edge of the bed, enduring spasms of abdominal pain. As the nausea overwhelmed her and the vomit splattered on the floor, Deputy Martin's concentration was on his radio. Word came back from headquarters he was to stay put and watch the house while a search warrant was processed.

*   *   *

Processing of the search warrant for Charlene Renberg's house was not the only task Mitch Wakeman called in and assigned to his staff. He simultaneously instructed the agency's principal legal advisor to coordinate with Chief Division Counsel in the San Antonio field office the preparation of a skeleton of probable cause for an application for electronic intercept of communications—more commonly known as a phone tap—on Sadie Harding's home telephone. He stressed the need to articulate the exigent circumstances, in particular as they related to the national security considerations of the case. Once prepared, the document would be faxed to Legal Counsel at headquarters. That would initiate preparation of a final affidavit to be forwarded to the U.S. attorney general, who would then authorize its presentation to the Foreign Intelligence Surveillance Act court, the half-dozen judges who review such applications. Only after approval by the FISA court would an order be issued, authorizing a 30-day telephone surveillance of the subject specified in the application.

Wakeman's reasoning was simple. Renberg was likely to surmise that he had been double-crossed by Harding. It was not far-fetched to hope he might call her, if nothing else to say he knew what she had done, and that he had survived her betrayal. Tracing his call might prove to be the best chance they had to find him.

*   *   *

When Renberg heard Sara Kinser follow her mother into the kitchen, he slipped into the bathroom and locked the door. He was going to have to come out and meet Sara, but he wanted to take a look at himself first. It wasn't the prettiest of sights. The combination of shaved head and scratches would raise anyone's suspicions, but there was nothing he could do about either.

"Kyle?"

It was Connie, and she was approaching the bedroom.

"I'm in here," he replied. "I'll be out in a minute."

Running was still an option. There was a window he could easily squeeze out of, but what good would that do? They'd call the police and he'd be back to square one. At least here there was a computer, and it was him, two women and a baby. Two hours ago he would have taken that without batting an eyelid. Besides, he was assuming Sara knew about him and would recognize him. There was a chance she didn't or wouldn't. All else considered, River Oaks was still his best bet. He would go out and meet her and take his chances.

He flushed the toilet. He splashed cold water on his face and patted it with a towel. Then he straightened up, took a couple of deep breaths, and decided it was time.

They were standing at the foot of the staircase. Sara, with the baby in her arms, had her back to him and was talking to her mother in a hushed tone. She swung around sharply when she realized he was behind her.

"Kyle, this is my daughter, Sara," Connie said.

"Hi, Sara," he said amicably. "It's a pleasure to meet you."

"Hello," she replied, staring straight at him. If she made an effort to hide her shock it was a dismal one, for he was left with no doubt. She had recognized him.

"We were worried about you driving out there," he said. "I guess it's not as nasty now as it was earlier."

She started up the stairs. "Excuse me, I need to change Laura's diaper. Mom, could you come up and give me a hand?"

No doubt whatsoever. It didn't take two people to change a diaper.

When Connie followed her up the stairs Renberg went to the computer. There was a screen saver on the monitor and he moved the mouse to bring back AOL. From upstairs, there was only the sound of a door being closed.

"Jesus, mom! That's him, the guy the cops are after!"

They were in the master bedroom and Sara was beside herself. She put Laura in her cot and turned to her mother.

"Are you sure?"

"Yes, I'm sure!" Sara hissed. "He's shaved his head and beard because his picture is in the paper. Canoeing, my ass!"

The older Kinser put a hand to her mouth. "Oh my god!"

Sara grabbed the bedside phone and dialed 911. Renberg was waiting. As soon as the Compaq Phone Center window popped up on the screen with 911 in the DIAL NUMBER box, he clicked on the HANG UP button. 911 appeared again, and again the computer responded to his click by hanging up the line. He waited ten, fifteen, twenty seconds. When they made no further effort to dial out he skipped across the dining room to the kitchen door. He could still see the computer screen, and he stood at the door, watching, listening and waiting.

Upstairs in the master bedroom, Sara Kinser's anxiety turned to panic. "He's done something to the phone line!" She glanced at Laura, then turned to her mother. "Where's the gun?"

"In my closet," Connie replied, petrified at the thought they might have to use it.

"Give me it."

Connie ran into her walk-in closet and reached under a sweater on the top shelf. She came out and handed Sara a black 9mm Smith & Wesson semi-automatic.

"Is it loaded?"

"No. The bullets are in my dresser."

"For Christ's sake, mom! Where?"

Connie rummaged through a drawer and found them. Sara immediately snatched the box from her mother's hand, ripped the cover off, and spilled the bullets out onto the bed. She grabbed a handful and, as her mother watched in horror, started filling the clip. Neither of them noticed the door handle turning.

He was next to the cot in a flash. By the time they reacted Laura was already in his arms.

"No!" Connie screamed, lunging for the baby.

Sara slid the clip into the handle and pointed the gun at Renberg's head. "Put her down!" she shrieked, stepping towards him.

He swerved to one side to avoid Connie and they saw the knife. It was in his right hand, two inches from Laura's throat.

"Stay back!" he warned. Laura started crying, and Connie and Sara froze.

"Put the gun down."

Sara's eyes were on her baby. "Okay."

"*Put it down!*"

"Okay!" She laid it gingerly on the bed cover. "Don't hurt her."

Connie stepped back towards Sara, begging him to put Laura down.

"Get away from the bed," he ordered, gesturing with his head. "Do what I say and nobody will get hurt."

"Please," Connie pleaded, "We'll do-"

"Shut up, mother!" Sara hissed, pulling her mother away from the bed.

Renberg circled around and picked up the gun. "Now listen to me. I don't want to hurt any of you. You just need to stay out of my way, and everyone will be fine."

"What are you going to do?" Connie whimpered.

"Shut *up*, mom!"

"I just need to use the computer," he replied. He turned to Sara. "Where are your car keys?"

She shrugged her shoulders. "I put them down when I came in. In the loft, maybe."

"Alright. I'll be out of here soon. Don't make any trouble for me and you'll all be okay."

"We'll do whatever you say."

"Good. You do that, and nobody will get hurt."

Sara glared at him hatefully. Laura continued to cry.

"Connie, I'm going to have you tie up Sara."

"Please…"

"Get me some pantyhose."

"Do it, mom," Sara said coldly. "Do what he says."

Connie went to the closet. "On the carpet," Renberg said to Sara. "Face down, hands behind your back."

Sara did as she was told. When Connie came out of the closet with the pantyhose, Renberg instructed her to bind Sara's hands together. He had her use several double knots, and made her redo two to get them tighter. The procedure was repeated for Sara's feet. Laura's crying was a constant reminder of what was at stake for the Kinsers, and Connie followed his instructions as best she could. When he was satisfied Sara was adequately restrained, it was Connie's turn. He had her bring out more pantyhose, then made her assume the same position on the carpet as Sara. Reminding them he still had the knife and the gun, he set Laura back down in the cot. He first bound Connie's hands, then her feet. He added a scarf to Sara's hands, told them he'd be right back, picked up Laura, and went downstairs.

A quick search in the garage netted nothing by way of rope. He grabbed the rose scissors from the garden tools rack and headed back into the kitchen. He snipped the power cords off the microwave, the toaster, and the electric mixer, then did the same with the four table lamps in the great room. He took the cords upstairs and used them to better secure Connie's and Sara's hands and feet. He ignored Sara's protests that her hands were hurting because the wire was so tight. He gagged them using hand towels and medical tape from the bathroom. While waiting a few moments to ensure they could still breathe, he removed the clip from the gun and filled it to its fifteen-bullet capacity. He stuck a pacifier in Laura's mouth, left her in the cot, left the bedroom door open, and dropped back downstairs. He made a quick stop at the front door, long enough to lock it from the inside. Then, ever aware the clock was ticking, he sat down again at the computer.

* * *

"Anyone home?" Shirley Mathis shouted.

A zipper came down the tent's front section and a man's head appeared, disappeared, then reappeared with a hood on. The zipper came down further and the man stepped out into the rain. A woman peered out from the tent behind him. Late twenties, early thirties, Mathis estimated.

"I'm looking for a suspect last seen in the campground about an hour or so ago. White male, twenty-nine years old. About six-one, a hundred and eighty-five pounds with black hair and blue eyes."

"We haven't been out of the tent since the rain started," the man said. His female companion nodded.

Mathis frowned and gazed past them further into the campground at a couple more tents that were visible downstream. "Well, if you come across anyone fitting that description we'd appreciate it if you'd call 911."

"We'll do that."

Mathis raised the window and revved the engine. The man turned back towards the tent, anxious to get out of the rain. Mathis suddenly lowered the window again. "Say, how did you get here?"

The man turned and was about to say something when he suddenly stopped. He pointed to the riverbank. "The canoe! It was right there! It's gone!"

Mathis got out of the Blazer. "What canoe? Where?"

"Right there next to the water," he said, leading the way. The woman came out of the tent and followed him. "It was right here!"

They all looked around, but there was no sign of it.

"What kind of canoe?"

"A two-seater. Wooden. Red."

"When was the last time you saw it?"

"Just before the rain started. Since then we've been in the tent."

Mathis took one more look around and headed back to the Blazer. She punched one of the preset frequency buttons on her transceiver and brought the microphone to her mouth.

"4307, Hays County Sheriff's Office."

"Unit calling, please identify agency."

"State Game Warden."

"Go ahead, 4307."

"I need to advise other units and agents I'm at a campground on the south bank of the Blanco, about two, two and a half miles east of Hidden Valley on Flite Acres. Someone fitting the suspect's description hitched a ride over here and was last seen about forty-five minutes ago. A canoe is reported missing and may have been taken by the suspect.

Unless there've been other sightings to indicate otherwise, we might want to concentrate the search downstream of this location."

"Ten four, 4307."

Mathis set the microphone down on the seat next to her and stared at the river. If Renberg had taken the canoe, he could conceivably be miles away by now. They needed to get downstream of him, and Parks and Wildlife had a resource the other agencies lacked, one tailor-made for the situation. She reached for the microphone again and called her supervisor in the Temple office.

"4307 to 4304."

"Go ahead, 4307."

"There's a good possibility the suspect in the FBI manhunt is in a canoe on the Blanco river, somewhere between Wimberley and San Marcos. Any jet ski units nearby?"

"There's one at the Guadalupe near Canyon Lake. He could get to the Blanco in…say fifteen minutes."

"Have him work upriver from San Marcos. We're looking for a red wooden canoe."

"How do the low water bridges look?"

"There's only two or three downriver from here, and the water's rising. By the time he gets to them they should be passable."

"Ten Four."

Mathis eyed the two other tents she could see further downstream in the campground and hit the gearshift lever. It was likely their occupants hadn't seen or heard of Brad Renberg, but it was against her nature to leave any stone unturned.

CHAPTER THIRTEEN

"There's good news and bad news," Harkutlian said over the phone, well aware which of the two Stan Daulton would want to hear first. The President was about to tell him when Harkutlian pre-empted him. "The bad news is, they had the son of a bitch cornered, but he managed to get away. One of the FBI men took a bullet in the process. It was friendly fire, not Renberg. Anyway, Renberg got away."

Daulton shook his head and bit his lip. "Now tell me something good."

"Well, we know Renberg hasn't read the memo yet."

"How's that?"

"When they surrounded him it was at the house of another ex-hacker, someone who was in the same gang as Renberg a few years back. Apparently Renberg was there alone, working the computer. It looks like the e-mail Harding sent him was encrypted, and according to the FBI, he'd been unable to decrypt it. They're still after him, of course, but in the meantime a court order is being processed to block his access to his e-mail. With a little luck, that'll happen—or they'll catch him—before he gets his hands on another computer."

"Outstanding," Daulton said. "Way to go."

"It's not over yet, mind you. We won't know for sure until they catch him. What happened with the CIA?"

"I've discussed the matter with Wilson. He's going to take care of it."

"Good."

"What else can I do?"

"Just keep your fingers crossed."

"How do the others feel about your approach? Denying everything if the story breaks."

"Roone and Bob have their reservations," Harkutlian replied, "But they don't have any better suggestions so they'll go along with it. Lee, on the other hand, could be a problem. He's brooding."

"Lee's a soldier. I'd be surprised if he wasn't troubled."

"We're all troubled by it. As we were in April. But when you consider the 37,000 troops stationed over there, you'd think he'd be okay."

"Leave Lee to me," the President said. "I'll talk to him tomorrow. In the meantime, let me know if there are any further developments."

*   *   **

The Americans weren't going to come.

The Korean picked at his breakfast in silence. His wife sensed it, but it was not her place to ask. She watched and waited. When he pushed the plate away she removed it off the table and brought him Ttog. The rice cake was his favorite confection, but there was no acknowledgement. He was there, but his mind wasn't.

The doubts had surfaced two years ago. It was a crisis of confidence. At least that's how it had started. Then his confidence had collapsed, and with it his faith.

His mind wandered back through generations and centuries, back to the third millennium BC, when fishermen migrated to the peninsula from the north and settled close to the rivers and the coast, searching, as man has done throughout history, for a better life. Then the hunters followed in the seventh century BC and laid the great dolmens. He thought back to the 2nd century BC, to the state of Choson in the northwest, to the great capital that evolved into the present-day city of

Pyongyang. He reflected on the three Korean Kingdoms of centuries past—Paekche in the west; Silla in the southeast; and Koguryo in the Yalu River basin in the north. He nodded at the thought of the years of warfare that had led to the unification of Korea under Silla. The peace that had followed ushered in an era of great cultural enrichment and technological innovation. A further century of fighting had ensued before the ruling clans of Silla relented to the state of Koryo.

It had all been, always, for a better life.

Centuries of struggle. Manchurian invasions, Mongol campaigns, military overlords, and the Yi Dynasty. Then, in the nineteenth century, the first treaties with western nations. Indeed, the very first, in 1882, was with none other than the same United States which he had believed would help him.

He rose from the table, picked a newspaper off a chair and sat down.

They would start a war, of that he was sure. Other than subjugation, it was the only way out. They had seen the collapse of communism in the Soviet Union, and the spillover into Eastern Europe. They had preached and pointed and pontificated to each other and declared that it *hadn't* all been for the better.

Then the floods, which had only made matters worse. It was no longer a matter of economic reform. Now they were desperate. The population at large was on the verge of famine.

All for a better life? All for nothing was closer to the truth.

He had been sure the Americans would come. He had felt certain the videotape would lure them. He had been wrong. With their help, he might have gotten his family out. But five months had passed, and it was clear he was on his own.

The Korean put on his reading glasses and unfolded the newspaper. Tomorrow, he would lead the delegation to Beijing. He would not be coming back.

*   *   *

The Korean's wife wasn't the only woman wondering what had her husband so preoccupied. Clean on the other side of the world, in the comfort of her home in Fort Meyer, Virginia, Nancy Trujillo had similar concerns. Sensitized as she was to her own husband's moods, she knew that whatever was gnawing at him had to be potent. Unlike the Korean's wife, Nancy Trujillo had probed. Just the stress of the job, he'd said, but she didn't buy it. He'd been chairman of the Joint Chiefs of Staff for four years now. What was different about the last two days? Anxieties over the election? That was eight weeks hence and the polls looked great. It couldn't be another woman. Lee wouldn't.

"Where are you going?" she asked as he put on a windbreaker.

"Just out for a walk," he replied.

It was most unusual. He never went out for a walk alone.

"Would you care for some company?"

His smile was contrived. "Uh…no thanks. I need to think. Let the air clear the cobwebs."

"Are you sure? I won't interrupt."

"Thanks, honey. I need to be alone."

"I love you."

He hesitated at the door. "I love you too. I love you very much."

"Lee…"

He latched the door behind him and she stood at the window, watching him walk away. She felt a powerful urge to run after him, to touch him, hold him, comfort him. When he disappeared from view she drew the shades and went to check if the children were done with their supper.

His face was tense and sullen, a mirror of anger and despair. He'd argued all along against rejecting the Korean's approach outright. But they'd insisted, and he hadn't argued forcibly enough. He'd relented and they'd prevailed and now it was all about to hit the fan.

General Lee Trujillo kept his chin down and walked at a moderate pace. He had neither the will nor the drive to walk faster. Besides, he was in no hurry.

Thirty-seven years of dedicated service. It had all started at the Army Command and General Staff College at Fort Leavenworth. Then Fort McNair, and the National War College. The Reserve Officer Training Program at Yale had led to the Air Force. 2,600 flying hours. 156 combat missions over Laos and North Vietnam. And two years in the camp. The worst two years of his life.

Ed wasn't a military man. And the President had never served. They couldn't possibly know how it felt. You had to have experienced it.

It was a clear night, a touch of chill bringing out the evening joggers en masse. Trujillo turned away from the bustle towards the sanctuary of the woods. The soldier in him was at peace, now that he'd decided. The husband and father in him, not so. Nancy, Joseph and Andrea deserved better. Ultimately, he'd failed them, too.

Everywhere he looked there were fingers, and they were all pointing. He was the principal military advisor to the President. To the Secretary of Defense, and the National Security Council. They were talking denial. They were talking about the election, about what was important for the party. Four more years. Of what? Four more years of denial? For General Lee Trujillo, they sorely missed the point. They had yet to mention honor.

The joggers went about their way, striding, pacing, counting miles in their zones, one and all oblivious to an old soldier's lonely struggle with shame, duty and honor. So it remained until the calm was shattered by a solitary gunshot that rang out from the woods.

CHAPTER FOURTEEN

The Buckley Amendment to the Federal Privacy Act imposes restrictions on unlimited access by law enforcement agencies to academic records. This increases the legwork—literally—for the likes of Special Agent Deborah Burke, who might otherwise have investigated over the phone. As it is, she had to rush down in person to the registrar's office at the University of Texas before it closed for the day. She presented the appropriate identification and submitted a written request for the information she needed.

It may have taken the better part of half an hour, but her efforts were not in vain. Brad Renberg's application record included the name of his father, one David E. Zuber. It was the same name Special Agent Burke had found entered for "husband" on Mary Renberg's marriage license, details of which she'd culled from a database before she'd left the office. The problem was, the dates didn't gel. Brad Renberg was born in 1967. But Mary Renberg and David Zuber were married in 1979. Why had Brad's mother and father waited until their son was twelve years old before getting married?

That was the question Deborah Burke pondered as she drove back to the office from the University of Texas. It was still unanswered when she presented the information to Mitch Wakeman.

*   *   *

I've found what you've been looking for.

The answer had to be there, somewhere. He'd tried everything he could think of and nothing had worked. With PGP it was either home or square one, and Renberg was at square one.

Damn you, Richard. You know how this shit works. Why didn't you write it down for her?

Sadie couldn't have been lying. How would she have possibly known how to lie? Richard had used the sentence in the voice message. She wasn't with him at the time, so she hadn't heard the message. It *had* to be real.

The voice message...

He stared at the sentence again, then looked left and right, searching for the phone. He pushed the chair back and jumped up. He was at the top of the stairs in two blinks of an eye. The cordless phone was on the coffee table next to the ottoman. He grabbed it and ran back downstairs, dialing the number as he went.

"Zube, answer your damned phone. I found what you've been looking for, man! Check your mail and call me."

He listened to it over again, then a third time. He played it over and simultaneously read the words on the screen. He listened and heard and stared and read, over and over.

I've found what you've...

I have found what you've...

I have found what you have...

He sighed out loud. He'd tried them all, in upper and lower case, in plain and Italics.

I've found what you been...

Nope. The *you've* was clearly audible. It had to be something else.

I've found what...

Wait a minute. Wait just a minute!

I found what you've been looking for?

I found...?

I found?

It sounded exactly like *I've found.*

"I've found what you've been looking for," he said out loud. "I found what you...I've found. I found."

He pulled the keyboard towards him, the excitement surging once again. At the pass phrase prompt he held his breath and typed:

```
I found what you've been looking for
```

The screen responded with:

```
Just a moment....Pass phrase appears good.
Plaintext filename:  korpen
C:\WORK>
```

It felt like a massive valve had opened, spewing adrenaline into his bloodstream. The sense of relief was unbelievable, the release overwhelming. He would have leaped and hooted and hollered, but it wasn't yet time. Six different fingertips touched six different keys as he typed KORPEN. The screen instantly filled with text. Legible text!

The rest of the world ceased to exist as he started reading.

```
             UNITED STATES OF AMERICA
               DEPARTMENT OF DEFENSE
      Memorandum
      TO:       Secretary of Defense
      FROM:     Deputy Secretary of Defense
      SUBJECT:  Brief of 4.12.96 meeting with Sec
                State, CJCS
      DATE:     April 12, 1996
      The meeting was called by the Secretary of State
      to apprise the Department of Defense of recent devel-
      opments in the Korean peninsula.
          Since the onset of your illness last week, North
      Korea has publicly and vociferously renounced key
      aspects of the 1953 Korean peninsula armistice
      arrangements, punctuating its dissent with the
      following actions:
```

—On March 29, North Korea's deputy armed forces
minister, Kim Gwang-jin, declared that war on the
Korean peninsula was a virtual certainty.

—On April 4, Pyongyang announced it will no longer
maintain the Demilitarized Zone, and that North
Korean Military (KPA) personnel would no longer
carry the required insignia inside the DMZ. On the
same day, the speaker of the Supreme People's
Assembly, Yang Hyong-sop echoed the sentiments of
Gwang-jin, stating that war on the peninsula was
"…only a matter of time."

—Between April 5 and April 7, 300 heavily armed
KPA soldiers were sent into the DMZ at Panmunjom
three different times, once each day, in open violation of the armistice accord.

Seoul's response has been relatively muted. While
the South Korean defense ministry raised its vigi-
lance level from Watch Con 3 to 2—the effect being
more frequent analysis of intelligence reports—the
South's armed forces' level of alert has not been
raised. Seoul's rhetoric has largely been limited
to warning Pyongyang against further provocation.

The assessment of State and Defense Departments
analysts is that there is no imminent threat of war
on the peninsula. There has been neither a build up
of North Korean forces, nor any sign of military
maneuvers to suggest preparations for an attack.
Rather than considering the situation a credible
threat to the peninsula's status quo, the developments are viewed as yet another attempt by
Pyongyang to extract more concessions from the
United States.

You are aware of the Agreed Framework that the
Korean Peninsula Energy Development Organization
(KEDO) negotiated with North Korea. In return for
supplying North Korea with two new light-water
nuclear reactors and interim fuel oil, KEDO secured

a commitment from Pyongyang to freeze the North's nuclear program and allow international inspection of the its nuclear waste sites. You are also no doubt aware that the Framework has proven tougher to implement than it was to sign. In the past few months Pyongyang has continued to balk at the Framework's terms, constantly making new demands that stall the Framework's progress. Witness Pyongyang's refusal to accept South Korean-built light-water reactors and the frequent obstruction of regular scheduled international inspections. The latest episodes in the DMZ fit North Korea's pattern of trying to wring ever more concessions from the U.S. and the international community, be it in the form of economic aid or increased diplomatic recognition. Pyongyang's ultimate goal is to replace the 1953 armistice with a bilateral peace treaty between Pyongyang and Washington, a scenario we have always unequivocally rejected.

It is against this backdrop, and at the same time as the saber-rattling was being reported by the international media, that another situation developed, this of a more covert nature and bearing special sensitivities with regards to potential repercussions for the United States government.

As you know, in response to North Korea's demand for an exchange of full diplomatic recognition between Pyongyang and Washington, a demand made and rejected during KEDO's negotiations for the Agreed Framework, State recently proposed the establishment of a US liaison office in Pyongyang. James Stafford, a senior diplomat with extensive experience in Southeast Asia, has been tentatively appointed to head the proposed office. During a visit to Pyongyang last week, Stafford met several times with a high-ranking member of the Central Committee of the Worker's Party, and one of the North's renowned ideologues, Kim Kwang Soo. According to Stafford, on the one occasion when the two men were alone for a few minutes, Kim expressed a desire to defect to the US. He requested political asylum and asked for Stafford's help in getting him and his family out of North Korea. In return, Kim claims he can provide the US with irrefutable evidence of two surviving American prisoners of war still being held in North Korea. Kim claims the evidence will include recent video footage showing the two men are still alive. To lend credence to his information, Kim offered Stafford the names of the two American POWs, Douglas C. Strams and William D. Pickard.

Upon his return to Washington last Tuesday, Stafford reported this information to the Secretary of State in a personal, one-on-one briefing. The secretary duly apprised CJCS and I, in my capacity as acting Secretary of Defense, of the situation.

Considering the sensitivity of the subject matter, as well as the recent flurry of media speculation about whether American POWs were knowingly abandoned in North Korea, and in light of the oft-stated Defense Department position that we have no clear evidence of any Americans being held against their will in North Korea or elsewhere, I believe the ramifications of Stafford's information cannot be overstated. While CJCS suggested it might behoove this administration to quietly investigate Kim's claims, I am in concurrence with the Secretary's arguments against pursuing them.

The line dividing the Korean Peninsula is currently the world's most volatile flashpoint, and it is clear that any serious embarrassment of the regime in Pyongyang could conceivably be as catastrophic as a collapse of the North's economy. State Department and Pentagon intelligence analysts have warned it could spark a war of far-reaching and potentially disastrous consequences.

On the domestic front, disclosure of Kim's information—assuming there is substance to it—would be of no beneficial consequence. The issue would destabilize the nation by seriously eroding the voting public's faith in the institution of government. And this being an election year, the fallout would doubtless provide potent ammunition for the Republicans, who have long maintained that our current strategy of constructive engagement vis-a-vis North Korea is misguided.

My own research of Pentagon documents indicates that Strams and Pickard were indeed among the 900 or so American servicemen known by Armed Forces officials to have been captured alive by the North Koreans at the end of the war. Pentagon records further show that neither man was included in the prisoner exchanges that preceded the armistice. Nonetheless, the Secretary of State, CJCS and I feel, as I am sure you will, that the strategic considerations outlined above dictate only one course of action. In light of the potential consequences of the alternatives, the consensus opinion is that dismissal of Kim Kwang Soo's claim and rejection of his appeal, while exercised with disinclination and reluctance, would be the lesser of evils.

CHAPTER FIFTEEN

On the outside, Brad Renberg's demeanor was calm. His chest expanded and contracted with every breath. He blinked, and tapped his finger against the mouse to scroll through the text. But otherwise his body was perfectly still.

On the inside, the music was deafening. A symphony of emotions that numbed his senses even as it kindled his spirits and stoked the sweet spot of his soul.

He eyes were riveted to the screen. If it turned out to be a hoax, Richard Harding's demented notion of a cruel joke, he'd kill him and burn him and sprinkle his ashes in a cesspool.

But how could it be? There was the Ten Most Wanted list and the FBI and it all made sense because it was real. It *had* to be real.

He stirred as Laura's crying brought him back to earth. He considered turning off the baby monitor, then changed his mind. If he couldn't keep an eye on the Kinsers, an ear was the next best thing.

He left Netmail's site and typed:

`http://lcweb2.loc.gov/pow/powhome`

It was an address etched into his brain like no other. AOL's *Please wait while that site is contacted* message appeared. Seconds later he was online with the Library of Congress, Federal Research Division, POW/MIA Database. The screen welcomed him to the Vietnam-Era

Prisoner-Of-War / Missing-In-Action Database. He'd read it before, many times, but he read it again, relishing the new perspective. He read that the database contained 131,403 records. He read that it had been established to assist researchers interested in investigating the U.S. Government documents pertaining to U.S. military personnel listed as unaccounted for as of December, 1991. He read that the title of the collection was *Correlated and Uncorrelated Information Relating to Missing Americans in Southeast Asia.* The screen told him that researchers using the database could identify documents of interest by using search terms such as last names, country names, service branches, keywords, and statements such as "downed over Laos." He clicked on *Search: POW/MIA Database.*

```
THE FEDERAL RESEARCH DIVISION POW/MIA DATABASE.
     The retrieval system used on this database is
Inquery, developed by the Center for Intelligent
Information    Retrieval    at    the    University    of
Massachusetts, Amherst.
     Enter as long a query as you wish.
     Press the RUN button to start the search.
```

He entered *Strams* and clicked on RUN.

```
     No records were found for the search.
```

He tried *Pickard* and fared no better. Doubts about the authenticity of KORPEN began to nudge his mind when he remembered something. He went back to the top of the page and clicked on *Important Information.* The new screen told him that to facilitate use of the Library of Congress POW/MIA Database, it is essential to understand the genesis of the database and its contents. He scrolled downwards through the text until he found what he was looking for. His memory had served him well. Under the heading of *What is NOT in the Library of Congress POW/MIA Database* the first entry read:

```
     POW/MIA information on World War II, Korean
Conflict   and   the   Cold   War   unaccounted   for.
Documents   pertaining   to   these   conflicts   are   the
```

responsibility of the Archivist of the United
States. For further information please call the
Textual Reference Branch, National Archives at
(301) 713-7250.

He clicked on BACK a few times, returned to AOL's NetFind screen, typed *NATIONAL ARCHIVES* in the search box, and clicked on FIND. After a few seconds NetFind reported it had found 2,910,768 documents about national archives. A listing of the first ten, sorted by relevance, appeared on the screen. None of the titles suggested anything that appeared remotely connected to what he was looking for, an impression quickly confirmed by the summaries below each title. The only summary containing the words "National Archives" was that under the title *Genealogy and the American Civil War,* and Renberg didn't waste any time reading it. Instead he went back to the primary NetFind screen and entered *Korean War POW/MIA Database* in the search box.

This time NetFind found 1,920,529 documents, and of the first ten that were listed, there were several that looked promising. He clicked on the seventh, the title of which was *Korean War MIA/POW.* The home page was presented as a help desk containing multiple links to other web sites related to Korean War MIA/POW issues. Renberg ignored the first, an MIA mission statement, and clicked on the second, titled *Advocacy & Intelligence Index for Prisoners of War—Missing in Action.* It turned out to be someone's personal opinion of the ineptness of the government's lies regarding the issue, followed by a series of quotations of various government officials, all proclaiming solidarity with those who had served and not returned, and with their families. Other quotations reaffirmed the government's solemn commitment to see the MIA issue resolved, down to the last American soldier.

Renberg had seen and heard it all before. He was beyond scoffing at lies. He clicked back to the help desk and scanned the other links. Just like the effort to decrypt KORPEN, this was all going to be trial and error. And just like with KORPEN, he had no choice but to plod on. There was nothing else to do but click on another heading and see what lay in store for him. He chose *KOREAN WAR / VIETNAM CASUALTY LISTS* and prayed that he was getting warmer.

*   *   *

When the call crackled over Mark Grant's radio, the game warden was well within earshot, casually securing the jet ski to the trailer harness behind his vehicle. The heavy rain had kept him off the water most of the day, so the combination of clearing skies and new instructions was a welcome stimulant. Like all law enforcement personnel on duty in the central Texas region that afternoon, Grant was well aware of the FBI-led manhunt in progress just a few miles northeast of his location. To get a piece of that action suited him just fine. He checked his watch against the dash-mounted clock and reported he could be in San Marcos by 6:45. It would leave him almost two hours of daylight, ample time to scout the Blanco between San Marcos and Wimberley.

*   *   *

"Are you watching the news?" The President's voice was low, monotonous, distraught, and it put a lump in Harkutlian's throat.

"No," the secretary of state replied. He immediately assumed that the details of Robert Carlson's memorandum had just been broadcast to the nation.

"Turn on *CNN*."

Harkutlian grabbed the remote off his credenza and poked the power button. It was a breaking story, transmitted live from the scene of some woods in Fort Meyer. The body being wheeled on a gurney into an ambulance was covered head to toe with a white sheet. It was too premature to rule out foul play, the reporter said, but all the signs strongly suggested the chairman of the Joint Chiefs of Staff had shot himself.

"Pathetic fool!" Harkutlian groaned, shaking his head in perverse anger at the news. "Of all the mindless, asinine…"

He sighed with disgust at the TV as he began to calculate the ramifications. For once in his life, Ed Harkutlian found himself struggling for the words to adequately articulate his revulsion.

    *   *   *

Once she had his name, Austin FBI Special Agent Burke expanded her search to include details of David Zuber. A birth certificate was on record at the Bureau of Vital Statistics, as was, much to Burke's surprise, a death certificate. The surprise was compounded by two items of information. The first was the date. David Zuber had died in 1980, just one year after marrying Mary Renberg. Brad would have been thirteen at the time. The second was the cause of death. According to his death certificate, Brad Renberg's father had committed suicide.

Deborah Burke's search was far from over. She ran down her checklist and split the database resources into two sets, one for her to handle, the other to be pursued by the investigative assistant. Of those that were her responsibility, Burke started with military records. The repository was the National Personnel Records Center in St. Louis, Missouri. Burke knew it to be a 7 to 4 operation that would respond after hours if circumstances warranted the effort, so she enlisted the help of the FBI Resident Agency in St. Louis. She was informed that the right person would be contacted and summoned back to the Center to check the records as soon as possible. She was advised to expect up to a two-hour delay.

    *   *   *

His break came when Renberg clicked on *Korean War Project*. The home page he accessed listed a Dallas post office box address and telephone number, and as the other sites before it, numerous links to other Web sites. At the top of the list was *KIA/MIA Database*. He clicked and waited. A message appeared to the effect that the database was based upon two source files compiled from the original Department of Defense Form 1300's and to date included the 33,642 official declared dead by hostile means. It requested the user type in the last name only on the first try. Renberg's fingers flickered across the Keyboard as he typed *STRAMS* and punched the enter key.

His heart pounded against the walls of his chest. The name *DOU-GLAS C. STRAMS* flashed at the top of the screen, next to the words *Status Summary:*

> 1st Lt. Douglas C. Strams, USAF: Downed on a 29 January 1952 bombing mission over the DPRK. The Pentagon thinks he may have been shipped to the Soviet Union.

"It does, does it?" Renberg sneered, a glint in his eye. He clicked on BACK and entered *PICKARD*. Once again the database spat out a summary:

> USAF Capt. William D. Pickard—16th Fighter-Interceptor Squadron, went down while flying a Lockheed F-80C in a bombing mission in November, 1951. Known to be alive as of May 17, 1953.

Renberg sighed deeply and stared at the screen. It was unbelievable. After all these years, after everything he'd tried, there it was. In plain English, in black and white. And it was Richard Harding who'd found it! It was just, plain, unbelievable.

What were the bastards going to say now?

He slid down a couple of inches in the chair, suddenly aware that his backside ached. The sound of Laura's crying rang in his ears. She hadn't stopped crying, but his intense concentration on the monitor had for all intents and purposes blocked her out. He jumped out of the chair and ran upstairs. Connie and Sara Kinser were still bound and gagged on the floor. A quick inspection revealed Sara had almost freed her hands. Despite her attempts to resist him, he undid the knots and re-tied them. Then he pulled the tape off her mouth.

"For God's sake, have a heart," she pleaded. "Just let me hold her for a few minutes."

"I can't do that," he replied calmly. "I have a big heart. But there's one more thing I need to do before I leave you, your kind mother, and your beautiful baby alone. Please bear with me."

"Bear with you? Can't you see-"

The tape went back over her mouth, snuffing out her protests. When he tried sticking a pacifier in Laura's mouth she promptly rejected it and continued to bawl.

"Okay," he said, reaching into the cot. "Come here." Feeling distinctly awkward, he picked her up and held her against his chest.

"It's okay, Laura. Please stop crying." He patted her gently on the back and walked towards the window. The rain had all but stopped, and from his elevated vantage point he could see Flite Acres. If they did a house-to-house it was only a matter of time before they checked the River Oaks Lodge.

Laura surprised him with a loud belch.

"Is that what the problem was?"

She did it again as he took her back to the cot. He laid her on her back and tried the pacifier again. This time she took it.

He paused in the loft, his attention on the river. The water was faster now, rougher and angrier than it had been before, and he didn't care to think what might have happened to him out there. He skipped back downstairs, knowing what needed to be done, but unsure of exactly how to do it.

*　　　　　　　*　　　　　　　*

Shirley Mathis' hunch was good. Besides Wilhite and the couple who had lost the canoe, none of the other campers had seen Brad Renberg. It looked like he'd hitched the ride with Wilhite to the camp ground, then taken the canoe. The question was, how far had he gone?

Mathis picked up speed as she approached the mud pit at the exit from the campground. As the mud got deeper and the Blazer felt like it was bogging down, Mathis flexed her foot on the gas pedal and tugged at the steering wheel with a sawing action. Her momentum carried her through and she emerged safely on the blacktop beyond the gate.

She knew Flite Acres continued downstream for a few more miles. Was he already beyond the point where the road dead-ended?

She reverted to two-wheel drive and turned right on Flite Acres. While the road still ran roughly parallel to the river, there was now a greater distance between them, enough so that she soon lost sight of the water. Her only recourse was to turn on every driveway that snaked away to the right off Flite Acres, and follow it all the way to the end in order to check out the river. That made sense, except for the fact Renberg had a forty-five minute lead on her. She decided to do it in reverse. It seemed more reasonable to go as far as she could straight down Flite Acres, then turn around and check the river wherever she could on her way back.

According to her odometer, the end of the road came just 4.8 miles later, at a gate with a *PRIVATE PROPERTY—NO TRESPASSING* sign. A black metal mailbox next to the gate declared the address to be 3700 Flite Acres. The gravel road on the other side of the gate curved off to the left, to a large ranch house that appeared to sit farther away from the water than the road was. Unless the river took a big left turn too. Mathis got out, opened the gate, drove past it, stopped long enough to close it again, then proceeded towards the ranch house. With the track being gravel, there was mercifully no mud to contend with.

The river had indeed curved to the left, and Shirley glimpsed it when she neared the house. The woman who came to the door hadn't seen or heard anything unusual, but she hadn't spent the afternoon with her eyes glued to the river either. She invited the female game warden to go see for herself. Mathis did so, on foot, and long enough to conclude that for Renberg to have negotiated his way through this particular stretch of turbulence, he would have to be a competent canoeist. She ventured all the way down to the water's edge and checked in both directions. There was no sign of Renberg, or anyone else for that matter. She thought about how soon the jet ski might start making its way up the river. She turned and headed back to the Blazer.

At that precise moment, some sixteen miles down river of Shirley Mathis' position, Parks & Wildlife Game Warden Mark Grant had just finished strapping on his PFD. With a quick glance at the clearing sky, he carefully eased the jet ski off its trailer, into the swelling waters of the Blanco.

*   *   *

When the call from Denver came through, Steve Vogel expected to hear that the court order was now in the hands of agents on their way to Netmail's offices. He was pleasantly surprised to find that Denver was ahead of him.

"It's done," Matt Jordan said. "We served the order. Renberg can't get to his mailbox anymore."

"How long ago was that?" Vogel asked.

"I just heard."

"Good. Do *we* get to see what's in his mailbox?"

"We should. I just thought you'd like to know *he* can't get to it anymore."

"Yeah, that's good, thanks."

"What else can we do for you?"

"That should do it. I appreciate your help."

"No problem."

Vogel was pensive as he put the phone down. To the best of his knowledge, Renberg hadn't yet decrypted the message when he'd fled from Pendergraft's place. That was over two hours ago, and they still hadn't found him. If he was out there waiting to get to a computer before he could retrieve the message again, then they'd scored a direct hit. If he'd already found a way to retrieve it, they were back to square one. They wouldn't know for sure until they caught him.

He used his cellular to call FBI Austin. When he learned Wakeman was at the County Sheriff's in San Marcos, he got the number and called there.

"At least there's a little less time pressure to catch him," Vogel said. "I've had his access to his e-mail blocked."

Wakeman was still smarting. "How do you know he doesn't spread his e-mail around to several addresses?"

"I don't, and he might have. At least we've blocked his access to the one we know about, the one he was using at Pendergraft's place. How are things on your side?"

"We've learned he has an aunt who lives here in San Marcos. We're watching the house and waiting for a warrant."

"No sign of him around Wimberley?"

"He hitched a ride with someone, and it looks like he may have stolen a canoe and made his way out on the river. We're still working with the same perimeter on the roads, and a Parks & Wildlife jet ski is on its way up the river."

"Any of our boys still around here? I need a ride."

"I'll tell the dispatcher."

"Thanks. Uh…Mitch?"

"Yeah?"

"How's Juan?"

"Last I heard he was in surgery. But it doesn't look good."

Vogel was about to say his fingers were crossed when he was pre-empted. Wakeman had abruptly hung up.

*   *   *

Shirley Mathis couldn't know for sure if Renberg had slipped through the containment perimeter by way of the river. If he had indeed been the man Wilhite drove to the camp ground, and if he had in fact

stolen the red canoe, and if he was possessed of enough skill to negoti-
ate the canoe through the turbulent stretches, then he was gone. In that
case she could only hope the jet ski would be on the river in time to
intercept him. She felt good about the first two ifs. Put together, Wilhite's
passenger and the canoe's disappearance were quite a coincidence, and
like any good law enforcement officer, Mathis viewed coincidence
through a thick shroud of suspicion. But did Renberg know what he
was doing in a canoe? In her years with Parks & Wildlife, Mathis had
seen, first hand and on numerous occasions, what the mixture of water-
craft, a novice and rough water could produce. Until she heard that the
jet ski—or one of the other patrol cars—had Renberg, she had to check
the river, whenever and however she could.

She drove back along Flite Acres from the ranch at 3700, and it was a
good quarter of a mile before she came upon the first track running left,
towards the river. It wasn't until she turned onto the gravel that she read
the sign at the side of the road. About a yard square, it was suspended
under a crosspiece supported on either side by two round wood posts,
and it welcomed visitors to the River Oaks Lodge.

CHAPTER SIXTEEN

The clock on the Volkswagen's dash read 6:32 when Sadie Harding pulled into her parking spot at the Whisper Hollow apartments. She unbuckled the seatbelt, set the parking brake and killed the engine. As she got out of the car and locked the door, she instinctively glanced around the parking lot before making her way up the stairs to the second floor. There was no way for her to notice the eyes that keenly watched her every move from behind the tinted glass of the blue car parked innocuously across the driveway.

It was the first time she had been in the apartment since the FBI had paid their visit the day before. Richard's room had been thoroughly turned over, but hers showed evidence of only a perfunctory search. She was relieved to find her cocaine was still in its usual place, wrapped inside pantyhose in the bottom drawer of the dresser. She kicked off her shoes and turned on the TV. She was still on edge from the afternoon's action, and anxious to find out if the FBI had succeeded in catching Brad. She didn't feel too good about what she'd done, but if it was Brad Renberg who'd gotten Richard into this mess, then he deserved whatever was coming to him. For her part, she could always deny having anything to do with his capture. If he linked it to her, then hey, she didn't know she was being followed. He was the one who asked her for the key, and she delivered it.

She knew she'd missed the evening news reports, but flipped through the local channels anyway. When it became clear she would have to wait till the late news at ten, she turned the TV off and started the water running in the bath. She was in her bedroom, just starting to undress, when she heard a knock on the front door. Sadie stiffened and stood still. A few seconds later there was another knock, this time louder.

"Sadie, it's Kelly. Kelly Calloway."

Still Sadie didn't move. Kelly was Brad's friend. Did this have anything to do with that afternoon?

"Sadie, Please open up." Another knock. "I need to find Brad. It's urgent."

Sadie hesitated for a moment, and Calloway knocked again. Sadie stepped out of the bedroom and into the living room. "This is really a bad time…"

"I'll just be a minute," Calloway insisted. *"Please!"*

It occurred to Sadie that Brad Renberg might be outside with Kelly. She still didn't know for sure that they'd caught him. What if he'd found the device she'd planted on the seat and gotten away? There was potential for some real nastiness here.

"I can't open the door. What do you want?"

"It's urgent that I find Brad."

"I don't know where he is."

"Well if you hear from him, please tell him I need to speak to him. It's urgent. Can I give you a phone number?"

"I doubt I'll…" Sadie stopped short in mid-sentence. There was something distinctly fishy going on. "How do you know where I live?" she demanded.

Now it was Calloway who seemed to hesitate. "I…I know from Brad that this is where Richard lives. And Brad mentioned you and Richard share the apartment."

The answer sounded lame to Sadie. "Yesterday I told you I was staying at Michelle's. Why did you come looking for me here?"

"I called Michelle's and no one answered. I'm desperate to get word to Brad. I gave him Michelle's number yesterday because he wanted to talk to you. I was hoping you'd know how I can reach him."

It was plausible, but Sadie was still suspicious. "Well I don't know where he is, and I doubt I'll hear from him. Try his pager."

"He's not answering his pager."

"I can't help you."

"Can I just leave a number with you in case you hear from him?"

There was no harm in that. She wouldn't have to open the door. "Hold on." She waited a few before adding: "Go ahead."

Calloway called out the number.

"Got it," Sadie lied.

"Thanks. I really do appreciate it."

There was silence, then Sadie heard Calloway going down the stairs. She waited to see if there was any other sound, anything that might indicate someone else was out there. She heard nothing. She went straight to phone in the kitchen and called Michelle. The call was answered on the third ring.

"Michelle, it's me."

"Hey."

"How long have you been at home?"

"What, here? All afternoon. Why?"

"Have you been answering your phone?"

"Yes. Why?"

"Did you step out at all? Could the phone have rung without you hearing it?"

"I've been here all afternoon. I answered every time it rang. Why?"

"Kelly Calloway was just over here. She claims she called your place and nobody answered."

"She didn't call here. I'm pretty sure of that."

"Hmmm."

"What's the big deal?"

"Never mind. I'll talk to you later."

Sadie was deep in thought when she hung up. Something wasn't right, but she couldn't quite put her finger on what it was. She went to the bathroom and checked the temperature of the water in the bathtub. It was going to be hell waiting for the ten o'clock news.

＊　　　　　　　　　＊　　　　　　　　　＊

The Explorer parked in the driveway suggested there was someone home, so Game Warden Mathis was surprised when the doorbell went unanswered. She tried ringing it again, with the same result. She could see no one through the glass door, but there was a staircase, and the folks could be upstairs and hard of hearing. Besides, it was a lodge, and *Welcome* was etched into the glass pane on the front door. Mathis turned the handle and pushed.

It was locked.

She cupped her hands around her eyes and peered in through the glass. This was a nice, upscale place, about the most impressive she'd seen in Wimberley. She stepped left, towards the window next to the garage. It looked in on the kitchen and a dining area, the two separated by a counter. There was still no one to be seen, but Mathis did note the blank computer monitor in the hutch on the desk between the dining room and the living room. She also noted the keyboard drawer was open and the chair was back, away from the desk.

She went back to the Blazer and honked the horn. When there was no visible reaction, she reached for the Glock 40-caliber semi-automatic handgun at her hip and walked back to the lodge. She went around the side, to the right of the front door, and looked through the windows. She stepped up onto the porch and walked around to the door leading to the living room. Her back was to the river when she turned the handle. This one wasn't locked, and Mathis cautiously stepped inside.

"Hello?" she shouted out loud. "Anyone home?"

Nothing. Not a sound. Only that of the water gushing behind her. "Hello?"

As she considered going upstairs, a number of scenarios crossed her mind. Just because a car was parked outside didn't necessarily mean someone was there. Whoever the Explorer belonged to could have gone off with someone else in another car. What if someone was upstairs, asleep? Then again, it could be a couple, too caught up in each other to answer. How would she look, barging into the bedroom with a gun? There was an invasion of privacy issue here, a line she was reluctant to cross.

She stepped out onto the porch again and glanced at the river. Too many unknowns for comfort. She had to guard against overreacting and endangering the lives of innocents. But things didn't feel right, and the nagging suspicions were powerful.

She took the three steps off the porch onto the grassy bank, and started towards the river. She looked back at the River Oaks Lodge several times but it was as eerily quiet as before. No one showed. Not even a pet.

At the water's edge she checked the river in both directions. Here, too, the water was rough. There were rocks and boulders littering the surface and she again wondered how good a canoeist Renberg was. She turned to go back, then hesitated. It was the old leave-no-stone-unturned thing. She stared hard at the lodge, then started walking upstream along the riverbank. There was another house not too far upstream, but her attention was on the water, the rocks, and the two banks. She covered over fifty yards, and again was about to turn back, when something caught her eye. Now she ran, twenty more yards, until she could see it clearly. Something was wedged between two rocks, something red, and the way it had splintered suggested it was wood. She couldn't be sure it was part of a canoe, but she didn't need to be. She turned and sprinted for all she was worth back towards the lodge.

       *   *   *

Brad Renberg was near panic when he burst into the bedroom. The adult Kinsers were still on the carpet, bound and not going anywhere. He reminded them he had the gun, told them he would use it, and demanded they not make a sound. He made sure Laura had a pacifier in her mouth, and prayed she'd keep quiet. Then he slid over to the window to check out the intruder.

He'd scrambled upstairs at the first sound of the approaching vehicle. The only thing he did on the way was smack the big power knob on the monitor. Now he was aghast to see the vehicle wasn't a civilian one. He couldn't make out the wording on the insignia on the door, but it didn't matter. The body that stepped out was uniformed—light brown pants and shirt, a western-style straw hat, a badge on the left breast and...*breasts?* A female!

She disappeared from view below him at the front door. The doorbell rang, and Renberg motioned with the gun at the Kinsers. He crept over and checked that the tape over their mouths was secure. The bell rang again. Connie looked at him with petrified eyes and he brought his index finger to his lips. Sara struggled. He grabbed a handful of her hair and she stopped. He tiptoed over to the door, cracked it open, and listened for a sound from downstairs. There was none, so he crept back to the window. He was watching when the officer went back to her Blazer and honked the horn. He was still watching when she took her gun out and came back towards the lodge.

He held the bedroom door ajar, listening, watching. There was no sound from downstairs. No breaking glass, no forced entry. Then he saw her. She was outside, walking around the side of the house. Then she was on the porch. He cussed himself for not checking that *all* the doors were locked. He watched breathlessly as she tried the door to the living room. He turned hollow with fear when it opened.

He still had no proof. It was hopeless without proof. He couldn't let them take him. Not yet.

"Hello? Anyone home?"

Renberg held still.

"Hello?"

Laura was sucking on the pacifier. He aimed the gun at Sara and she understood. He peered out of the crack in the door again in time to see the officer step back out onto the porch. He watched with relief as she stepped down onto the grass and started towards the river. He let her get to the water's edge before he slipped down the stairs and sneaked out onto the porch.

*   *   *

Shirley Mathis ran as fast as she could. He was there, she was sure of it now. He'd come on the river and the Explorer belonged to someone else.

Did he have hostages?

She couldn't do this alone. She needed back up, lots of it, and *now*. She hurried up the grassy bank and ran along the side of the lodge towards the Blazer.

"*Freeze! I'll shoot!*"

It was visceral and it came from behind her and she froze.

"Don't make me shoot you!" There was a soft thud as he jumped off the porch onto the muddy ground behind her.

She didn't move a muscle.

"Slowly, real slow, put the gun down."

She bent at the waist and laid it on the ground.

"Straighten up. Stand up and step away."

She took two steps.

"Further."

She took two more.

"Put your hands up."

"Don't be-" she started.

"Quiet!" he hissed. "Do as I say!"

As she raised her hands Renberg stepped forward and picked up her gun. "Now, very slowly, turn around."

Her movements were slow and deliberate as she turned to face him. He slipped her gun into his belt. The gun in his hand was pointed straight at her chest. His eyes flickered down to the badge on her shirt. Parks and Wildlife Game Warden. "How many more of you are out there?"

"Every officer in the county's looking for you, Brad. You can't-"

"Take out your handcuffs."

"Listen to me, Brad…"

"Your handcuffs."

She started lowering her hands.

"One hand only," he said. "Real slow."

She used her right hand to pull the snap on the holder at her waist.

"Take them out."

She withdrew the handcuffs slowly.

"Hold them out in front of you. Now turn around, bring your left hand down, and put both hands behind your back where I can see them. Slowly."

She turned around so she was facing away from him.

"Put the cuffs on and lock them."

"You'll never-"

"Shut up. Do it!"

The handcuffs went on. First the right hand, then the left.

"Shrink them down."

The teeth clicked as she tightened the cuffs around her wrists.

"Lie down. Face down."

She got on her knees and eased herself down on her side before rolling over onto her stomach. Renberg put his foot on her back and checked that the handcuffs were tight.

"Where's the key?"

"In my pocket."

"Which one?"

"Front left."

He rolled her over. With the gun at her throat, he searched the pocket. He found one key and held it up. "Is this it?"

"Yes."

He searched through her other pockets. There was nothing else she could use to free her hands, so he helped her up.

"Don't make things worse for yourself, Brad."

"Let's go," he said, pushing her towards the lodge. "Around the side."

He let her lead the way, prodding her onto the porch and through the door into the living room.

He wasn't sure where to put her. Upstairs was getting crowded, and he'd feel safer with her downstairs, where it would be easier to keep an eye on her. The question was where?

He ruled out the kitchen. If any more unwanted visitors showed up, they'd be able to see her through the window. He could disappear upstairs in a hurry, but not if he had to worry about moving her up there too. The same reasoning ruled out the living and dining rooms. The downstairs bedroom also had windows and opened onto the porch, but it was a bedroom, and bedrooms normally had shades.

"In that first door on the left there," he said.

He still needed a way to immobilize her, and the bedroom provided no answers. He needed something solid and fixed that he could tie her to. Neither the bed nor any other item of furniture appeared heavy enough.

He gestured towards the adjoining bathroom. "In there." An exposed pipe or one of the bathroom fixtures, maybe. He found the answer in the shower. Four feet up the wall, next to the shower fixtures, there was a porcelain soap holder with a handle. It was glued in place on the wall amongst the tile, and Renberg hoped it would take more physical strength than she had to tear it out.

"Into the shower."

"Right into it?" she asked, puzzled by the order.

"Right into it," he confirmed.

Once she was in he said, "Stick your hands out towards me, and don't try anything stupid."

Keeping the gun leveled at her head with his right hand, he used his left to slip the key into one side of the handcuffs and unlock it.

"Take your hand out and slide it through the handle on the soap holder."

"My hand?"

"What?"

"You want me to slide my hand through there?"

"Don't get cute," he replied. He removed the key and stepped back beyond her reach. "The cuffs."

"Through there?"

"That's what I said."

With the gun still pointed at her head, she did as she was told.

"Now put it back on."

When he heard the clicks he leaned over and checked the cuffs. They were secure enough, but the soap holder was iffy. Porcelain was brittle. She might hurt herself in the process, but it was conceivable she could break it. It was a risk he would have to take. He still needed time on the computer, and while she might break free of the wall, she couldn't do so without him hearing her. Besides, she'd still be handcuffed, and he had the guns.

"Okay, listen. I don't have a thing in the world against you. You have a job to do, and so do I. If you try anything, I can hear you. Don't make me hurt you."

"They'll be coming, Brad," she called out as he left her standing in the shower. "You'll never make it out of here."

On the first part, she was right, of course. He couldn't escape feeling she was just the first drop through the crack in the dam. It was only a matter of time before she didn't respond on the radio and they came looking. As to whether or not he could survive this...

It all depended on how much time he had.

He ran upstairs and checked on the Kinsers. Connie and Sara were still on the carpet and the knots were still tight. Laura was in her own little world. She didn't seem to miss the pacifier, which lay next to her head in the crib. Renberg let her be. He glanced out the window and cursed softly.

He stepped over to Connie and pulled the tape off her mouth. "Where are your car keys?"

"Please don't leave us like-"

"Where are the keys?"

Sara was trying to protest, but the words were muffled.

"In the kitchen," Connie said. "On the wall, next to the garage door."

He secured the tape back on her mouth and was downstairs in a flash. He found the keys on a rack and hurried into the garage. He backed Connie's Cadillac out and parked it in front of Sara's Explorer. Then he ran to the Parks & Wildlife vehicle. The keys were in the ignition, and he quickly pulled the Blazer into the garage and closed the door. As he was stepping out of the Blazer, a voice came over the radio. It was a two-way conversation, unrelated to him, but it gave him an idea. He turned the volume up and rolled down the windows. Then he wedged a broom between the kitchen door and its jamb so that the door stayed partially open when he released it. Now, from his position at the desk, he would be able to hear what came over the radio.

He could hear the game warden jerking the handcuffs against the soap holder. He'd hidden her car, but if anyone came, she could still attract attention by screaming. He ran upstairs and grabbed the roll of medical tape he'd used on Connie and Sara. He found another hand towel in the downstairs bathroom. She tried to resist, but gave up when he pulled on her hair. He put the folded hand towel over her mouth and secured it in place by wrapping several feet of tape around her head.

"I wouldn't tug too hard on those cuffs," he said, stepping back. "You'll break bones before anything else." With that he left her and returned to the computer. It had been nearly twenty minutes since she'd pulled up to the River Oaks lodge. If not for her, he might have had a lot more accomplished by now.

CHAPTER SEVENTEEN

Mark Grant's passion for the outdoors matched his dread of a desk job, and being a Texas Parks & Wildlife Game Warden was the answer to both. To spend his days skimming across rivers and lakes on a jet ski was a dream come true. To get paid for doing so, a fantasy realized. The rain had swollen the river, leaving it bloated with mud and silt, but far from slowing Grant down, the conditions only fed his gusto. Expect him in a red canoe, the dispatcher had said, between San Marcos and Wimberley, probably further up river, closer to Wimberley. All the more reason to gas it, Grant figured, as he guided the Yamaha WaveVenture 1100 against the flow, employing all 110 horses to attack the river head-on.

The river ran east from Wimberley for approximately six miles before curving southward for another six to San Marcos. Grant knew he'd reached the halfway point once he was following the sun. Nine minutes had elapsed since he'd left San Marcos, and he reasoned that if Renberg were still on the river, it wouldn't take another nine for their paths to cross. He had his gun and his radio. He instructions were to observe and pursue, radio in his position, and await the arrival of backup units before moving to apprehend the suspect. The clouds were behind him now and there were blue skies above. He was ready.

Grant was not the only person with an eye on the clearing skies. Some twenty-five miles to the north, a helicopter pilot attached to the

Texas Department of Public Safety was also satisfied the worst of the weather was behind them. His chopper was equipped with Forward Looking Infrared Radar and night vision capability, but he was still anxious to get to the vicinity of the search before sundown. He gave his civilian-clothed passenger a thumbs-up signal, and gently eased his baby up off the tarmac.

*　　　*　　　*

Renberg brought up AOL's WELCOME TO THE INTERNET window and typed:

    www.infospace.com.

Under a banner proclaiming Infospace to be the ultimate directory, the homepage listed several options, and Renberg clicked on YELLOW PAGES. From the next menu he picked BUSINESS BY NAME. In response to the name prompt he entered *The Washington Post.* He typed Washington, D.C. for the city and clicked on LOOK IT UP.

Eight seconds.

    There are no entries that match your search
    criteria.

He deleted Washington, D.C. from the CITY bracket, and put it under STATE.

    There are no entries that match your search
    criteria.

"Bull*shit!*"

He deleted "The" from the name bracket and tried again. This time five listings appeared on the screen, the second of which was identified as the telephone number for the Washington Post newspaper. Renberg scribbled down the ten digits and returned to Infospace's homepage. He clicked on WHITE PAGES, then PHONE NUMBERS. The next screen declared itself the most comprehensive telephone directory on the Internet, and claimed listings for more than 112 million people in the US. Renberg responded to the PEOPLE SEARCH prompt with Stafford for the last name, James for the first, and Washington, D.C. for the state. Two listings appeared. One was for a James S., the other a James D. Renberg jotted both down with their respective numbers. At the menu on the left of the screen he clicked on GOVERNMENT. That gave him six options, the first two of which were GOVERNMENT EXECUTIVES and FEDERAL LISTINGS. It was fifty-fifty, and he chose the latter. Now the options became four, one for each of the branches of government, and one for REGIONAL OFFICES. He opted to check the Executive Branch. His next choice was between the Executive Office of the President and any one of thirteen departments. He chose the Department of State. Much to his aggravation, the listings that appeared were for offices and services, but not for personnel by name. He went back three pages and tried GOVERNMENT EXECUTIVES. The search of government officials by name or title was more to his liking. He tried James Stafford and this time found only one. It was the "D".

"Hellllo, James D. Stafford," he murmured as he struck a triumphant line through the "S" on the notepad. There was a glint in his eye as he noted Stafford's phone number. "You bastards can run," he sneered, "but you sure as hell can't hide."

          *   *   *

Hays County Sheriff's Deputy Hale Martin was reflecting on the monotony of watching a house when the Toyota pulled into the driveway. He immediately entered the license plate number into his mobile data terminal for a vehicle check. The driver stepped out of the Toyota, and glanced worriedly at the patrol car on the street. She was halfway to the front door when the information appeared on Martin's screen. The Toyota was registered in the name of Charlene Renberg. There were no outstanding warrants, no violations of any kind on record. Renberg and her Toyota appeared clean as a whistle.

Martin jumped out after her as she fumbled with her keys.

"Mrs. Renberg?"

She looked over her shoulder nervously and slid a key into the lock.

"May I ask you a couple of questions, ma'am?" He caught up with her as she pushed the door open. "Have you seen or heard from Brad today?"

It was only when she stepped inside that she turned to face him. "Brad?"

It wasn't just fear Martin saw in her eyes. It was alarm. "Your nephew, ma'am."

"No I haven't."

"Who is that in the house with you ma'am?"

"It's not Brad," she replied, stepping back, "and I don't know where Brad is. Leave me alone."

Martin stood his ground as she slammed the door. He shook his head once and turned back to his car. It wouldn't be long now before they had the search warrant.

Charlene Renberg watched through the window as the deputy walked back to his patrol car. She'd heard about Brad on the news, but her first thoughts were for her sister. Even before she entered the bedroom she knew from the stench that her concern was justified.

She had taken care of Mary long enough to know all the signs. The vomit, the disorientation, the weak and rapid pulse, and the sickly sweet odor of acetone on Mary's breath all pointed to one thing. Charlene ran to the kitchen in a panic. When the 911 operator responded to her call, she blurted out the address and pleaded for an ambulance.

"Oh, Brad," she wailed as she dialed his pager. "What the hell have you done?"

Sheriff's Deputy Hale Martin heard the ambulance being dispatched on his radio and immediately smelled a rat. He radioed in that he was outside the address and there was no sign of any medical emergency. He told his dispatcher to get word to the FBI man that Charlene Renberg had requested the ambulance, and that he, Martin, thought it might be a trick to get Brad Renberg out of the house.

Moments later Charlene Renberg was feverishly counting the insulin doses in her refrigerator when Mitch Wakeman, the Hays County Sheriff and four of his deputies hustled into their vehicles and sped off towards her house.

*   *   *

The swollen river allowed Mark Grant to get his jet ski past the low-water bridges with no problem. When he started passing houses on the river, he knew he was close to Wimberley. Considering the time that had passed since the jet ski was requested, chances were that Renberg was actually downstream of him by now. He steered the craft around and started cruising back down the river. He radioed in his status and requested the dispatcher coordinate him with Mathis' position. When nothing came back and he pressed again for the information, he was informed that Mathis was not responding. For the first time the element of fun Mark Grant had associated with the afternoon's proceedings began to diminish. It was to wane some more a few minutes later. He was maneuvering his way through a rough section, choosing his lines early and scouring the river and its banks for any sign of Renberg, when he spotted the debris. It wasn't much—it looked like it might be a single piece of red wood that the force of the water had wedged tight between two rocks. He circled around to get a closer look. It was wood, and it was red, and that was all he needed to see. He stood up on the jet ski and craned his neck. There were no other signs of debris, and he didn't recall having seen any drifting down the river further downstream. He radioed in to the dispatcher and asked when she'd last heard from Mathis. The dispatcher informed him that the last time Game Warden Mathis had called in, she'd reported being at 3400 Flite Acres. Grant knew he was close to Flite Acres, but he had no idea where 3400 was. There was one way to find out. He could see two houses, one a short distance upstream, and the other, a grand-looking log structure, further away in the other direction. He guided the jet ski over to the north bank, killed the engine, and disembarked. He tethered the craft to a tree trunk and started towards the closer of the two houses, the one upstream from where he stood.

*   *   *

Secret Service Special Agent Noel Markovski was still working the houses east of Hidden Valley on flight acres when he heard the request. They wanted someone to pick up the FBI's Steve Vogel, who was still at Pendergraft's house, and in need of a ride to San Marcos. Markovski was aware of the commotion surrounding Renberg's aunt's house in San Marcos. If San Marcos was where the action was, then that was where he needed to be. He radioed in that he was on his way to pick up Vogel, and raced back to 2411 Spoke Hollow.

Vogel was waiting impatiently. As soon as he'd loaded Pendergraft's computer into Markovski's Jeep, they set off for San Marcos. Markovski drove like his life depended on it and got them there in eight minutes. They learned en route that Wakeman was on his way to Charlene Renberg's house, and the dispatcher gave them directions. They arrived to find the party in full swing. The ambulance was in the driveway, behind the Toyota. Wakeman's car and three Sheriff's Department vehicles were scattered on the street. Neighbors on both sides were out on the sidewalk, gawking. Markovski screeched to a halt and left his Jeep partially blocking the street as he followed Vogel inside the house. They were just in time to see an elderly woman being lifted onto a stretcher. A paramedic was telling his colleague that there were no signs of edema or pulmonary congestion, and that an IV of NSS was in order to combat the ketoacidosis. Wakeman explained they were looking at Renberg's mother, who was on the verge of slipping into a diabetic coma.

The paramedics had their hands full with Mary Renberg. They would later comment, however, that they had never before been in a situation where the law enforcement personnel had been so suspicious of the ambulance, and its reason for being there.

*   *   *

It started as a distant buzz, and it caused Renberg to snap his head up and take his eyes off the screen. He held his breath as he tried to identify the source. When it grew louder he jumped out of the chair and ran to the front door. Just as he got there he realized it was coming from the other direction. He ran through the great room, past the fireplace to the glass door at the porch. By now it was clearly coming from the river, and he guessed it was a boat. A few seconds later he saw it—a jet ski, driven by a man wearing an orange lifejacket. Renberg moved back, away from the glass. As the jet ski proceeded up the river and out of sight, he opened the door and stepped out onto the porch. He stood there, listening, waiting for the sound to fade away. It got lower, but to his dismay, it didn't fade out. The note of the exhaust dropped, meaning the craft had slowed down, then the revs held constant at idle speed, an indication it had stopped. There were trees blocking his view up the river, but Renberg decided to hold his ground rather than risk being seen if he left the shelter of the porch. Moments later the engine abruptly died, and his curiosity got the better of him. He skipped down the wooden steps and cautiously made his way towards the water, seeking the cover of the largest trees as he went. He was only twenty yards from the water when he saw it again. The man was tying the jet ski to a tree. Renberg picked his way from one tree to another and moved closer. He was soon close enough to see the man had a wireless radio in his hand. Then the lifejacket came off, and Renberg saw the man's clothes were the same light-brown color as the game warden's uniform. And when he noticed the unmistakable outline of a hip-holster, Renberg decided he'd seen enough. As the game warden walked off in the direction of the house further upstream, Renberg hurried back to the lodge as fast as caution would allow.

*   *   *

Mark Grant, too, was exercising caution, but in his case it meant having his gun out and ready as he approached the house. He circled around to the front and saw what Brad Renberg had found earlier that afternoon. A dark interior, a locked door, and a Honeywell sticker warning of an intrusion alarm system. It all suggested that Renberg's presence at this particular address was unlikely. If Renberg had tried to seek refuge here, he would have tripped the alarm. The brass number plate above the door read 3000. Grant was sure it was Flite Acres. And the dispatcher had said Shirley Mathis had last called in from 3400. The way addresses went in these parts, that was probably the next house down the road, the other one he'd seen from where he'd stopped on the river. He retraced his steps back to the water. As he passed the jet ski he radioed in his position to San Marcos. The dispatcher confirmed she'd still heard nothing more from Shirley Mathis. Grant notified her he was on his way to investigate what he believed to be 3400 Flite Acres.

*   *   *

Shirley Mathis was not a religious woman, but when she first heard the buzz of the jet ski she instinctively started to pray. She heard it fade, then abruptly stop, and she prayed a little harder. She heard the porch door open and close, and guessed Renberg was out there, watching. She thought desperately of how she might warn Grant and alert him that Renberg was there. She had been gagged, and her mouth was taped, so she couldn't scream or shout. The only other option was to rattle the handcuffs against the porcelain soap holder. But Renberg would hear that and react, and Grant wouldn't, unless he was right there in the lodge, which he wasn't. She slumped her shoulders and prayed ever harder.

*   *   *

Renberg knew he didn't have a second to waste. He accessed the *Infospace* website again and looked up the telephone listing for Terri

Rait in San Antonio. Then he dialed the number on the phone, praying he would be in luck.

"Hello?" It was a female voice and Renberg recognized it.

"Terri, It's Brad."

"Brad! Wha-"

"Is Chris there?"

"Uh…yeah." She sensed the urgency.

Pendergraft took the phone. "Brad! Where are you?"

"Chris, listen. I don't have much time. I'm desperate, and I need your help. There's something I need you to do."

"What?" Pendergraft sounded hesitant.

"Write this name down: James Stafford. S-T-A-F-F-O-R-D."

"Got it."

"Here's his phone number." He gave Pendergraft the area code and the seven-digit number.

"Got it."

"And this is a number for the Washington Post." Another ten digits.

"This going to get me in trouble?"

"No. Just don't go back home yet. The FBI followed me there. But you're not involved. Just listen."

"I'm listening."

"Here's what I need you to do…"

*   *   *

Mark Grant approached the lodge as stealthily as he could, staying low, and using the trees for cover as he closed in. He had already assumed the worst: that it was 3400 Flite Acres, that Renberg was there, and that he'd somehow managed to overpower Shirley Mathis. He was still mindful of his instructions: establish visual contact with the suspect, then radio in and await the arrival of backup units before moving to make an arrest. At this point, the first order of business was to confirm that this was indeed 3400 Flite Acres. If it was, and there was a Parks and Wildlife vehicle outside, he was prepared to skip the visual contact part.

When the trees thinned out he plotted his approach through the bushes and shrubbery, again seeking whatever cover would minimize his exposure. His route brought him up towards the side of the house. He paused a few times, straining his ears, seeking any clue as to what might be happening inside. There were none. Everything was still and quiet. At one point, as he crept around the side towards the front driveway, he was only a matter of yards from where Shirley Mathis was standing in the shower. But he made no sound, and neither knew the other was there. He came around the corner of the house and saw the cars. There was a Cadillac and a Ford Explorer, but no Parks and Wildlife vehicle. Grant relaxed some as he sensed he might have been wrong about the address. He looked for a number on the house, but found only the word of welcome etched into the glass on the front door. He dropped his guard further, stepped to the front door, and turned the handle. When the door didn't budge, Grant knocked on the glass.

Renberg was startled. He dropped to the floor and slid on his belly to the kitchen. From there he crawled into the garage, taking care not to let the door slam behind him. As Grant knocked again, Renberg stuck the gun into his belt and pried open the garage window. He went through headfirst and pulled his torso and legs through. He landed in a heap on the soaked turf, next to the electrical panel. He pulled himself up and took the gun out from under his belt. He stood there for a few seconds, his back straight against the wall, his head still as he listened for any sound that might tell him what the game warden was doing. Hearing nothing, he inched his way towards the porch, away from the driveway. When he ran out of wall, he took one last glance around him, then sprinted into the cover of the shrubs at the side of the house.

*   *   *

Shirley Mathis jumped at the sound of the first knock. She didn't know whether to hold still and let the situation play itself out, or rattle the cuffs and hope Grant would hear her. She wasn't even sure it was Grant knocking, and if it was, and he heard her, what would he make of it? Renberg would likely also hear her. Would that help or hinder Grant, or whoever else was at the door? She didn't know what to think. There was one thing she knew for sure—her current position was untenable. She was helpless, and she had to do *something*. When she heard the knocking again, she swept aside all considerations of the consequences, and rattled the handcuffs against the soap holder as hard as she could bear.

From where he stood outside the front door, Grant heard something. No one came to the door, so he moved to his left and peered through the windows. He tried the kitchen window, but it was latched from the inside. Suddenly he heard a baby cry out. It came from inside the kitchen, and it perplexed him that he couldn't see a baby, until he saw the monitor. As his suspicions grew again, he continued on towards the garage, looking for an open door or window. He walked around and found one at the back of the garage. He was trying to decide whether he had enough probable cause to justify climbing through, when he saw the Parks and Wildlife Blazer parked inside. Now there was no holding back. In an instant he was through the window and creeping into the kitchen. He swung his gun around in all directions as he entered the dining room. Now he could hear the baby crying upstairs, and another racket coming from his right, beyond the great room. He moved furtively, sticking close to the walls, past the staircase, still with his gun at the ready. He hesitated for a moment outside the bathroom. The rattling was coming from just inside the open door, now accompanied by what sounded like muffled moans. He took one large step and swung into the bathroom behind his gun, his right index finger resting tensely on the trigger. He almost squeezed it, but the sight of Mathis jerking her arms against the wall held him back in the nick of time.

"Jesus Christ!" he exclaimed as he ripped the tape off her mouth.

She spat out the hand towel. "It's Renberg! He's here!"

Grant rummaged through his pockets, found his key, and unlocked Mathis' handcuffs. "Where?"

"I don't know," she whispered as she shook her hands. "I heard you when you came up the river and he did too. I heard him open the door."

"Where's your gun?"

"He's got it."

"Your rifle? Shotgun?"

"I left them in the truck."

"What about the baby?"

Mathis shook her head. "I don't know. He could be upstairs with hostages."

"Okay. Let's check for the rifle and shotgun."

He led the way back into the corridor. Mathis was right behind him. The baby's cries became more persistent. Grant waited at the garage door as Mathis looked in the back of the Blazer. She found both the Remington 12-guage slide-action shotgun, and the .223 caliber Ruger mini-14 rifle.

"Both here," she whispered. She reached for the Ruger. "Let's radio in. If he's upstairs with hostages-"

"Do it!"

Mathis was requesting assistance on the radio when she and Grant heard the engine. She dropped the mike and they ran through the kitchen and dining room into the great room. They burst out of the door onto the porch, just in time to see Renberg race off down the river on the jet ski. Seconds later, while Shirley Mathis issued urgent pleas through her wireless radio's microphone, Grant ran upstairs and freed a badly shaken Sara Kinser and her near-hysterical mother.

★ ★ ★

Mitch Wakeman was taking no chances. Earlier that day, he'd experienced first-hand Brad Renberg's cunning at eluding certain capture when cornered and surrounded. As the DPS helicopter hovered overhead, and the paramedics loaded Mary Renberg onto the ambulance, Wakeman divided his attention—and the men under his command—between the ambulance and the house. He wasn't yet ready to concede that the medical emergency was authentic. As far as he was concerned, it was just as likely a ploy to divert everyone's attention long enough for Brad to make yet another escape. So Wakeman ensured that enough sheriff's deputies were stationed around the house to preclude anyone getting out unseen. He positioned men around the ambulance too, just in case. When it was ready to pull away, Wakeman personally checked to make sure the paramedics were who they were supposed to be. Charlene Renberg insisted on accompanying her sister to the hospital. And for his part, Wakeman insisted that the ambulance be escorted front and rear by sheriff's deputies. As the convoy pulled away, Wakeman decided he had sufficient probable cause, and led the assembled lawmen into Charlene Renberg's house.

The search was quick, thorough, and disappointing. Just as Wakeman begrudgingly concluded they were barking up the wrong tree, the county sheriff received confirmation of same from his dispatcher. Two deputies stayed behind to watch the house. The remaining lawmen—eleven in all, including Wakeman, Vogel and the Secret Service's Markovski—scrambled under the county sheriff's direction towards all points between San Marcos and Wimberley with vehicular access to the river. An urgent call went out for additional men and additional boats to hit the water, and the DPS chopper was dispatched to scout the Blanco from the air.

*   *   *

It was closing in on eight in the evening when FBI Special Agent Deborah Burke heard back from St. Louis.

"We ran that check on David Zuber," the voice on the line said.

"Did you find anything?" Burke asked.

"I'll say."

"Tell me."

"This thing's loaded."

"How's that?"

"Go park in front of your fax machine and see for yourself."

Burke was next to the machine when it started humming. She finished reading the first sheet and was anxiously awaiting the second when it rolled off onto the collection tray. She snatched it up and devoured it.

A single "Uh oh," was her first reaction to the military service summary. Then she ran to her desk, reached for the telephone, and dialed Mitch Wakeman's number.

CHAPTER EIGHTEEN

Brad Renberg's mind was racing as fast as the jet ski, which was at full speed. They would be after him in no time. They would have heard and seen him so they knew he was on the river, and they knew which direction he was heading in. Only he didn't know where they were. There could be other jet skis or boats waiting around the next bend. It was impossible to guess how much time he had, or how much distance before he ran into them. Of the two, it was time that was most critical. Pendergraft needed time, how much, Renberg couldn't be sure. So he had to disappear, probably for several hours, and hope that the stars lined up for Pendergraft, and ultimately, for him.

Staying on the river was out of the question. It flowed into San Marcos, and they surely would be waiting. It was almost eight and the sun had just dipped over the horizon, so he would soon have the cover of darkness. 3237 and 150 were to the north, 12 to the south, and I-35 due east. When he'd studied the map of the surrounding area the day before at Pendergraft's house, he'd noted several roads between the Blanco and 12. From where he was on the river he couldn't be more than six to ten miles from blacktop. Depending on the terrain, and how quickly he could move in the dark, a three or four hour walk. It was doable.

He pushed on for two more minutes until he saw the cliffs. They weren't huge—maybe thirty feet high—but they were right up against the river. It was as good a place as any. With the throttle open as far as it would go, he sped down the river until the cliffs were to his left, then veered the craft around sharply and steered it straight at them. He barely had time to jump before the jet ski rammed into the solid wall of limestone. He was underwater when it exploded, but he surfaced in time to see the aftermath of the collision. Debris from the jet ski littered the river and smoke billowed from the fragmented remains of the gas tank. He dived underwater again and started swimming towards the opposite bank. He surfaced a few feet from the bank and found a spot to pull himself out. It was only then that he noticed the gun was no longer under his belt. It had to have fallen out when he'd jumped off the jet ski. It crossed his mind to dive back in the water and see if he could find it, but he realized that would be hopeless. He set the thought aside and started running away from the river, in a direction perpendicular to its flow. He covered nearly four hundred yards before he first heard the helicopter.

*   *   *

According to the county sheriff, there were several points of paved access to the river between San Marcos and Wimberley. A few were north of San Marcos, the closest being two miles west of Kyle, with another further north, about a mile off Farm Road 150, some three miles west of Mountain City. The sheriff led the way to the first, followed by Wakeman and Vogel in Wakeman's car. Markovski tailed one of the deputies to the second. Two other deputies sped off towards a third, which was at a point very close to the lodge at 3400 Flite Acres. They had barely left San Marcos when Wakeman's cell phone rang. He flipped it open and brought it to his ear. It was Special Agent Deborah Burke, and she had the beef. Wakeman's expression turned sullen as he listened to what she said.

"I see," he murmured, pursing his lips. "Are you sure?"

"What?" Vogel asked anxiously.

"Okay. Good work, Debbie. I'm going to put Steve Vogel on the line. Tell him what you told me."

Vogel snatched the phone to hear for himself. He listened solemnly as Burke retold the story. "Can I get you to fax that to headquarters?" he asked when she was done. He recited a number, then flipped the phone shut and shot a glance at Wakeman. "No wonder!" he said. "That's one hell of chip on the son of a bitch's shoulder!"

Wakeman nodded silently. Vogel handed him back the phone, then used his own to dial the ten digits that would connect him to the FBI's Economic Crimes Unit chief.

In light of what he'd just learned, Wakeman's comfort level with the law enforcement manpower currently employed in the hunt for Renberg sagged. This case was no longer about a hacker meddling with computers just to prove he could. As Vogel apprised headquarters of the latest developments, Wakeman placed a call of his own, to his immediate supervisor, Sam Holsten, the assistant special agent-in-charge of the San Antonio field office. Holsten had left his office two hours earlier, but he immediately returned Wakeman's page. Their conversation was terse and to the point. Holsten quickly agreed that Wakeman's request for extra manpower was justified, and took upon himself the task of mobilizing every available agent in San Antonio, Dallas and Houston to join in the hunt. Wakeman was left assured that within thirty minutes, somewhere in the range of one hundred FBI agents would be on their way to San Marcos.

*   *   *

Renberg took shelter under an oak tree as he watched the chopper get closer. It swooped in quickly towards the smoke and circled the crash site. He had come upon the cliffs just in time. There was no doubt the chopper was panning across the river, looking for him. Thirty more seconds on the water and they would have met. It wouldn't be long before they started combing the surrounding area. The chopper dropped down for a better look. Renberg figured they'd concentrate on the river for a while, before starting to circle outwards when they didn't find him. Now was the time to distance himself from them. He turned his back to the commotion and ran for all he was worth.

He tried to maintain a southeasterly heading, modifying his direction in spurts only as necessary to stay under the cover of the trees. He soon slowed down, as his body reminded him to pace himself. The run turned into a spirited jog, and although he was breathing hard, he resisted stopping. It was easier to endure the fatigue, now that he knew. Just like with hacking, it all came down to motivation. Ability meant nothing without the desire. And now, now that he finally had something against the bastards, his motivation knew no limits. The top immediate priority was to buy Pendergraft some time. Not long, considering the wealth of knowledge and assistance Chris could tap from the underground. Then, after all these years, he would hopefully have them. His spirits soared, and he pushed himself like never before.

*   *   *

When the dispatcher relayed the helicopter's observations, the sheriff pulled over and let Wakeman come up alongside him. They briefly exchanged opinions before making U-turns and burning rubber back towards San Marcos. Wakeman asked the Secret Service's Noel Markovski and the deputy he was following to continue on to their river destination, while he and Steve Vogel followed the sheriff through San Marcos and onto Ranch Road 12. A few miles west of San Marcos they hung a right on County Road 226. The sheriff told Wakeman it ran in a northwesterly direction to the Round Rock Ranch, through which they could take a gravel road to a point on the river very close to the cliffs where the jet ski had crashed.

"We don't have but twenty minutes of daylight left," Wakeman noted, "if that."

"Son of a bitch," Vogel cussed. "I'll need to see a body before I'll ever believe he perished in the crash."

Wakeman still wasn't over Vogel's role in Juan Camacho's death, and he didn't fancy an extended conversation. But in his own mind, he didn't disagree. Renberg had proved to be as slippery as an eel. And there was nowhere eels were more adept at disappearing than in the water.

     *   *   *

The verbal briefing that FBI Economic Crimes Unit chief Scott Berger received from Steve Vogel prompted him to request an immediate facsimile of David Zuber's military service record. Vogel relayed the instructions to Deborah Burke, who acted on them without delay. All in all, from the time Burke first saw the record, it took less than thirty minutes for a copy to land in the tray of FBI director Brent Zarbach's fax machine, who in turn wasted no time in relaying the information to Edward Harkutlian. The secretary of state was already in a foul mood, still privately seething over Lee Trujillo's wayward decision to break ranks with the rest of the group. What Zarbach had to say only compounded Harkutlian's ire.

"Whatever files Harding copied better not have anything to do with American prisoners of war," Zarbach stated flatly.

An alarmed Ed Harkutlian subconsciously tightened his grip on the phone. "Why do you say that?"

"Because there's more to this Renberg fellow than meets the eye."

"I'm listening."

"Renberg's father is David Zuber."

Harkutlian instinctively swallowed against the dryness in his mouth. "Who the hell is David Zuber?"

"David Zuber," Brent Zarbach went on, "was born in nineteen forty-six. He was drafted in sixty-six, at age twenty. To the best of our knowledge, when he went to Vietnam, he left behind a pregnant fiancée, Mary Renberg. Two months after he started his tour of duty he was captured and taken prisoner by the Viet Cong."

Harkutlian's heart skipped a beat.

"Because of his mechanical expertise," Zarbach continued, "he was allegedly often led out of the camp—under heavy guard—to repair disabled Jeeps. At least he claimed he was. On one such foray in seventy-seven, he supposedly managed to slip a note to a foreign journalist in Hanoi. When the note was forwarded to the U.S. military, it was apparently ignored. In seventy-eight Zuber passed another note to a Norwegian member of the World Bank, who in turn informed the International Red Cross. The following year the American government negotiated his release from Hanoi. That makes Zuber the only American POW to be returned by Vietnam after nineteen seventy-three. When he came home he was thirty-three, and he'd been held for thirteen years."

"Sounds like a happy ending." Harkutlian knew he was being optimistic. Every instinct his body possessed told him there was more.

"Only that's just the beginning," Zarbach said. "When he got back here, Zuber claimed that before being released he had been subjected to electric shocks that were designed to confuse him and scramble his memory. He claimed Hanoi didn't want him exposing the locations of their POW camps, something he insisted on ranting and raving about. His behavior, and his constant insistence that other US POWs were still alive over there, made him an embarrassment to the military brass over *here*. Within a week of his return, the government branded Zuber as a traitor who'd stayed behind in Vietnam of his own accord. He was summarily court-martialed for collaborating with the enemy, demoted from private first-class to private, and given a dishonorable discharge."

Harkutlian was stunned. For the second time that evening, he was completely lost for words.

"But that's not the end of it," Zarbach added. "Right after his court-martial, David Zuber and Mary Renberg got married. Less than a year later, Zuber put the barrel of a gun in his mouth and pulled the trigger."

But for Harkutlian's raspy breathing, the line went quiet. Zarbach let the silence hang.

"So Brad would have been fourteen at the time," Harkutlian finally noted.

"Yes," Zarbach replied. "This confirms what I suspected earlier. What we have here is not just Joe hacker pulling a prank. Renberg has an axe to grind with the government. The first time he was caught busting into Pentagon computers he was using the handle *Zuberman*. This guy has a motive behind his actions. And, more than likely, a specific intent. Revenge can be one hell of a driver."

Harkutlian had never felt so vulnerable. Several times over the past thirty-six hours he'd consoled himself with the thought that things couldn't get much worse. And every time he'd thought that, he'd been proven woefully wrong.

"What's the word from Austin?" he asked, trying to mask his trepidation. "Still no sign of him?"

"I'll call for an update and let you know. Last I heard he was still on the run. Until I hear otherwise, it's safe to assume that's still the case."

"Thanks, Brent. I'll be waiting to hear from you."

When he put down the receiver, Harkutlian didn't wait to hear from anyone. He immediately called the President and shared with him the FBI's latest findings. He asserted to the President that there was an urgent need for the two of them to meet immediately with Roone Hackelman and Bob Carlson, to ensure that they all agreed upon a common strategy.

The President unhesitatingly concurred. He asked Harkutlian to hold while he called the other two and summoned them to the White House. Then he got back on the line with his secretary of state and confirmed that they were on their way.

*   *   *

The reality of Renberg's physical condition caught up with him just in time. He had put over half a mile between himself and the river when the combined strain on his legs and lungs forced the issue and slowed him to a walk. He came upon the fence just moments later. It was a multi-strand barbed-wire fence, the sort used all over Texas to demarcate boundaries of the ranches that dotted the countryside. With the rapidly fading daylight, he might have failed to notice it on the run. He shuddered to think what the consequences could have been. Running into the thorn bush would have seemed like a cakewalk in comparison to the wire's shredding potential. Relieved as he was that his lack of fitness had probably averted a disaster, he was just as buoyed by what the fence implied.

A ranch meant a ranch house, ranch equipment, ranch hands, and, in all likelihood, means of transport of one sort or another. He grabbed one of the wooden posts and, using the wire strands for footholds, climbed up and over the fence to the other side.

He guessed the average size of a ranch in Texas to be 1,500 to 2,000 acres. An acre was just over 43,000 square feet, which, divided by nine, came to just under 5,000 square yards. With 1,760 yards to a mile, a square mile was approximately seventeen squared, with four zeros on the end. Seventeen squared was 289, so a square mile was about 2,900,000, say 3,000,000 square yards. Dividing that by 5,000 gave 600. So there were about 600 acres per square mile, or three square miles to the average ranch. Basic electricity classes had taught him not only the importance of the square root of three, but also its numerical value, 1.732. That meant that each side of a roughly square average-size ranch was between one-and-a-half and two miles long. It was not unreasonable to assume the ranch house would be somewhere close to the center of the property. That meant it probably wouldn't be more than a mile away. If his numbers were close, rather than having to walk for two hours to get to County Road 12, it was possible he could hit a ranch house in closer to fifteen minutes.

He knew his math was good. And he discovered how good his judgment was at the crest of the next hill. Off in the distance to his left—north, since the sunset was behind him—he made out a small cluster of buildings, not but a third or maybe half a mile away. There was no more need to run. A brisk walk would get him there in minutes. And far from being a hindrance, the descending cover of darkness would actually help him get close undetected.

He was surprised once and startled once in quick succession as he picked his way through the trees. The surprise came when he suddenly happened upon a stretch of blacktop. It seemed like the road came out of nowhere, ran straight as an arrow, and went nowhere. It didn't go in the direction of the buildings, yet there didn't seem any reason for it not to. There was no apparent natural obstacle, like a lake, that it would have had to be routed around. Renberg crossed it and pushed on towards the ranch house. He didn't understand it, and it didn't occur to him that private landing strips were a common feature of Hill Country ranches.

What startled him was something far less glamorous. He had just turned to look back after crossing the blacktop, when a sudden movement not ten feet away scared him near to death. He froze, momentarily paralyzed with fear. It happened again before he realized what it was. He counted six cows in all as the relief gushed through him. In less pressing circumstances, he might have appreciated the lighter side of the encounter. But considering the situation, the last thing on his mind was humor. With his cattle radar now in active mode, he pressed on towards the ranch house.

He got within one hundred yards before he could make out three separate buildings. The main ranch house was the most prominent, a single-story structure with a fenced garden. Off to one side was a large barn with a cattle fence enclosing a pen containing four Hereford cows. Renberg first heard, then saw, a small group of men sitting on a bench in front of a shack behind the barn. When he got closer he heard them speaking Spanish. Ranch hands, he guessed. What interested him most, however, was the three-quarter-ton Chevy pickup parked between the barn and the ranch house. Chances were good the keys would be in the ignition, but there was one drawback. A trailer was hitched to the pickup, a cumbersome-looking contraption that was sure to make a getaway attempt slower and noisier than it had to be. Lights were on in the ranch house and the shack, but it was now quite dark where Renberg stood, and his presence had as yet gone undetected. He crept towards the barn, following a circuitous route that shielded him from the view of the men outside the shack. He slipped through the cattle fence, past the cows, which remained surprisingly unperturbed by his presence, and into the welcome shelter of the barn.

It was even darker inside the barn than outside. Renberg stood motionless by the gate to the cattle pen, waiting for his eyes to adjust. Even when they did, he still could barely see anything. There was a strong aroma of hay and cottonseed cake. He fumbled along the wall, feeling his way towards the main door. As he got close he stumbled against a large rubber wheel and felt the rear end of a tractor. A means of transportation if all else failed, but hardly one to get excited about. He'd never driven a tractor before, and even if he was to get it to a road, it would be far too conspicuous. His best bet was going to be the truck. If he could unhitch the trailer, and if the key was in the ignition—the bigger of the two "ifs"—then he might be out of there in the time it took anyone to react. The truck was in full view of the ranch hands outside the shack, some twenty yards from the barn door. But the absence of exterior lights on the barn meant the cover of darkness again played to his advantage. He pushed the barn door the few inches it took to enable him to squeeze through. Then, keeping his head down, he sprinted across to the trailer. There was no change in the voices from the shack, but he held still and waited a few seconds. It was a sixteen-foot stock trailer with solid front and sides, and a steel gate at the back. Unfortunately, it was much heavier-looking up close than from a distance. He felt around the hitch and found the receiver. It felt very solid, and he doubted he could disengage it. But it wasn't yet his biggest concern, and he let it be. He crept along the side of the truck to the passenger cab. The windows were up, and the interior was too dark for him to see the ignition. The cab light would come on if he opened the door, and again, one of the ranch hands might notice. His options were few, so he risked it. The truck wasn't locked, and the light did come on, but there was no key in the ignition. He lifted the handle and pushed the door back to where it latched halfway, enough to kill the light. Just as he was contemplating pushing on towards 12 on foot, the front door of the ranch house swung open and the burly figure of a man with a cowboy hat in his hand stepped out onto the porch. Renberg slipped back to the end of the trailer and scurried back to the barn. The man put his hat on, adjusted it with a little tug, and strode purposefully towards him.

Renberg squeezed in through the door and shrunk back against the wall. The barn door was pushed wide open, and with the flick of a switch the barn was flooded with light. Renberg held his breath and cowered behind the door. The man walked a few paces past the tractor and grunted as he heaved something up. Then he walked back outside. He left the light on and the door wide open. Renberg heard two soft thuds, then he heard the truck door open and shut. Seconds later there was the sound of the ignition turning and the engine cranked to life. Renberg crept around the door and peered outside. The man—the ranch foreman, Renberg guessed—pulled the truck forward a few feet, then reversed it towards the end of a ramp at the corner of the barn. He corrected his line once, then backed the trailer up all the way to the edge of the ramp. As he turned the ignition off, one of the ranch hands walked over. The foreman got out of the truck and swung open the gate at the back of the trailer. He was joined by the ranch hand, who asked in heavily accented English if he needed help. The foreman replied that the cows were to be auctioned in the morning, but he was transporting them tonight. The two men climbed through the wooden fence into the cattle pen. Renberg crept back along the wall to the door that led from the barn to the pen. He watched as they herded the four cows through the loading chute, up the ramp, and on to the trailer. The gate was swung shut with a clang. The foreman asked the ranch hand to turn off the light in the barn, and climbed back into the cab. Renberg slipped out into the cattle pen as darkness returned to the barn. The truck's engine roared to life again and Renberg watched as its brake lights glowed. He never would remember consciously making the decision. As he heard the clunk of the truck's forward gear engaging, he dashed through the darkness up the loading ramp. The truck had barely started pulling away when he leaped off the edge of the ramp, over the gate and into the back of the trailer. His foot caught the top of the gate and he landed hard on the baseboard, his tumble softened only by the numbing rush of adrenaline.

The engine strained against the weight of the trailer as the truck picked up speed, its driver unaware that his passengers now numbered five.

*　　　　　*　　　　　*

Secret Service Special Agent Noel Markovski was in a quandary. He'd heard the report of the jet ski crash, and he was aware that Wakeman and Vogel had changed direction. He knew they were on their way to hook up with the DPS chopper. But Wakeman had specifically instructed him to press on with one of the sheriff's deputies to Farm Road 150, and from there to the point where the road met the river three miles west of Mountain City. Wakeman's logic was they would be downstream of the crash site, in position to intercept Renberg if the crash turned out to be just a ruse to divert everyone's attention. But what riled Markovski was the fact that boats were already heading up the river from San Marcos. Markovski could see no point in him being somewhere on the river bank—a "just in case" position—as long as there were boats on the water. He wanted to be where the action was, and he couldn't help but wonder if Wakeman wasn't purposely trying to distance a member of a rival agency from the focal point of the hunt. Wakeman was acting like the FBI was the lead agency here, that all others were subservient to his command. That might sit fine with the local and state agencies, but the brass at the Secret Service would surely scoff at the notion.

The more Markovski thought about it, the easier the decision became. He didn't even bother to communicate his intentions to the dispatcher in San Marcos, or to the deputy up ahead. At a break in the oncoming traffic, he slowed down, made a three-point turn in the middle of the road, and raced towards San Marcos to get back where his own superiors would want him, smack in the thick of things.

*   *   *

Brad Renberg's introduction to the delicate charms of bovine etiquette was as sobering as it was sudden. Of the four cows in the entourage, three faced the front of the trailer, while the fourth restlessly started its journey in reverse. As Renberg crawled towards the cover of two bales of hay up front, it was that last heifer which assumed the responsibility of welcoming him aboard. The emission was short—a semi-liquid burst of no more than three seconds in all—but the aim could not have been truer. It was a darkish-brown, sludgy excretion that splattered in flight and covered a space the size of a dartboard by the time it landed. Renberg's saving grace was his posture—face down and on all fours as he crawled to the front of the trailer. He was hit on the back of his head and neck. In the few disorienting seconds it took for the initial shock to subside, the odor manifested beyond any doubt the nature of the strike. He retched and sprang away in convulsive disgust as he realized what had happened. When another cow took her cue and followed suit, dumping her issue towards the back of the trailer, Renberg was mercifully already clambering over the hay at the front, well out of range of her trajectory. He wiped his hand down the back of his neck and immediately regretted doing so. As the trailer bumped along down the caliche gravel road, he resorted to holding his nose and breathing through his mouth while rubbing himself against the hay. He was still doing so when the pickup suddenly slowed and pulled to the right. Renberg figured that by standing, he might just about manage to see over the walls of the trailer, but he would then risk being seen. He tensed, played it safe, and stayed low. The gradual illumination of the track behind the trailer made clear the reason for the slowdown. Another vehicle was approaching in the opposite direction. As the pickup slowed to a stop, Renberg hastily arranged the bales of hay end-to-end, so he could hide between them and the solid front of the trailer. The cows shifted restlessly as a car pulled to a stop alongside the truck.

"We're looking for a suspect last seen trying to make a getaway on the river in these parts," a voice said. "Have you seen anyone who doesn't belong?"

"I sure haven't," the foreman replied. "What kind of suspect?"

"We need to use the property to get to the river."

"No problem." The Mexican ranch hands were all legal.

The engine revved and the vehicle moved on by. When it passed, Renberg peered over the hay. Its rear was illuminated by another set of headlights, and he saw it was a County Sheriff's patrol car. The second car drove by, then it suddenly stopped and reversed back towards the truck. Renberg pulled his head back down behind the hay.

"Special Agent Wakeman, FBI," the driver said. "What's in the trailer?"

"Cows."

"Do you mind if I take a look?"

"Hell, no," the foreman replied.

Renberg heard first one, then a second car door open. He held his breath, curled up as snug as he could get against the front of the trailer, and pulled tight on the bales of hay.

CHAPTER NINETEEN

When Secretary of State Ed Harkutlian was ushered into the Oval office, he was confronted with a palpable air of doom and gloom. His counterpart from Defense, Roone Hackelman, had arrived moments earlier with his deputy, Robert Carlson, and the President was briefing them on the FBI's latest findings. Stan Daulton stopped in mid-sentence long enough for the door to close behind Harkutlian.

"I was just telling Roone and Bob what we've learned about Renberg," the President said. "I got as far as the court-martial. You're the one who heard it from Brent, so why don't you take over from there."

"There's not much left," Harkutlian said, his tone devoid of compassion. He backed his frame down on a sofa across from where Hackelman and Carlson sat. "First they slapped Zuber with a dishonorable discharge. Then he married Mary Renberg. Then he committed suicide."

Silence permeated the room. Roone Hackelman had been on the edge of the sofa, leaning forward towards the President's desk, resting his elbows on his knees as he listened. He unclasped his hands and slid back all the way. Stan Daulton came around the desk and sat next to Harkutlian, whose gaze was fixed on Carlson. The deputy secretary of defense averted his eyes.

"That changes everything," Carlson rued. "This makes it a whole different ball game."

"There would never have been a ball if it wasn't for your memo," Harkutlian quipped.

"Let's not be pointing fingers," Hackelman said, pre-empting Carlson's response. "For the record, I'm saying right here that at the time, Bob's memo was appropriate and in line with established communication protocols."

"Roone got the only hard copy," Carlson added, bolstered by Hackelman's support. "And I swear on the life of my children, I deleted that file from the computer. I didn't ask Ellen to do it, I did it myself."

"You *thought* you deleted it," Harkutlian noted curtly.

"I *know* I deleted it!" Carlson replied, his voice rising in anger. "I wiped it off the hard disk and then I checked the directory and it was gone."

"Not gone enough," Harkutlian retorted.

"Alright, alright," Stan Daulton said. "Recriminations will get us nowhere. We need to decide how to manage this thing. And it starts with us all sticking together."

"The damage is already done," Carlson brooded. "Lee's dead, and–"

"Lee was stupid," Harkutlian hissed. "I, for one, have no sympathy for him. What he did was *his* choice, and it was a selfish, stupid thing to do."

Carlson's eyes widened at the remark. His face turned crimson and he got up off the couch. "I'm not going to sit here and let you talk–"

"That's *enough!*" Daulton jumped up and wedged himself between Carlson and Harkutlian, who was rising to meet Carlson's challenge.

"Hey!" Hackelman yelled, now also on his feet. "Settle down, guys!"

They all became aware of two Secret Service men that suddenly materialized next to the President. "It's okay," Daulton said, nodding to reassure them. "It's okay. I'll take care of this." They retreated a step as Hackelman pulled Carlson back to the couch. Stan Daulton gestured with his head to Harkutlian, who, still glowering, also took a step back. Daulton nodded again to the agents. They took a moment to satisfy themselves that the situation posed no threat to the President, then made themselves scarce. Daulton waited until they closed the door behind them before turning back to Harkutlian and Carlson.

"What the hell has gotten into you guys?" he said incredulously.

Both where bristling and neither said a word.

"Calm down, Bob," Hackelman ordered. He turned to Harkutlian. "We're going to cut the bickering and deal with the situation, okay?"

"Yeah, sure," Harkutlian replied, his face as flushed as Carlson's. "As long as tempers stay under control, there'll be no problem."

Carlson nodded sullenly. "Lee was a good man and a good friend."

Harkutlian remained impassive until he realized that all eyes were on him. "Sure," he murmured.

"I think an apology is in order for the way you spoke of Lee," Daulton pressed.

"We all need to speak our minds," Harkutlian replied.

"And show respect for the dead," Daulton insisted.

"Fine." He pursed his lips. "I apologize."

"Good," Daulton said. "Maybe now we can focus on what we're going to do about Renberg."

"There's only one way we're going to deal with the situation," Harkutlian asserted. "We have to deny it."

Carlson looked across at Daulton. "I think we should at least *consider* explaining it," he said. "After all, we acted in good faith. The primary rationale was saving lives."

Hackelman was quick to respond. "Well, the problem is not the decision itself. Yes, it might be unpopular, but it's probably defensible. The problem is it makes liars out of us all. Either for representing to the nation that we've never had any knowledge that American servicemen are still alive out there, or," he looked pointedly at Harkutlian, "just as bad, for failing to come forward when we've had evidence to the contrary."

"Nobody here ever saw any evidence," Harkutlian retorted.

"Evidence was offered," Hackelman snapped back. "We declined to consider it. The memorandum establishes that."

"Which is exactly why our only recourse is denial," Harkutlian insisted. "Look, the FBI has blocked Renberg's access to his e-mail. The word is he hasn't read the darn thing. But even if he has, what proof does he have that it's real? We're talking about a document that contains no signatures. Anyone can type something like that and put it on a computer. Renberg's family background works against him here. The guy has a huge chip on his shoulder. He'd love to make the U.S. government look bad. But he lacks a shred of evidence to support his claims. It'll be just like the TWA missile theory. Yeah, it's possible. But all it boils down to is some jerk sticking something on the Internet and saying there it is. In the face of denial, you either have proof or you're spewing hot air."

"I agree with Ed," Stan Daulton said. "Defending this is going to be impossible. Like you said, Roone, at the very least the three of you have been lying to the nation. And even if we paint it like I didn't know about it, I *still* look bad. I can just hear the Republicans: If three—four, counting Lee—members of his administration are up to something like this without him knowing, Jesus, what else is going on that he's unaware of? Who the hell's in charge over there?"

The office went quiet. Carlson was thinking one lie leads to another, but the others were right. There was no proof.

The silence was broken by one of the President's phones. He strode to his desk and picked it up. "Put him on," he said. He looked back at Harkutlian. "It's Brent, for you."

Harkutlian got up and took the receiver. The other three watched with anticipation as he listened to what the FBI director had to say. He told them even as he put the receiver down.

"They found him again, and again he got away. This time he used a jet ski on a river. A few minutes later the jet ski crashed and exploded. There's a chopper, boats, and a ton of men out there, but so far, there's no sign of a body."

*   *   *

When Mitch Wakeman and Steve Vogel stepped out of the car, the sheriff reversed his own vehicle back towards them to see what the delay was. He pulled up just as they came around the back of the trailer. The ranch foreman got out of his truck. Wakeman's flashlight illuminated the four cows, now shifting towards the front of the trailer and beginning to show signs of distress.

The sheriff got out of his car. "What's the deal?"

"Just checking," Wakeman replied. "It looks alright. Just cows and hay."

"And cow shit," Vogel noted dryly.

As if to confirm the observation, one of the two cows yet to empty her bowels on board obliged her audience with a fresh load.

"Let's go!" Vogel groaned.

The sheriff turned his back on them.

Wakeman panned his flashlight around the trailer one more time. The odor wafted towards him and he stepped back in disgust. He turned the flashlight off and followed Vogel back to the car. The foreman chuckled to himself and climbed back into the truck. Four doors slammed, engines revved, and the gathering broke up.

Renberg waited longer than he felt he had to before emerging from behind the hay. "Cow shit, alright," he mumbled to himself, suddenly finding new respect for the commodity. "Way to go, girls."

A few minutes later the pickup rumbled over the pipes of a cattle guard and through an arched gateway. The gravel gave way to blacktop and the transition smoothed out the ride. Renberg figured it wouldn't be long before they hit 12. He wondered whether they would turn left, towards San Marcos, or right, further into the Hill Country. He had the answer a couple of miles later, when the truck turned right. There was a fair bit of traffic on 12, which only added to Renberg's anxiety. With the load of the trailer behind it, the truck was slow, especially when climbing the hills. Renberg found himself hiding behind the hay again as one car after another pulled to within yards of the back of the trailer. While they waited for a break in the oncoming traffic, the cars washed the trailer with the glare of their headlights. All it would take to expose him was for one of the cows to move one of the bales. It was a precarious situation, but apart from hanging onto the bales like they were made of gold, there was not much Renberg could do.

Things improved a few miles down the road, at the Wimberley junction. The foreman slowed down and signaled left, then drove across the oncoming traffic lane and pulled up at the gas pumps outside *Jak's* convenience store. Renberg was familiar with *Jak's*. A no-alcohol-sales ordinance had been in effect in Wimberley since way before Pendergraft moved there, and *Jak's* was where Pendergraft and his visitors bought their beer.

The foreman got out of the truck and pumped gas. When Renberg heard him replace the nozzle in the pump, he was ready to make his move. He gave the foreman time to walk to the store, then he stood up and surveyed the scene. There were two cars parked in front of *Jak's*, but the truck was the only vehicle at the pumps. To the left of *Jak's* there was a small, abandoned shack that had once been the original store before the larger replacement was built. A restaurant, *Crowley's*, sat to the left of the shack. Renberg noted the payphone on the wall on the far side of *Jak's*, facing away from the shack and *Crowley's*. The set up was adequate for his needs. He needed to get out of the trailer, and the shack seemed a good place to hide out while he bought some time.

He was about to go for it when another car pulled up to the front of the store. The foreman reappeared and started walking back to the truck. Renberg crouched back down in the trailer. When the foreman climbed into the cab and gunned the engine, Renberg seized his chance. He jumped out of the trailer and walked off in the direction of *Crowley's*. The truck pulled away from the pumps. Renberg kept his head down and kept walking. The truck accelerated onto the road, and Renberg veered to his right, away from *Crowley's*, towards the shack.

He was out in the open and completely exposed. The area was illuminated by lights mounted on the store, on the restaurant, and under the canopy over the gas pumps. Renberg heard voices and was aware of two people coming out of the store. They got into a car and started the engine. He kept walking, around the side of the shack to the back of the buildings. Here there were no fixtures, only the welcome relief of darkness. He looked out at the road in time to see the truck and trailer turn right at the junction and descend on 12 towards Wimberley.

The shack was boarded up on all sides, and it was clear that pulling a board off with his bare hands was going to be impossible. Short of having a crowbar to work with, there was no way he was going to get inside. But he was still better off in the shadows than in the trailer or on the ranch. Here he was miles from the river. Not entirely out of the proverbial woods, but well away from where they were looking for him.

He sat down and leaned back against the shack. The strain of being on the run was taking its toll, and he willed himself to keep things in perspective. He was running from the law in his own country. If they caught him, he was still guaranteed due process. He couldn't imagine how it must feel to be in a jungle, surrounded by an enemy, and staring at untold years in a POW camp.

His thoughts were interrupted when a back door at *Crowley's* suddenly swung open. In the light that spilled out, Renberg saw the apron-clad figure of a busboy emerge. He pulled a dolly-mounted waste container out behind him and wheeled it to a garbage dumpster set some twenty yards back from the restaurant. Renberg sat motionless as the busboy lifted a hinged plastic cover up and let it fall back against the top of the dumpster. He removed two white trash bags from the container and heaved them over the side. Then he flipped the dumpster's cover shut and went back inside *Crowley's*.

Renberg stared at the dumpster. He got up and crept towards it. He had spent time in dumpsters before. On a few, unforgettable occasions, he, Pendergraft and other members of Triple D had resorted to what hackers unaffectionately call dumpster diving. It had mainly been outside various engineering offices of Southwestern Bell Telephone Company, and they had gleaned mountains of information from discarded network and systems design manuals. Information that had enabled them to manipulate computerized telephone company switches with ease and, initially at least, impunity. Granted, they had been relatively clean dumpsters, typically filled with discarded documents and paper, not soiled napkins and greasy food waste. Still, a dumpster was a great place to hide. Besides, he was already half-covered with cow manure. How was a little ketchup going to hurt? He pushed the cover up, climbed over the side, and gently eased himself down onto the trash.

*   *   *

The gravel road snaked through the *Round Rock Ranch* for just over a mile past the ranch house, until it dead-ended at the river. They were a good six hundred yards from the crash site, but Wakeman, Vogel and the sheriff could hear the chopper and see the beam of its searchlight as it hovered over the cliffs. They made sure that both cars were locked, and with two flashlights between the three of them, they picked their way along the riverbank on foot. As they arrived across the water from the cliffs, they were joined by two of the boats that had sped up the Blanco from San Marcos. A third was already there, its spotlight combing the trees and shrubbery on both banks for any sign of Renberg. On their way there, all three boats had recovered bits and pieces of debris that they'd found floating down the river. But there had been no sign whatsoever of Renberg. No limp body in the water, no item of clothing, nothing. There was not even a hint of blood on what was clearly the point of impact against the cliffs. Wakeman ordered one boat to stay at the scene, and the other two to cruise in opposite directions and check both the river's surface and its banks.

"What would you do if you'd just taken the jet ski and you knew the game wardens had heard you?" he asked the sheriff.

Vogel was quick to reply first. "I'd get the hell off the water, is what I'd do. After creating a diversion."

The sheriff nodded.

Wakeman was already flashing his light around the trees behind them. "Let's get all the men we can over here," he hollered. "And I need that chopper's night vision in wide arcs on both sides. Unless he's found in the water, he's out there somewhere."

The sheriff echoed Wakeman's words to the men on the boat, who instantly broadcast his instructions over their radio.

*   *   *

The stench was patently unbearable. On the trailer, even with the wind swirling around him, the smell of the cow dung had been bad enough. But now, in the cramped and confined space of the dumpster, embellished as it was with the foul odors of kitchen waste, it was more than Renberg could stand. He peered over the side, then jumped out and slipped furtively back to the shadows behind the shack. He didn't feel quite as safe here as in the dumpster, but it was a necessary compromise. If a few minutes in the dumpster had proven to be unbearable, a few hours was definitely out of the question.

It was as he was hoping it wouldn't take more than a few hours that the first doubts began to surface. His thoughts went back to the FBI at Pendergraft's house, and how they could have possibly known he was there. It was either Sadie, or it had to be Pendergraft. Neither made much sense, but it *had* to be one or the other. Nobody followed him there from Austin, he was sure of that. And he didn't make any calls from the house, so there was no possibility of a phone trace. He'd met Sadie at Dripping Springs and Driftwood, and no one had followed him back from there. There *was* the outside chance she'd planted a bug on the bike, he had to acknowledge that. If so, she had knowingly done it for the FBI, but if that were the case, would she have given him the right key from Richard? He was at a loss trying to explain it. Unless it hadn't been Sadie at all...but Pendergraft.

The notion mesmerized him. On the surface, it was unthinkable. But it was, even if remotely, possible. He had to acknowledge that. There was a chance, an outside chance, perhaps, but a chance nonetheless, that it was Pendergraft who had betrayed him. He didn't want to believe it. How could it be? They were like blood brothers. Comrades in arms. It was the stress of being on the run that was getting to him, putting crazy ideas in his head. It had to have been Sadie. Richard had squeaked. He'd told them where he'd gotten the dialups. Sadie went to see Richard, and they'd cut a deal with her. Plant a bug on Renberg, then get the hell out of the way. That *had* to be it.

But what if it wasn't? What if it had been Pendergraft? Here he was, depending on Pendergraft to set them up for him. If he couldn't trust Pendergraft, who could he trust? And in truth, given the situation, was it right to trust anyone other than himself?

The more he thought about it, the more the doubts nagged, and the clearer it became. The answer was no. He shouldn't—he *couldn't*—trust anyone else. Not with this. Not now. He had to do it himself. That was the only way he could be sure. And he'd been a fool to think otherwise.

So it was back to square one. He needed to get to a computer. He had to get back to Austin and sneak into Taylor Hall. They wouldn't look for him there because they wouldn't think he'd dare go back. But he had to do it. It was the only way.

His concentration was broken by the crackle of a wireless radio. A mobile unit, the kind in service vehicles and police cars. He ventured a peek around the side of the shack. A state trooper had just pulled up in front of *Jak's*. His window was down and the radio was chattering away. Renberg heard the cop say something into his microphone. Then he got out of the car. Renberg was thinking trash dumpster again, when the cop stepped inside *Jak's*. For one insane moment, Renberg considered hijacking the car. Then he came to his senses. He couldn't hijack a police car, or any car out there. It would be missed before he got a mile down 12. They'd have a welcome party set up for him before he reached San

Marcos, let alone Austin. He slipped away from the shack, back to the shelter of the tree line behind the buildings. A couple of minutes later the patrol car drove off. Renberg crept along the tree line behind *Jak's*, sticking to where the shadows were darkest. He emerged at the far side of the store and, resisting the urge to run, made his way as casually as he could to the payphone.

He was now out of the shadows and in full view of the cars on the road. The best he could do was turn his back and hope no one paid him any attention. He still was averse to involving Kelly, but there was no other way. They had agreed she'd leave a number in his voice mailbox. He hoped desperately that she'd done so. Using the calling card numbers he had long ago committed to memory, he dialed into his voice mail and listened anxiously as a recorded voice told him he had one message. He played it back and felt a flush of relief. He memorized the number, then hung up and immediately dialed it. Kelly answered after the first ring.

"Hello?"

No voice had ever sounded more comforting. "Kelly, it's me."

"Oh!" she shrieked. "Thank God! Are you okay?"

"I'm fine."

"I've been sick with worry!"

"No, I'm fine, really."

"Where are you?"

"I'll get to that. Where are you?"

"I'm with a friend. It's okay. She's cool."

"Does she have a car?"

"Yes."

"Can you use it?"

"Yes. Why?"

"I need you to come and get me."

"I...God...of course! Where are you?"

"Make sure you don't use *your* car. I don't want anyone to follow you."

"Okay! Tell me where you are."

"Go down 35 to San Marcos. It's about twenty, twenty-five minutes. Get off at San Marcos and follow the signs to Wimberley. That'll take you through San Marcos and out on the other side on 12. Make sure you get on 12. If there's any doubt, ask for directions."

"Wait…I'm writing this down."

"About seven or eight miles down 12 you'll come to a junction with a sign indicating a right turn for Wimberley. Right there at the junction, just before the turn, there's a convenience store on the left. It's called *Jak's at the Junction*. There are a couple of gas pumps outside, and a restaurant next to it called *Crowley's*. You got that?"

"J-A-C-K-S?"

"No C. J-A-K-S."

"Got it."

"Right there between *Jak's* and *Crowley's* there's an abandoned little shack, all boarded up. I'll be waiting behind the shack. Come around to the back. If there are any cops out front, wait until they go away. Go into *Jak's* or something. Just wait until it's clear."

"I'm leaving now."

"Be real careful. When you're on 12, if there are headlights behind you, let them pass."

"I understand."

"Thanks, Babe."

"For God's sake, just sit tight. I'm on my way."

The line went dead. He hung the receiver back on the hook and slipped back behind the building. He hated getting her involved, but there really was no other way.

*   *   *

Mitch Wakeman's physical fitness served him well as he ran back to his car. He grabbed his phone off the front seat and placed two calls.

The first was to the Austin Police Department, and he requested that a team of divers be ready to start searching the riverbed at the break of dawn. The second was to the Texas Department of Corrections in Gatesville. His request that their tracker dogs be immediately dispatched to San Marcos was met with an apology. The dogs were currently in a van, en route from Huntsville to Gatesville. They had just left, and could be diverted to head directly to San Marcos, but it would be two to three hours before they got there. He asked that they be sent anyway, and hung up wondering whether it wasn't an exercise in futility. In two or three hours it was doubtful there would be a trace of a scent left for them to track.

The lights of several more vehicles were bobbing and bouncing as they approached along the gravel road. Wakeman watched as the first two skidded to a stop behind his. Two more, still a few hundred yards away, were now driving through the dust kicked up by those that had gone before them. When Secret Service Special Agent Markovski pulled up to the gathering in his Jeep, the crowd of lawmen around Wakeman numbered seven.

Markovski was relieved to see Wakeman. In his rearview mirror it was beginning to look like every law enforcement officer in the state was descending on the *Round Rock Ranch*. Even if the arrest was ultimately made by an officer of another agency, Markovski was intent on making sure the Secret Service showed a presence when it happened.

"I need a couple of units posted at the ranch entrance to keep the media at bay," he heard Wakeman say.

Not me, Markovski thought. Local boys can handle that. Wakeman had started issuing orders on how the newcomers would join the search when Markovski's phone chirped. He barely heard it over the din of the chopper circling overhead, the beam of its searchlight boring through the darkness like a giant laser. Markovski stepped back from the group and snapped the phone up off his belt. His eyes never strayed from Wakeman as he brought the phone to his ear. He held his head low and covered his other ear to block out the ambient noise. He listened for a few moments, then turned his back on the group and repeated the words *"Jak's…Crowley's."* Scant attention was paid him when he climbed back into his Jeep, maneuvered a quick three-point turn, and headed back up the dirt road towards the ranch house.

In the dark sky above, the chopper was sweeping around in ever-widening arcs. Its night vision system and infrared radar picked up an assortment of deer, cattle and lawmen, but smelled not a whiff of the wanted fugitive.

*   *   *

It all happened very suddenly, a few minutes later. It had just occurred to Renberg that he'd forgotten to ask Kelly what kind of car she'd be driving. But it was over ten minutes since he'd spoken to her, and too late to call back. By now, she was surely well on her way down I-35.

He was sitting on the ground, leaning his back against the shack, his exhaustion compounded by anxiety. He couldn't see the *Crowley's* front door, so he wasn't aware of the man who pulled into the parking lot and walked into the restaurant. Renberg had no idea of the words the man had with the manager, or the subsequent discussion the two of them had with the chef and the busboy. And when the man walked out of the restaurant and crossed past the front of the shack to *Jak's*, Renberg's mind was on how he was going to get back into Taylor Hall.

He jumped when the busboy suddenly flung open the back door and fell through it, landing in a heap on the ground. He was startled to see the chef come out after him, holding his clenched fists up as the two shouted insults at each other. Renberg stared at the untimely commotion and pulled himself to his feet. His attention was squarely on the brewing fight, and he never sensed the movement behind him. All he felt was the cold barrel of a gun that was jammed against the back of his neck.

"Freeze! Secret Service! Get your hands up!"

He started bringing his hands up in bewilderment. Before he knew it his feet were kicked out from under him and he was on the ground, face down, his arms being wrenched behind his back. He was still disoriented with shock when handcuffs were slapped on. A skilled pair of hands patted up and down his body, between his legs and over his ankles. Then he was jerked back to his feet. The chef helped the busboy up, and it was their turn to gawk.

Noel Markovski swung Renberg around and hit his face with the beam of his flashlight. He found a dazed expression, no hair, and no goatee. But there was no doubt it was Renberg. Markovski pushed him around to the front of the restaurant and shoved him into the Cherokee's cargo bay, a compartment separated from the passenger seats by a thick wire mesh barrier. Renberg was aware of the tailgate being slammed shut. The chef and the busboy came around the corner of the building to watch what was happening. Markovski climbed into the driver's seat and started the engine. He recited Renberg's Miranda rights, then smacked the gear lever and pulled away.

As they sped off down 12 in the direction of San Marcos, Markovski confirmed the triumph to the Secret Service office in Austin. He reported to Special-Agent-In-Charge Manny Schweitzer that Brad Renberg was in his custody, and that he was now bringing him in.

CHAPTER TWENTY

Brad Renberg was not the only one floored by the sheer suddenness of the arrest. The news also took Lawrence Luenberger by surprise, although his reaction was on the opposite end of the emotional spectrum to Renberg's. The head of the Electronic Crimes Branch of the Secret Service's Financial Crimes Division listened to Manny Schweitzer's account of the details with mounting glee, then issued some simple instructions.

"Not a word to anyone until we're absolutely sure it's him," Luenberger warned. "Get him into the office, and make sure no one other you and your men see him. Let the FBI chase a dead end for a while. Markovski's visual ID is fine, but I want a fingerprint match before we break the news."

"Understood," Schweitzer replied. "We should have it within the hour."

*   *   *

Renberg's mind was a medley of panic and confusion.

How could it have happened?

It had to be the call to Kelly. They knew she had warned him the day before, when they were waiting at his apartment. The bastards had guessed he might contact her. They'd figured that by leaving her be, she might unwittingly lead them to him. That had to be why they never arrested her. They had followed her to her friend's place and tapped the phone line. They would have had time. And now they'd be waiting for her at the junction.

He cursed himself a million times. He should never have called her. All it had taken was one moment of weakness, one instance of terrible judgment.

"What the hell did you do?" Markovski suddenly blurted out. "Swim through a pile of cattle shit?" All four windows came down.

Renberg closed his eyes. A tortuous stream of images flashed through his mind. There was the thirteen-year-old boy, thrilled to be meeting his father, his unseen idol, for the first time.

The hearings…the court-martial…

The broken hero. His father was sitting on the ground, leaning back against the wall, his hands holding the shotgun to his mouth as his toes pushed a pencil against the trigger.

That was the day his mother died too. He'd always said the bastards had killed them both.

The car phone rang, jerking him back to the present. Markovski answered and conversed in the hands-free mode.

"Where are you?" Renberg heard Manny Schweitzer ask over the speaker.

"I'll be on 35 in about six minutes," Markovski replied.

"Have you told San Marcos or the FBI that you have him?"

"Not yet."

"Good. Don't. Luenberger wants to wait for fingerprints, so keep it quiet."

"Got it."

Markovski's wireless radio started crackling as he hung up the phone. It was the dispatcher in San Marcos, and her broadcast was directed at the field units of all agencies involved in the search. She announced that word had just come from the Hospital. Four hours into the operation to save his life, Agent Juan Camacho had just succumbed to his injury.

"Man, you're in a shit pile worth of trouble," Markovski said, turning his head to the side as he addressed Renberg. "On top of all the other stuff, now you've got the death of an FBI agent to answer for."

"I didn't kill anyone," Renberg replied, shaken by the charge.

"Come on, man, I was there. You set your dog loose on him. You're going to get nailed for that."

Renberg was stunned. For all his scheming and conniving, this was not a variable he'd factored into the equation. This was murder. Manslaughter at best. And an FBI agent to boot. Shit pile was the truth. Only now it had suddenly gotten deeper.

He thought desperately about what he could do. The fact was, he didn't know for sure if it was Sadie Harding or Chris Pendergraft that had betrayed him. If it was Pendergraft, then it was all over. But what if it *was* Sadie? What if he'd been wrong suspecting Chris? Then the only difference between now and a few minutes ago was that now they had him in the back of a Jeep. He ran through who knew what—what he knew, what he knew they knew, and what he hoped they didn't. His only option was to bluff. There was just one, tiny opening, and it was his only chance. He had one more move to make, or the game really was all over. First he needed to stall, for time was still the key.

"Get word to the President," he said to an astonished Noel Markovski. "Tell him I know about Strams and Pickard."

"What the hell are you talking about?" Markovski replied, glancing at Renberg in his rearview mirror.

"Didn't you say you were Secret Service?"

"What does—"

"Do it!" Renberg shouted. "Tell him I know about Strams and Pickard! Tell him to run that by the secretary of state!" He toned it down and took a deep breath, well aware of how desperate he was for

Markovski to comply. "Tell him he can either talk to me tonight, or try to explain to America tomorrow."

*   *   *

The meeting had already broken up when the President received the call. He first heard out the director of the Secret Service, then he overruled him.

"Where is he now?" Daulton asked.

"They're taking him to Austin," was the reply.

"Have him brought here ASAP."

He slid the receiver back on the hook and grappled with a swell of dread. So Renberg had read the memorandum. Hello, worst case scenario. Harkutlian's argument about proof was about to be put to the test. If Renberg's ammunition was the memo, then the White House was in the clear. There was nothing that pointed at anyone other than Trujillo, Hackelman, Harkutlian and Carlson. Renberg had to believe that. According to the agent in Texas, Renberg had asked that the President be told to run it by the secretary of state. The only reason he'd ask that would be so the secretary of state could explain to the President what Strams and Pickard were all about. Renberg wouldn't have asked for that if he thought the White House knew.

Stan Daulton called Ed Harkutlian and Roone Hackelman and told them to scuttle their plans for the evening. There were still some unanswered questions, but it looked like push was coming to shove.

*   *   *

Renberg was sitting up in the back of the Jeep when they reached the airport. Special Agent-In-Charge Manny Schweitzer was waiting, as was Special Agent Randy Dawson. They held open a chain-link gate bearing an *AUTHORIZED PERSONNEL ONLY* sign long enough for Markovski to drive through. He, in turn, stopped long enough for them to climb in. Schweitzer pointed out the chartered jet and Markovski wasted no time.

"We've got you a change of clothes," Schweitzer said, turning towards Renberg. "There's no shower, so you'll have to make do with the regular facilities. Make it easy on yourself and don't cause any trouble."

Markovski and Dawson were assigned to accompany him on the flight. Once the jet reached cruising altitude, they removed the handcuffs and held the restroom door open and watched as he cleaned himself up. He changed into what they gave him—a clean shirt and a pair of jeans that was two sizes too large. When he asked for news of his mother, they assured him she was fine. Then he asked how they'd found him, and they smiled and shook their heads. After that the fatigue overcame him and he surrendered to the deepest sleep.

        *   *   *

They woke him up at a few minutes past two, just before they landed. A dark car with tinted windows was waiting on the tarmac and the three of them were whisked away.

He was dropped off at the south portico, the low-key private entrance used by the President and his family. Two Secret Service men from the White House protection detail removed his handcuffs and escorted him through to the West Wing. He never knew how many metal detectors he passed through, let alone where they were. Before he approached the final door, they had established over and again that he was clean. The handcuffs went back onto his wrists, and suddenly he was there.

The President was at his desk, sitting straight-backed in his chair. Harkutlian stood at the edge of the desk, his hands on his hips. Hackelman and Carlson were on the sofa to the President's right. Renberg stood at the door and met their gazes in turn. Robert Carlson's was the only face he didn't recognize, but he had no doubt who it was.

"Come on in, Brad," Stan Daulton said, gesturing at the sofa to his left. "Sit down."

It was nothing he could ever have practiced for, nothing he had ever foreseen. He glanced behind him as the door was closed, then turned back to face the President. "I prefer to stand."

"Suit yourself," Daulton replied stoically. He glanced across at the other three, then looked back at Renberg. "That's quite a chase you put on. A lot of good men are still out there looking for you."

Renberg chose his words carefully. "A lot of good men have been...still out there...for way too long."

Hackelman shifted his weight on the sofa, while Carlson braced himself for the impending confrontation. Harkutlian was still as a rock, his eyes pasting Renberg with scorn.

The President cleared his throat. "Yes, well, I guess it's up to us to decide what we're going to do about that." He brought his fingers together to form a spire in front of his mouth.

"What did you tell the *Washington Post*?" Harkutlian growled.

It took Renberg a second to realize what that meant. Pendergraft! So it *was* Sadie who'd betrayed him. He could have whooped and hollered, but he had to stay in control of his emotions. "Not enough," he replied, reciprocating Harkutlian's disdain. "Not yet."

"The man from the *Post* mentioned Strams and Pickard." Harkutlian insisted.

Renberg's heart sang. "They don't know what it's about," he asserted, suddenly buoyed by the discovery that the calls had been made. "I didn't give them first names, or the context. But I sure as hell got your attention."

"I wouldn't read too much into that, son," Harkutlian quipped. "If it were up to me, your ass would already be a jailhouse treat."

"It's not up to you," Renberg replied defiantly. "Because my ass isn't the only one on the line here."

"Alright," Daulton interjected, sensing Harkutlian's mounting anger. "So you got our attention. What do you want?"

Renberg scanned the faces before him with unconcealed contempt. He would have loved to do some real damage, but his hand was forced by the death of the agent in Texas. He turned to address Daulton. "I want to propose a deal."

"A deal?" Daulton said, as if the thought had never occurred to him. "Why should we deal with you?"

"Because unless I stop it from happening, a copy of Carlson's report will land on the desk of every newspaper editor in the country before the sun rises."

"So?" Harkutlian smirked. "Do you really think anyone's going to believe it? All you've got is a document off a word processor. Anyone with a little imagination could have produced it."

The hatred Brad felt was visceral, but Harkutlian was right, of course. "That's fine," he replied calmly. "You tell the country what you know, I'll tell what I know, and people can decide for themselves."

Hackelman shifted his weight on the sofa again, and the attention turned to him. "And, exactly what is it you know?" he asked.

Renberg's eyes stayed on Harkutlian. "Like I said, you'll have to take your chances with that. You'll *all* have to take your chances with it."

"I vote we kick his ass out of here right now," Harkutlian hissed.

The President tapped his fingers against each other. "Wait a second," he said. "Just out of curiosity, what's this...deal...you're proposing?"

Renberg looked at the President and responded evenly. "I have a list of conditions. You agree to them, nobody gets a word."

"You're in no position to set conditions," Harkutlian snarled. The President put a hand up towards him. Harkutlian wanted to say more, but the President's move restrained him.

Daulton turned back to Renberg. "What conditions?"

Renberg heart was racing. The moment he'd dreamed of for years was finally at hand.

"Do you know who David Zuber is?"

The President took his time before answering. "We are aware of what happened to your father. A terrible thing, I might add."

"Then we'll start by clearing his name." It was clear Renberg wasn't asking. He was demanding. "A posthumous rescindment of the court-martial would be in order."

The President didn't react.

"And his remains will be moved to the Arlington National Cemetery," Renberg added sternly.

Daulton leaned back in his chair and clasped his hands together over his stomach. "I think what happened to your father is wrong. We can't bring him back, but we might do what we can. What you're asking for is within the realms of reason."

Renberg breathed a little easier. "There's also my mother. She lost her benefits after the court-martial. She deserves to have them re-instated."

Daulton thought it over before replying. "I don't necessarily disagree with that."

There was silence in the room. It was clear his audience anticipated more.

Renberg swallowed hard, then continued. "We need some new laws," he asserted. "Laws that would make it a crime for anyone to withhold information relating to the status of a missing person."

Harkutlian scoffed at the notion. "Now you're pushing your luck."

Again the President put up his hand. Harkutlian shook his head. There was a disgusted look to him as he took a seat on the vacant sofa across from Hackelman and Carlson.

Stan Daulton eyed Renberg pensively. "Go on."

"You will arrange for hearings," Renberg said, "to investigate all that's known about whether or not the government knowingly left men behind. De-classify all documents relevant to the issue. Get everything out in the open."

The President frowned. "That would be a matter for congress."

"You can get it started," Renberg insisted.

Daulton shrugged his shoulders. "Maybe."

The President wasn't disagreeing. The fact emboldened Renberg. "Then, of course, there's the question of what will happen to me."

"You've only broken God knows how many laws," the President observed.

"But no one outside of a few Secret Service men and the four of us here knows I was arrested."

Daulton caught Renberg's drift. He just wasn't quite sure of the destination. "So?"

"As I understand it, the Secret Service guys see and hear all sorts of things that go with them to the grave. All it would take is a word from you."

Daulton raised an eyebrow. "And the rest of the men out there looking for you?"

Renberg's response was calculated. "They'll never find me. I drowned in the river."

Again Harkutlian shook his head. Hackelman and Carlson weighed Renberg's demands and waited to see how the President would react.

"Where would you disappear to?" Daulton asked.

"You can arrange that, too. There's the federal witness protection program. I'm a witness to some federal activity you wouldn't want me describing in court. I think I qualify."

The President rose from his chair and walked around to the front of his desk. He leaned back against the edge of the desk and folded his arms. "Are you sure you don't want to sit down?"

"There's more." Renberg said, ignoring the question.

"Why should we sit here–" Harkutlian started.

"Let him speak," Daulton said, quieting Harkutlian. "Let's see what else Mr. Renberg has in mind."

The President was inclined to deal. Renberg could feel it. It was a question of how far he could push. "I don't want any trouble for Kelly

Calloway," he said. "She had no idea what was going on. I pulled her into this without her knowing what it was all about."

"Who's Kelly Calloway?"

"A friend of mine. An innocent bystander."

The President shrugged his shoulders. "Innocent bystanders have nothing to worry about."

"No. Don't give me that. I asked her to help me and she was going to without knowing what kind of trouble I was in or why. She's probably been arrested. I want her let go. None of this is her doing. She didn't know a thing about it."

"Fair enough," Daulton said. "I guess that–"

"I'm not done yet. Richard Harding read the memo."

Daulton's eyes swung from Renberg to Harkutlian and back. "And what do you propose we do about him?"

"Limit his sentence to probation. He'll keep his mouth shut."

"How can you be so sure?"

"I'll make sure he understands it's the price of his freedom."

Daulton nodded slowly. "The flip side to all of this, if I understand you right, is that the memo disappears."

Harkutlian grunted in disapproval. Roone Hackelman and Bob Carlson continued to follow the proceedings on the edge of their seats.

"The memo disappears," Renberg confirmed.

"Let me ask you something, Brad," Daulton said. "Set aside consideration of conditions and a deal for a second. Don't you see that a war in Korea would endanger the lives of tens of thousands of Americans? Doesn't that count for anything?"

"That's not what this is about," Renberg replied.

"What then?"

Renberg measured his words carefully. "This is about the impunity with which elected officials lie to the people who elected them."

"Oh, give me a break…" Harkutlian groaned.

"This is about," Renberg continued, his voice beginning to crack with emotion, "a man who put his life on the line for his country, and came home telling of others who were still alive back there, only to be destroyed for the truths he spoke."

"It wasn't us who did that, Brad," Daulton pointed out.

Renberg gestured at all four of them. "This is about men like you, who write their secret memos, then turn around and solemnly declare that they have no knowledge that any American servicemen are still alive back there."

"Now listen here!" Daulton snapped. He pushed forward off the desk and raised a finger at Renberg. "I didn't know about Strams and Pickard, and I didn't know about the memo. If you've got reason to believe otherwise, I'll hear it now!"

Renberg's every instinct told him the President was lying. But there was no way he could prove it. KORPEN implicated the secretary of state, the secretary of defense, the deputy secretary of defense, and the chairman of the Joint Chiefs of Staff. It contained no reference to the President. Even if it had, Renberg still needed someone to meet his conditions and see that their provisions were implemented. And, far from incidentally, he needed to secure his own freedom. He needed a deal, and Daulton was the only man who could deliver.

"I stand corrected," Renberg conceded with a sarcastic grin. "Change that to men like them." This time he gestured with his head at the other three.

"This is ridiculous," Harkutlian muttered. "Why are we wasting our time here?"

Daulton ignored the remark and kept his focus on Renberg. "You realize," he said, "if we were to agree to your conditions, we'd have to wait until after the election."

"What do mean?" Renberg asked warily.

"Well, as regards you, your mother, your father, and your friends...this Kelly and Harding, we could move immediately. In fact, when it comes to you, we'd *have* to move immediately. You'd have to disappear tonight."

"Yes."

"But when it comes to passing new laws, convening hearings...well that takes time. Besides, if we were to put it all in motion now, we couldn't see it through if I'm not re-elected. Our priority right now has to be the election."

Renberg thought it over. The election was just weeks away. Daulton was right. The deal was with him, so he had to stay in office to see it through. "Okay," he agreed reluctantly. "I'll buy that. There's just one more thing."

The President sighed. "And that is?"

"I'll buy that you knew nothing about the memo." Again he gestured with his head at the other three. "What about them?"

The President looked over at the others. "What about them?"

There was an icy cool to Renberg's voice when he replied. "They've got to go. Trujillo too."

"Who the hell do you think you are?" Harkutlian started.

Hackelman broke out into a mocking laugh. "You have *got* to be kidding me!"

Carlson stared at Renberg. "You haven't heard, have you?"

Renberg looked over at him, but said nothing.

"Lee Trujillo went the way of your father yesterday," Carlson said. "He committed suicide."

Renberg *hadn't* heard. The last news he knew was the morning paper at Pendergraft's house, the one with his picture on the cover.

There was a prolonged silence in the room. Then Renberg looked back at the President. "They've got to go," he insisted.

Harkutlian had heard enough. "That does it," he barked, jumping up off the sofa. He took a few steps towards Renberg, who held his ground.

"You just pushed your luck farther than it can go, young man. Go tell the world about the memo. You'll never prove it's for real."

Stan Daulton quickly stepped in front of Harkutlian. "Take what you've got right now," he urged Renberg. "It's more than you could've hoped for."

Renberg stood fast and didn't flinch. He might well have taken what he had, but he was on a roll, and there was one more gamble he just couldn't resist. It was time to play the ace he wasn't sure he had. "I need to use a phone," he said to Daulton.

"Why?"

"I think you'll want to hear something."

The President's curiosity got the better of him. He waved of Harkutlian's protestations and offered one of the two phones on his desk.

Renberg noted it had a speakerphone. He had expected it would. He walked over to the desk and said a silent prayer as he dialed the number. The others in the room watched without a word.

Renberg held the receiver to his ear for over a minute, then he punched in four more digits, activated the speakerphone, and put the receiver down. His face gave away nothing.

There were three rings.

"Hello?" It was a girl's voice, one that nobody in the room recognized.

"Is this the Stafford household?" Only Renberg knew he was listening to Chris Pendergraft.

"Yes."

"May I speak to Mr. Stafford?"

"One second."

They could hear the girl call out to her dad. A few seconds later her voice was replaced by that of a man. "Hello."

"Mr. Stafford?" It was Pendergraft's voice again.

"Yes."

"Mr. James Stafford, of the state department?"

"Yes."

"My name is Walter Saranson, sir, I'm with the *Washington Post*."

There was an angry, confused scowl on Harkutlian's face.

"What can I do for you?" Stafford asked.

"I'd like to ask you about Strams and Pickard."

There was an eerie silence on the line.

"Mr. Stafford? Are you there?"

There was an audible click. The line went dead. Brad Renberg held his breath.

"What was that?" Stan Daulton asked.

Before Renberg could reply, the sound of another phone ringing came over the speakerphone. This time there were only two rings before the call was answered.

"Hello."

Harkutlian's eyes narrowed when he heard the voice.

"Ed, this is Jim." Another voice, urgent.

"Yeah, Jim."

Only Harkulian reacted. He grimaced and reeled backwards.

"You're not going to believe this," James Stafford was saying. "Someone just called from the *Washington Post*, wanting to ask about Strams and Pickard!"

"What?" Now everyone in the room recognized Harkutlian's voice.

"I hung up on him! What the hell's going on?"

"How do you know he was from the *Post*?"

"Because it *said* so on my caller ID! And he said he was from the *Post*! What's going on, Ed?"

"Son of a bitch!"

"How do they know about Pickard and Strams?"

"Of all the…Some son of a bitch hacker broke into a computer at the Pentagon and read a memo Bob Carlson had written about it."

"A memo? What memo?"

"And he copied it and got away."

"When?"

"Yesterday."

"What do you want me to do?"

"Don't answer your phone. We're going to deny it, is what we're going to do."

"Is that what's behind Trujillo's suicide?"

"Yes, Goddamn it, yes!"

"Oh, Jesus!"

"We've got to stick together, Jim! There's no proof the memo's for real. We're going to maintain it's fabricated. You got that?"

"Jesus!"

"Listen to me. Don't answer the phone or the door. Don't say or do anything until I call you. And this time make sure it's *my* name on your caller ID!"

The line went dead.

Renberg reached over and hung up the President's phone. In his head, there was the sweetest music imaginable. "You can get that number from phone records," he said. "But don't waste your time. Those recordings are also stored elsewhere."

Harkutlian's face had lost all color. The President pursed his lips, took a deep, disconcerted breath, and went back to his chair. Renberg stayed where he was, singing silent, gleeful praises to the heavens for blessing mankind with the likes of Chris Pendergraft.

A stunned silence resounded through the room. Finally, the President reacted. "You said copies of the memo would be distributed to the media unless you prevented it from happening."

Renberg's eyes were on Harkutlian. He willed himself to suppress a triumphant smile and turned to Stan Daulton. "Yes."

"What do you need to stop it from happening?"

Renberg shrugged a shoulder casually. "A computer with an Internet connection."

The President nodded resignedly. "After the election," he conceded softly.

"Sir?"

"That's the only way it can work," Daulton said. "If they go now, there will be questions."

Renberg thought about it for a moment, then concurred.

"After the election," the President said again.

Ed Harkutlian was already on his way to the door. He pushed it open, paused briefly, then turned around. First he looked at the President, then at Brad Renberg. He opened his mouth, then hesitated. There was an angry, spent look to his eyes as he turned his back and walked out of the Oval Office.

Epilogue

On September 6, 1996, Kim Kwang Soo entered the South Korean consulate in Beijing and requested political asylum. On September 8, an attempt by North Korean agents to penetrate the elaborate security net around the Sanlitun Diplomatic Compound was foiled by units of the Chinese Police. Five days later, Kim Kwang Soo was killed by a single bullet to the head while being transferred from the consulate to a waiting plane that was to fly him, via Manila, to Seoul.

The whereabouts of the videotape remain unknown.

*   *   *

It has been widely reported in the American print media that on September 16, 1996, a House National Security subcommittee convened hearings on whether the U.S. government knowingly abandoned American prisoners of war in North Korea. Newly declassified Pentagon documents were made public. They indicate that immediately following the prisoner exchange which preceded the signing of the armistice by the U.S., North Korea and China at the end of the Korean War, there was awareness, at the highest levels of the United States government, that over 900 American prisoners remained unaccounted for.

*   *   *

To this day, Mitch Wakeman and Steve Vogel refuse to believe that Brad Renberg died on the Blanco river. While the case was closed on orders from above, both men still dedicate much of their personal time to investigating Renberg's disappearance.

✶   ✶   ✶

Shortly after winning re-election in November, 1996, the President of the United States accepted the resignations of his secretary of state, secretary of defense and deputy secretary of defense, all of whom cited a desire to return to the private sector as the reason for leaving their government posts.

✶   ✶   ✶

Shortly after the Korpen affair, Chris Pendergraft received encrypted e-mail from Zuberman, requesting assistance in locating the whereabouts of one Kelly Calloway. Despite their combined best efforts, the two could not uncover a single shred of evidence that Kelly Calloway had ever really existed.

Although he never saw him again, Pendergraft still exchanges encrypted e-mail with Brad Renberg. Strictly on the basis of periodic references to local weather conditions, Pendergraft believes Renberg is living somewhere on the west coast of the United States.

✶   ✶   ✶

On February 10, 1997, the President signed into law the 1996 defense authorization bill. The bill contains a major revision to the Missing Persons Act, the first such revision since World War II. Among the changes is a stipulation that anyone withholding from the file of a missing person any information about the disappearance or whereabouts of that person shall be subject to a fine or imprisonment.

✶   ✶   ✶

And of all the different law enforcement officers involved in the search and capture of Brad Renberg, none emerged from the affair more highly commended than the Secret Service's Dana McLaughlan. In recognition of the versatility she demonstrated during her undercover investigation of the Austin-based cellular phone cloning ring, and the subsequent aptitude she displayed in her handling of Brad Renberg, McLaughlan was rewarded with a two-year stint in the most coveted and prestigious of special agent assignments: Protective Operations.

Her undercover identity of Kelly Calloway was never used again.

Printed in the United States
2320